A Man,
A Woman,
and a Cat

James J. Stewart

Table of Contents

1.
A Big Kitten

The sign said, "Stanley Mounce, DVM." As Bill Johnson pulled into the parking lot, memories of past visits flooded over him. He had not been there for more than four years. When he first got to San Diego twelve years ago, Dr. Stan had become his vet to take care of Bill's cat, Tiger. The last time he had been here, Dr. Stan had had to put Tiger down for him.

The pet carrier in the passenger seat of Bill's SUV was the same enclosed carrier, but he was not really sure what was in it. Whatever it was, it was too large for it and was cramped. The carrier was substantial enough for a small dog. It had a dark mesh at one end so the animal could see out, but from the outside, it was hard to see what was inside. Bill grabbed the handle as he got out of his SUV. Tiger had weighed a little over twenty pounds when Bill had him put down, but this creature seemed much heavier. Closing the door, he headed toward the entrance to the clinic.

It was early, and his car was the only one in the front parking lot. Inside, there were no other customers. Dr. Stan's receptionist and veterinary assistant looked up from her desk. "Good morning, Mr. Johnson! It's been a long time!"

He nodded. "Yes, it has, Sally. As I drove up, I was thinking it has been more than four years. How've you been?"

She smiled. "The same as always, but it's just Paul and I now with both our kids married and far away. I heard you lost your wife. It was breast cancer, wasn't it?"

Bill nodded solemnly. "Jody hung on and fought it for nearly three years. My parents came down from Fairbanks for the funeral, and of course all of Jody's family is still local here."

"So, your parents still have that walk-in clinic in Fairbanks?"

He nodded. "Jody's funeral was the first and only time they've left Alaska after Jody and I got married. I doubt they'll ever see this new pet of mine."

Sally looked at his carrier. "You said on the phone you think you've got some kind of cat, but you're not sure what it is. Is it friendly?"

Bill smiled. "She's very friendly and affectionate toward me, but I don't know how she'll act around other people. She wandered into my life just yesterday morning." The door opened next to Sally's desk, and it was the veterinarian. "Hey, Dr. Stan! Good morning!"

"Good morning, Bill! I understand you've got a bit of a mystery for me. Bring it on back."

Bill followed the vet down the hall and into an exam room, speaking quietly. "For some reason, she has adopted me. I think you'd better close the other door. She's been friendly and affectionate toward me, but I'm not sure how she'll behave toward other people."

"Okay." The vet closed the other door. "Put the carrier up on the table and tell me about her."

He lifted the carrier and put it on the table. Bill could feel the vibration of quiet purring. "Yesterday morning, when I went out on my porch to get my paper, out of the corner of my eye off to my left, I saw movement in a bush. When I looked directly at the bush, I caught a glimpse of orange eyes gazing at me."

"Orange? That's interesting. Then what happened?"

"As I approached, I heard what I at first thought was a gRowwl, but then I realized it was just purring."

"Okay."

"As I parted the leaves of the bush, I immediately decided that she was a large kitten of some kind. During these unusually cold winter nights of the past week, I've had a couple of nested cardboard boxes with a pad on the bottom near my back door as a shelter for small animals. Up until that moment, I had thought it was a little dog that had been staying there in that box. Maybe it wasn't."

The vet nodded. "Okay, let's have a look." He reached for the zipper, and Bill's new friend came out of the carrier and stretched. "Wow! She must be some kind of crossbreed. I've never seen an animal like this. Was she hungry, and have you named her?"

"In my fridge, I had thawed out a steak for fixing that evening. I put it in a cake pan and put it on the floor. She was definitely hungry. While she was eating, I pondered several names aloud. When I said the name 'Sheila,' she stopped eating, approached me, and stroked around my legs. Evidently, her name is Sheila."

The cat was staring at Dr. Stan. He looked at her. "I need to examine you, okay?"

She was compliant as he examined her. "Sheila, you certainly are pretty. You have a cheetah's head structure with appropriate face markings for that animal, but on your body, your spots on most of your body are a little less pronounced, and your fur is softer and more like that of a puma. If you are a cheetah – puma cross, I think you must have been born recently, perhaps at the beginning of this month, just from your size. We're going to license you and give you a couple of shots. I hope you won't mind when I take a blood sample in order to trace your origins." As he talked with her, he examined her all over and did all that was necessary. "If you're only three weeks old or so, I wonder where your mother is? There have been no reports of cheetah escapes from the zoo or anywhere else in this country. Where would a cheetah come from? That's a mystery, for certain."

As Dr. Stan examined her, another memory came to Bill. "Do you remember Evan Cokal and his cheetah?"

The vet nodded. "Sure! That cat's name was Sheila too. That's a strange coincidence, the two cats responding to the same name. When Evan died, Sheila his cheetah escaped from the shelter that was caring for her. The police searched the area for several days, but they never did find a trace of her. I suppose this kitten could be descended from her. I'll take care of the paperwork to have her registered legally with you. I'll want to see her about every month until she's finished growing. Meanwhile, maybe her mother will show up for a visit, though that might be scary."

Bill nodded. "No problem. Sheila's going to be a far more expensive pet than Tiger was, but that's okay. I can afford it. It's been mighty quiet around the house with Jody gone on to what my pastor calls 'the larger life.'"

"What church are you going to?"

"Four years before Jody passed, we decided to leave behind our 'Wild Bill and Jody' image and adventures. I designed some major buildings downtown while we were trying to get pregnant.

Part of our settling down was joining Torrey Pines Evangel Church in La Jolla."

"That's good to hear." The vet continued to examine Bill's new kitten, gave her some shots, and took a blood sample. "I notice here that, unlike a full-blooded cheetah, your Sheila can retract her claws. Still, she's going to need exercise to stay healthy. You may want to consider a large self-regulating treadmill for her. You may also want to get a child's sandbox as a litter box for her and keep her inside for now. When she's full-grown, you'll want to have a high fence for your back yard so your neighbors will feel safe. You'll have less liability too."

Bill nodded. When he lifted the flap on the carrier, Sheila immediately went inside, purring softly. "I think she's glad the exam is over."

Dr. Stan nodded. "Be sure to make an appointment for a month from now with Sally. I'll call you when I get a genetic breakdown of Sheila's blood." Bill picked up the carrier, but Dr. Stan wasn't done. "When Animal Control sees the paperwork I send in, they may want to issue a permit with restrictions for you. Keep an eye on your mail. There's one more thing you need to do, Bill. Stop at a pet supplies store and get a harness for her with a strong leash. Then you can walk outside with her. You may not be able to do it when she's full-grown, but for now it will be good for her to get outside, but she should live inside most of the time until you have enough fencing. Inside, she'll probably be better than any guard dog."

After Sally processed Bill's credit card for payment, he took Sheila out to his SUV and secured her carrier with the seat belt. "Okay, Sheila, after a short stop at the pet store and the meat market, we're going home. I'll go online to order you a sandbox."

"Rowwl," was his cat's soft reply.

Sheila had quite an appetite that first year, and she continued to be surprisingly tame. Bill special-ordered an extra-large treadmill. It was controlled by a row of infrared sensors that kept the cat centered on the belt, whether she was moving or not. If she stopped moving, it instantly stopped. It also had a special heavy-duty high-speed motor that would allow her to run exceedingly fast. Bill set it up in his great room, facing out toward his back yard, but it was well away from the window in case of nosey neighbors. Immediately Sheila began running on it, typically two or three times a day for ten minutes or so. From the first day, that seemed to be her favorite part of Bill's house. They stayed inside except when they walked at night. His neighbors were a mix. On one side, the owners were seldom home. On the other side, a young couple name George and Abby visited often and enjoyed Sheila as much as he did. The four of them sometimes walked together with the cat in the late evening.

Bill had a carpenter put a door designed for a large dog near the rear of the house in the laundry room. The door led to an enclosed ramp down into the basement. He put a child's sandbox down there filled with 100 pounds of cat litter. Amazingly, he didn't have to teach Sheila to use it. She knew what it was for, either by instinct or high intelligence. If Sheila's mother was the cheetah by the same name that Dr. Stan Mounce and Bill discussed, she must have been old when she gave birth to this Sheila. Even so, many generations of domestication and training behind her mother could explain Sheila's civilized behavior, and it might explain some of her other behavior as well. Amazingly, some basic commands, such as heel, relax, and protect, that had been used with her supposed mother, worked with this Sheila also.

Bill went online to the San Diego Union-Tribune, and he searched their digital records of past issues for all the articles involving Evan Cokal's Sheila. In addition to news stories, there was material from a Sunday magazine article on that cheetah, including an interview in which her owner talked about the commands that Evan Cokal's cheetah responded to.

When Bill told Dr. Stan about it at one of the monthly visits, he shook his head. "I can't explain it. There's absolutely no logic to either that cheetah's name or voice commands being passed on to your Sheila. The genetic test indicates that your Sheila is half cheetah and half puma. Her data was put into the Cokal Animal Genetics Database. You Sheila is not even closely related to Evan Cokal's cheetah. Although pumas are always wild and aggressive, cheetahs aren't that way towards humans. Still, she is amazingly tame as well. We have a major mystery on our hands. Pumas are found throughout most of North America, but cheetahs are found free exclusively in Africa. Here in the U.S., they're seen only in zoos. So, how did your beautiful cat inherit her cheetah genes? That's a major part of this big mystery."

Bill nodded. "Okay, so Sheila's mother was not Evan Cokal's cheetah, but was there anything else unusual in Sheila's genetics?"

"Her genetics are cheetah and puma, but there are some unusual markers that are not usually found in either species. I don't know why, and I don't know where these markers come from. While pumas can live twenty years or more, a typical cheetah's life expectancy is somewhat less. There is no way to determine how long your Sheila will live."

Taking Sheila home that day, Bill had a lot to think about. He made some changes to his home. Thinking that Sheila might like to stretch as other cats do, he had the carpenter who had installed Sheila's door put a foot-square post in one corner of the great room that went from the floor up to the first rafter of the open-beam ceiling. Before mounting it, he had him cover the post with industrial-grade carpeting. That turned out to be a good decision as Sheila grew heavier.

About six months after Sheila came into Bill's life, he came home from work one evening, and Sheila didn't greet him as usual. He looked all over the house, but he didn't see her sleeping anywhere. Going into the great room, he called out, "Sheila!"

"Rowwl," Sheila's reply seemed startlingly close.

He looked up. She was stretched out on one of the rafters up near the open-beam ceiling, almost invisible amid the shadows. "Do you like it up there?"

She stood up and jumped, landing silently next to him and purring softly. She stroked around his legs a couple of times, and then she walked toward the kitchen. He figured she was hungry. After putting a roast in her dish, he sat down on his sofa and turned on the news.

When she was finished with her meal, Sheila lay at his feet for several minutes, and then she bounded up the carpeted post again and stretched out on a rafter. "Do you like it there, upstairs, Sheila?"

"Rowwl," she softly responded, and closed her eyes. Bill wondered: *She seems to understand English amazingly well.*

When the newscast was over, Bill fixed himself some dinner, and then he went into his study to continue to work on a draft for a new building there in La Jolla.

A few months later a Sunday, Bill took pastor Ewart Scott and his wife, Rachel, to lunch after church. Right after they started eating, Rachel asked, "How's Sheila?"

Bill smiled. "She's growing rapidly. A couple of my clients met her when I had them over to my home on Tuesday. They were truly impressed with her, and there were no problems. I think I told you previously that her parents were a cheetah and a puma."

Pastor Ewart nodded. "Yes. After you mentioned Evan Cokal a few weeks ago, I looked him up in our church records. He was quite a prominent member of the church when he died suddenly twenty-six years ago. I never knew him of course, because I've only been here sixteen years. Rachel and I would like to meet your Sheila someday."

Bill nodded. "Check your calendar. Maybe next weekend we can have dinner out together, and then I will take you home to meet Sheila."

Rachel put her fork down. "That will be wonderful, but since you're taking us to lunch today, why don't you let us take you to that new Vietnamese place downtown?"

Bill nodded. "Okay." He took out his phone. "Both Friday and Saturday evenings are free for me next weekend. How about you and Rachel, Pastor Ewart?"

The pastor had his phone out. "Friday will be best. Rachel?"

She nodded. "I can't think of any conflicts."

Bill had a very busy week because the La Jolla City council approved his plans for a new City Hall, and He began talking to potential general contractors.

After a wonderful and filling dinner that Friday, Pastor Ewart and Rachel followed Bill's SUV back to his house. Going inside, they stopped in the doorway to the great room. "Sheila? I have some friends I want you to meet."

"Rowwl." The now large cat leaped down and paused.

Rachel's mouth was agape, and then she spoke softly. "That's got to be at least fifteen feet from up there! She's huge!"

Bill spoke in a normal voice. "Actually, it's more. The roof to the second story with its bedrooms over the garage and workshop is lower than this great room wing with its kitchen and my study. Sheila's grown considerably these first eight months, and she's still growing. Last month, the vet weighed her in at 165. Sheila, come on over and let them pet you." Her orange eyes focused on their faces, one by one, as she silently padded over, purring softly. "That's not a gRowwl. That's a purr, so relax. She knows she's intimidating, and she's relaxed."

The pastor and his wife were dumbfounded. He spoke quietly. "May we stoop down for a closer look?"

Bill smiled. "No problem."

When Rachel caressed Sheila's neck, that cat nuzzled her and licked her hand. Rachel continued to speak softly. "I did not know what to expect, Sheila, but you are so very beautiful!" Sheila nuzzled her again, still purring.

Ewart's voice was also quiet. "Do her muscles ripple like that all the time?"

Bill shook his head. "No, she's evidently just showing off." When Sheila heard Bill's voice, she looked up at him. "Sheila, you've been very good. Why don't you go back to your perch up above?"

She licked his hand, turned, and in a flash of speed she bounded across the great room and up the carpeted post. She strode across the rafters to the center of the room, and then she settled onto her favorite spot.

The Pastor was shaking his head slowly. "It must be her cheetah heritage. I could not have imagined any animal moving so suddenly and so fast."

Rachel nodded, saying, "Yes. That was amazing!"

As they moved toward the sofa, Bill pointed at Sheila's treadmill. "I had that treadmill customized for her to get exercise. Lately, Sheila's been running on it three to four times a day. She reaches speeds as fast as you saw and faster on it." He pointed across the room. "Any visitor who does not know otherwise would not know she lives here. That doorway with short hall leads to the laundry room, and a so-called 'dog door' in there leads to a ramp into the basement. There's a sandbox down there, and she also has a pad there where she can warm herself by the furnace if she wants to. If I finish off the basement someday, I may have to make other arrangements, of course. When she steps into her sandbox, an exhaust fan turns on for ten minutes."

Rachel started shaking her head, again. "As I said earlier, I did not really know what to expect. I don't see any hair on your furniture." She looked up toward the ceiling toward Sheila. "She is nothing like what I could have anticipated. She is delightfully beautiful and amazingly tame."

Pastor Ewart glanced upward and nodded. "Didn't you say that the vet says her father was a puma?"

"Yes, unquestionably, but the resulting hybrid is different in many ways from both pumas and cheetahs. For one thing, she is still growing, and she already weighs far more than any cheetah or puma. She's also stronger and faster. I have seen her standing right there," He pointed toward the end of the sofa, "and I saw her leap to that spot where she is now."

Rachel's eyes got big. "Really!"

"As I told you two some time ago, I thought her mother was Evan Cokal's pet cheetah, and that cheetah was more than thirty generations tame. Somehow, and our vet cannot explain it, Sheila knows human voice commands, but my beautiful cat is not even closely related to that other cheetah. When I was trying to choose a name for her, and I spoke the name I've given her, she immediately began treating me like an old friend. It was the same name of Evan Cokal's pet cheetah."

Pastor Ewart nodded. "While Rachel and I are here, I'd like to ask you an unofficial question."

"Unofficial?"

"Yes. As your pastor, I answer to the church's Board of Directors, but this is in no way an official question on the part of the church."

"Okay. Shoot."

"We're growing into the place where we soon are going to need to add another worship service. I'm personally interested in possible options to increase our seating capacity. You've been with us long enough to know the church pretty well."

Bill was thoughtful. "I can prepare some suggestions for you and the church's Board for no charge in about ten days. I'll come over during this coming week to take some measurements."

"That would be great! The Board meets a week from this coming Saturday for lunch. Would you need to meet with them?"

Bill shook his head. "Not necessarily."

The purring above them stopped. "Rowwl." Bill's cat spoke louder than usual. He looked up. What is it Sheila?" The doorbell rang. Bill looked at his watch. "I'm not expecting anyone."

2.
Dangerous Protection

As Bill walked toward the entry hall, he had an uncomfortable feeling. Looking through the peephole in his front door, he could see the face of his neighbor, Abby, and there were some people with her, but he could not see more. As he opened the door, Abby, quivering, said something about being sorry.

A man with her spoke loudly. "Back up!"

Instinctively, Bill started backing up, and in the corner of his eye, he was aware of Sheila crouching nearby on the floor in the kitchen. He had not seen her make a move or hear a sound from her.

Two men on both sides of Abby pushed her into Bill, and a third man slammed the door loudly. Abby and Bill continued to back up toward the great room.

Surprisingly, in another way, Bill saw Sheila moving towards the door. *Really??* Suddenly confident, he spoke more loudly than usual. "You men had better sit down on the floor right now, or in less than ten seconds, all of you could be dead."

The man who spoke earlier glared at Bill. "Very...."

"Rrooowwwllll!" Sheila was crouched and ready to spring.

The three men looked behind them as Bill spoke boldly. "She can kill all three of you before any of you can draw his gun." The first man started to move, and he had a gun pointed at Bill, who had not seen it previously. As the man began to turn, Bill shouted. "Sheila! Protect!"

During the next few seconds, everything was a blur. One man flew off to Bill's right. The man with the gun was flying in the other direction as his gun dropped to the floor, and the third man was kneeling with his arms folded over his head and neck. Sheila hopped up on the back of the man who had had the gun. The other two knelt with their hands in a defensive pose.

"Good job, Sheila! Hold." She didn't move a muscle except for her orange eyes scanning the scene. Abby was behind Bill with her arms around him like she was going to squeeze the life out of him. "Abby, everything is under control. You can let go."

Abby relaxed and looked off to the left. "Thank you, Sheila!"

"Rowwl." Her feline voice was softer.

"Amen to that!" Pastor Ewart was coming up behind Bill, but Rachel stayed on the sofa, her eyes wide. Ewart looked now at my gRowwl-like-purring cat. "I also thank you, Sheila." She blinked slowly in response, but held her position.

Bill took out his phone and dialed 9-1-1. "This is Bill Johnson at 4-2-1-1 Faculty Avenue. Three men forced their way into my home, but we have them temporarily under control. One or two of the men may need the paramedics." He paused to listen. "That's correct. 4211 Faculty Avenue. Yes, that is my correct caller ID. Thank you."

Bill put his phone away. "Sheila, you can watch them from above." Sheila stepped off the man, and in a moment's leap, she was glaring at the three men from about twenty feet above. Bill spoke to the man upon whom Sheila had been sitting. "Get up on your knees like the other two." As the man moved slowly, he let out a groan twice. "All three of you remain on your knees, with your hands behind your necks." Bill looked up at his pet. "Watch, Sheila."

"Rowwl." There was no mistaking the cat's confident voice.

"You men just saw how fast Sheila can move. If one of you makes a wrong move, from where she is poised, she can leap to the floor and kill all three of you just as swiftly as she disabled all three of you a few minutes ago. Do you understand?" All three nodded. The men were obviously terrified.

They could hear sirens in the distance. Bill turned to his neighbor, who had sat down on the sofa with Ewart and Rachel. "Abby, I'm afraid you had better stick around until after the police dismiss you. Do you want to let Ralph know what's going on?"

"He's working late this evening, doing some accounting of the investments of someone who lives near here. I'll tell him all about it when he gets home."

Bill nodded. "Okay." They heard a vehicle with a siren stop nearby. "I'd better get the door." The doorbell rang, and Bill went and opened the door.

"Mr. Johnson?" Bill nodded. "I'm Lieutenant Garvin, and this is Sergeant Forbes."

"Come in. Please come this way." As they entered the great room, Bill explained. "About five minutes ago my doorbell rang. Through the peephole, I could see my neighbor Abby's face" (she waved as Bill pointed), "but I could not see who else was with her. When I opened the door, these three men now on their knees forced their way inside and slammed the door behind them."

The lieutenant maintained a serious and professional tone in his voice. "Our radio call said that three men were under control. Who is holding them at bay?"

Bill pointed up at the rafters. "That's my cat, Sheila, holding them."

He looked up into Sheila's orange eyes. "Shit!"

"She is the reason I told the 9-1-1 dispatcher she should send paramedics to check the men out. I don't think any of them are seriously injured, but I'm an architect, not a doctor." Bill pointed. "The man on the sofa is Pastor Ewart Scott of Torrey Pines Evangel church, and the woman next to him is his wife, Rachel."

"Did these three say what they wanted?"

Bill shook his head. "No, Sheila did not let them talk much. That one," Bill pointed "showed a gun in his hand when I spoke to Sheila, and when he started to turn toward Sheila, she went into action. The gun is there on the floor where he dropped it while flying to where he is now." Bill pointed as the Lieutenant, putting on plastic gloves, went and retrieved the gun. He put it in a plastic bag.

They heard another vehicle with a siren arrive outside. The sergeants' radio made some sounds, and he responded, "10-4." He looked at his partner. "Backup is here, and paramedics are on their way."

"Good. Get these three cuffed and out of here."

"Right."

Lieutenant Garvin looked up at Sheila. "So, she's pretty dangerous?" Two uniformed officers came in, and they helped Sergeant Forbes take the three prisoners outside. The rest of them simply watched.

"In answer to your question, Lieutenant, Sheila is dangerous only when she has a reason. Would you like to meet her?"

He hesitated, and then he nodded. "Okay."

"Sheila, hop down and say hello to the Lieutenant." She leaped and landed silently less than a yard away from the officer. She was unruffled, but he was.

The lieutenant's mouth hung open slightly, his eyes wide. He gulped. "Whoa! You're huge!" He held out his hand, and she nuzzled it. "What is she?"

"Genetically, she's half cheetah and half puma. She showed up as a kitten in my yard several months ago. Where she came from is a mystery. I have a permit, and she's properly licensed. Relax, Sheila." Totally calm, she trotted over to the laundry room door and disappeared.

They watched her leave. "She is amazing." The lieutenant glanced at his partner. "We'd better get back to work, though. Those three men may also be responsible for two other home invasions in the past few weeks." The sergeant took out a pad and pen as the lieutenant continued. "We'll take statements from each of you."

It was almost an hour before all but one of the police left. A patrol officer remained behind to stay until the media people would leave. After watching the last police cars leave, Bill went inside. Abby was talking with the Scotts quietly.

Bill walked toward them but remained standing. "I'm hungry. Would anyone like a chocolate sundae or a banana split?"

Rachel looked at her husband. "I couldn't handle an entire banana split. Shall we share one?"

Pastor Ewart shook his head. "Even half of one would be too much for me. I could handle a single scoop sundae, though."

"Okay. How about you Abby?"

She looked at her watch. "Ralph will be home soon. I think...." The doorbell rang.

Bill turned and went to the door. Through the peephole he could see it was Abby's husband, and Bill opened the door. "Hi, Ralph. Abby and my other guests were just going to have chocolate sundaes with me. Would you like one?"

He grinned. "Sure! I never turn down anything chocolate!" As he went into the great room, Abby stood up, and they hugged. "Hey, beautiful. Laura and Ozzie say they'll join us tomorrow for lunch."

She smiled. "Great! Knowing them, they'll take us to either Piatti or The Cottage." Abby glanced toward the newcomer behind her husband. "Here comes Sheila."

The cat came through the laundry room door. "Rowwl."

Ralph knelt down. "Hi there, my friend! Are you being good?"

Rachel laughed. "Sheila has been very **very** good this evening, hasn't she, Abby?"

Bill interrupted them. "Abby, while you and the Scotts tell Ralph... You remember the Scotts, don't you, Ralph?"

"Sure!" He shook hands with Pastor Ewart.

"While you tell tonight's story to Ralph, I'll fix sundaes for all of us. Sheila, would you like a snack?"

"Rowwl." She trotted after him to the kitchen.

In Bill's walk-in refrigerator, he grabbed one of Sheila's select-grade roasts that was already thawed out. Back in the kitchen, he tossed it into the air, which she caught and took to her dish. Her purr was strong as she ate it.

It did not take Bill long to put scoops of ice cream into five bowls, and he put them on a tray with spoons and a bottle of dark chocolate syrup. As he returned to the great room, Abby was telling her husband what the lieutenant said when he first saw Sheila in the rafters.

Bill's cat padded softly and rapidly past him, climbed the pole, and returned to the rafters. Sheila was behaving like an extension of Bill or like a partner.

Ralph was smiling. "I remember the first time I saw Sheila! For just a moment I was frightened, but as she approached us with her purr, I relaxed. Now, miraculously, Abby and I see Sheila as simply part of our neighbor's family." He paused to put a spoonful of the sundae in his mouth. "This hits the spot, Bill. Thanks!" The others murmured their thanks as well.

Bill nodded. "You're welcome. One of the things I appreciate about you, Ralph, is that you're willing to go to people's homes with your accounting skills as you did tonight."

Ralph took another spoonful and nodded. "Abby goes out with me on these calls sometimes. She's a popular bookkeeper in this part of San Diego county." He looked over at the Scotts.

"Pastor Ewart, if the church ever has a need for my skills or Abby's, we'll not charge anything."

Pastor Ewart smiled and put down his empty bowl. "Thank you, Ralph. Right now, we've got a retired CPA as our Treasurer. Our Financial Secretary keeps the books for the Navy. We're truly blessed with whom we need, but if our situation changes, I'll definitely remember your offer."

Rachel put her bowl into her husband's. "It's getting late, Bill. It's been an unexpectedly memorable evening. She glanced at her husband. "I think it is time for us to head home."

They all stood up, and as the men shook hands, Abby and Rachel hugged. They all headed toward the front door.

Ralph looked at Abby and at Bill. "I think we'll call it a night too, Bill." They all said their good nights, and when Bill closed the door after them and locked it, Sheila strolled over to him. "Rowwl?"

"Yes, Sheila, I'm going to get a shower and crawl into bed. Are you going to spend the night in the rafters again, or are you going to crawl under my bed?" After rubbing her head against Bill's leg, she followed him upstairs into the bedroom. Later, as Bill drifted off to sleep, Sheila's orange eyes gazed out the window over the neighborhood as she purred softly.

For nearly two years after she entered Bill's life, Sheila continued to grow. Bill took her to the vet every month. With a small park in the neighborhood, about once a week, Bill got up before sunrise so that he and Sheila could walk together outdoors. Sometimes Abby and Ralph joined them on those walks.

3.
Unexpected Encounters

The vet did his monthly routine smoothly. "Sheila appears healthy and content, like a giant house cat. Is she still behaving as totally tame, like previously? Have you fenced your back yard?" Dr. Stanley Mounce finished listening to Sheila's heart and put away his stethoscope.

"There've been no problems with her. I decided such a fence would not look good in my neighborhood. My neighbors and I have a dog door between our yards, so Sheila has access to both yards. On the other side of my yard is my other neighbor's garage. The back of my yard is a cement block wall facing an alley. Sheila runs at least fifteen miles on her treadmill each day. She has her climbing post, and she likes to leap between the rafters of my great room. You'll have to make a house call sometime to see the setup." He put his hand on Sheila's head and scratched it. "Her sandbox is in the basement."

The vet nodded. "She hasn't grown any since last month, so let's make this second anniversary visit the final monthly one, unless there's a problem. Then she should come in annually."

Bill nodded. "Good! I'm going to consider this anniversary as her birthday from this day forwards. When I brought her to you the first time, you said you thought she was only two or three weeks old."

"That sounds good. We'll make her first visit her birthday. I like her harness. Where did you get it?"

Bill clipped a leash to the harness. "Six years ago, I designed most of the work done at the San Diego Zoo when they did some remodeling. I have a friend there who knows someone who does custom leather work. The leather straps are actually hollow, surrounding military-armor-grade steel mesh within the straps."

"It certainly is well-designed. It does not mar her fur at all, and she seems comfortable with it."

Bill nodded. "She does. This is going to be an interesting weekend for us – a change of pace. I have a friend who owns a motel in Winterhaven. After we spend the night there, tomorrow Sheila and I are going to go hiking in the Little Picacho Wilderness and on up into the Chocolate Mountains. I have not used all the commands that Sheila's mother knew, and this will be a chance to try out some of the others to see how Sheila responds. She continues to amaze me with her understanding of what I say to her. I need to get out of town because for more than two months, I have not had time for social life. I have planned this trip as a change of pace."

The vet smiled. "Sheila amazes me as she does you. That trip you're planning sounds like fun. I haven't been over to the Arizona border area for several years. Enjoy yourselves!"

A few minutes later, Sheila and Bill were on Interstate 8 and headed east. About a half hour west of Winterhaven, Bill saw a car pulled over with lights flashing. He opened the sunroof on his SUV so Sheila could watch, and he left the engine running with the air conditioning going after he stopped. The dash thermometer said ninety-one. Bill went to the driver's side door of the other car, and the window was rolled down. The woman looked vaguely familiar to him. "Hi! I'm Bill Johnson from San Diego. Do you want some help?"

"Hi. I'm Alex. I was supposed to be in Winterhaven fifteen minutes ago, but my car has died. I've got plenty of gas, so I don't know what's wrong. My cell battery is kaput, so I can't even call for help." She got out of her car, and suddenly Bill recognized her.

"Are you making a movie in Winterhaven? I don't recall anything in the news about a production out here."

"No, it's a TV pilot." Suddenly, her eyes got bigger. "What's that?" She pointed at Bill's SUV, where Sheila's head was above the roof, and the cat was gazing at them with her orange eyes.

"That's Sheila. She's my cat."

"Is she a cheetah? She has the markings."

Bill shook his head. "She's half cheetah and half puma. Would you like to meet her?"

Alex saw Sheila blink slowly, and her eyes got bigger. "I don't know.... Okay. Sure!" They walked back to Bill's SUV. "You don't have to let her out. Can I scratch her head?"

"Sheila, this is my new friend, Alex. She's an actress, and she wants to say hello." Bill paused. "Go ahead."

Alex reached up and petted Sheila's head. The cat was purring strongly. "Oh! Your fur is so nice and soft! A cheetah's fur is much stiffer and harsher. I worked with one once, a few years ago."

"Alex, I can call for a tow truck, but it could be an hour or more before it got here. Meanwhile, you'd bake in this heat. I can drive you into Winterhaven and to your set, and you can have a tow truck sent out to get your car. Sheila will stay in the back seat of my SUV."

Intrigued, the woman turned and looked at Bill. I'll go get my keys and my suitcase." She started toward her car.

"Sheila, you're going to have to move into the back seat."

Bill unlocked the passenger-side door as Alex approached. "Let me put your bag in the back. Sheila has moved to the back seat." He held the door open for her.

"Thank you."

Bill closed the door, went to the driver's side, got in, and got back on the highway.

Alex glanced back toward Sheila, who was still purring. "Is she dangerous?"

Bill smiled. "Only when it is necessary. I at first believed her mother was more than thirty generations tame and trained as a hunting cat. That cheetah, if she had been my cat's mother, was a gift from the last Shah of Iran to a man in La Jolla named Evan Cokal. I've since learned through a blood test that my Sheila's not related to that cheetah. According to our vet, the only thing we know about Sheila's father is that he was a puma."

"She's beautiful!"

"Thank you."

"You know I'm an actress. What about you??"

"I'm an architect. Tell me about this pilot you're doing in Winterhaven."

"Actually, we're only doing a few scenes in Winterhaven. This will take less than a week, and we might not use any of the material in the pilot. This pilot is rather risky and speculative. If it is sold as a series, the story line could go on for several seasons without having to create new material from scratch. This is speculative because the producers and director would rather it be sold as a movie franchise." She paused and decided she wanted to know more. "Does your wife live in San Diego?"

He took a breath. "She did. She died from breast cancer."

"I'm sorry."

"I'm getting accustomed to not seeing her, but in a sense, she'll always be with me because she shaped my life and helped make me who I am. Since Sheila showed up in my yard about a year ago and adopted me, it's been easier not seeing Jody every day.

They continued driving silently until they got into the outskirts of Winterhaven. "Where shall I drop you off?"

"Our temporary headquarters is at the Winterhaven Courtyard Suites."

"Excellent. The manager there is a friend of mine. Sheila and I will be there tonight. Tomorrow morning, we are going to go hiking in the Little Picacho Wilderness. We might even do a little climbing further north into the Chocolate Mountains. We'll go back to San Diego Sunday evening."

Alex pointed. "There it is!"

Bill nodded and pulled in at the entrance. "Hold on, I'll get your door." After getting her bag out of the trunk, he opened her door.

"Thank you very much. I hope to see you and Sheila later." She reached out and took her bag, and she quickly went inside.

Bill found a parking space nearby, and after getting his backpack, he put the leash on Sheila. "Heel, Sheila."

"Rowwl." She walked beside him to the doors and into the motel like a well-trained dog. As expected, their entrance invited a few stares of people in the lobby.

As they approached the front desk, Bill's friend was standing there. "Long time no see, Bob! Bill glanced downward. "This is Sheila."

"Hey Bill! It's been a few years, hasn't it! Hi, Sheila."

"Rowwl." She responded softly

Bob laughed nervously. "Is she dangerous?"

Bill smiled. "Only if she has to be."

Bob nodded. "I assume you have a permit for her. I'm giving you two a suite on the second floor. You're just here for one night, right?" Bill nodded. "Okay. Your credit card was charged when you made the reservation." Bob handed Bill an electronic key. "We've got celebrities here this weekend, making a TV pilot."

Bill nodded. "I know. The actress who checked in here a moment ago was stranded out on I-8, and I dropped her off. Will there be a problem getting a tow truck out there for her?"

Bob was now grinning. "So, you drove her in, huh? Do you like her?"

Bill nodded. "She's very nice."

"There's no problem getting a tow truck out there for her. You've been married quite a while though, haven't you?"

"I'm a widower. My late wife had breast cancer." Bill looked down at Sheila. "Hey, girl, let's go upstairs and get settled, shall we?" He looked back at his friend. "It's good to see you again, Bob."

He nodded. "It's good to see you too. Enjoy your stay. You too, Sheila."

"Rowwl." It was almost inaudible.

Facing a stairway and two elevators, Bill took the stairs two at a time. Sheila easily kept up.

At the top of the stairs, their door was at the end of the hall, and Bill was glad he had asked for the largest suite. It had two bedrooms and bathrooms, with a large lounge area. There was also a balcony with a small table and chairs. Bill could see the Chocolate Mountains in the distance. He unhooked Sheila's leash, and she started exploring. Bill went into one of the bedrooms and put his backpack on a chair. In the bathroom, he splashed his face with water, and then he drank a glassful. He went to the other bedroom, and Sheila was on the bed, her eyes closed. "Sheila?"

"Rowwl?"

"Do you need to use a sandbox?" She put her head back down and closed her eyes. Bill went back into the living area, went to the sliding glass door to the patio, and studied the landscape for several minutes.

The room's phone rang, and he picked up the receiver. "Hello?"

"Hi, Bill! This is Alex."

"Alex! This is a nice surprise. Aren't you working?"

"Everything's on hold until Monday. I'd like to show you my appreciation by buying you dinner. How about it? I'd love to feed Sheila too."

"Sure. I fed her a roast this morning. I suppose she won't refuse a steak for a snack."

"Excellent! We'll do room service, so we have privacy. I'm in 208. How about 6:00 PM?"

"We'll be there! See you later."

Bill went to his bedroom and stretched out to take a nap. The next thing he knew, Sheila was nuzzling his hand. He looked at the digital clock on the wall, and it said 5:30. "Thanks for waking me up, Sheila."

"Rowwl."

"Do you need a sandbox, now?"

She trotted towards the door, intelligently understanding. Bill got her leash and clipped it to her harness. Going downstairs, there weren't many people in the lobby. Only one woman turned to look at them. As they went out the automatic doors, the weather buffer area was very warm, but when they went through the second set of doors, they were hit with a wall of hot desert air. They quickly crossed the parking lot, and it was not hard for them to find a place where Sheila could do her business. It did not take long.

As they were crossing back across the asphalt toward the motel entrance, Alex was walking toward them. "Hi, Bill! Hi Sheila!"

"Rowwl." When Alex reached down, Sheila nuzzled her.

"My room is on this side of the motel, and I was having a cold drink on my balcony when I saw you two crossing the parking lot. I assumed that nature was calling your beautiful cat."

"Right." They silently went through both sets of doors. "In a place like Winterhaven, you have to love air conditioning!" He was glad to get out of the heat.

"Amen to that!" Alex pointed. "Are those the Chocolate Mountains in the distance?"

"Yes. We're at the southern end of the range."

"If you're going hiking out there tomorrow, I hope you've brought plenty of sunscreen!"

Bill nodded. "Definitely! I've also brought a lightweight umbrella."

"I'm sure that's a good idea. The rental-car company is bringing out another car to me this evening. I probably won't need it until Tuesday or Wednesday, though." They went up the stairs with Sheila between them. Alex stopped at the top of the stairs, and Sheila and Bill paused as well. Alex spoke quietly. "It's still early. If you want to wait and come to my room at six that's okay, but you're welcome to come now."

Bill looked at Alex and smiled. "That sounds good." As they stepped into her suite a few moments later, Bill took off Sheila's leash, and she went to the window and settled down. Sheila was becoming accustomed to Bill's habits and understood her place.

Alex went to a small refrigerator. "I don't do alcohol or drugs, but I've lots of soft drinks and tea. What would you like?"

"Ginger Ale will be fine."

"Do you like ice?"

"Please. Can you tell me more about this pilot you're shooting?"

"As I think I told you as we were driving in, it may be a pilot. It also might end up being a teaser or set of teasers for a movie franchise. They're working on financing a movie franchise." She handed Bill a tall and cold glass.

"Thank you."

"For the last three months, we've been shooting in a sound studio in Burbank. Before that, we did some shooting in Yosemite, up where the roads aren't open yet due to snow. When we leave here, we're going to spend one more weekend there in Yosemite Valley, but at a big hotel. Outside scenes will be shot in the early morning, and inside scenes will be shot in the middle of the night while the guests are sleeping."

"That sounds like a lot going into just a pilot."

"I hope it's not going to be just a pilot. I love the book it is based upon. It is Christian sci-fi fantasy."

"Has the book already been published?"

She smiled. "Oh, sure! *The Gaardian Saga* [© 2015] is available on Amazon. I don't suppose you have much time for casual reading."

Bill nodded his head. "Actually, I read seven to eight books a year, both fiction and non-fiction. Reading helps me maintain my sanity in this messed-up world of ours."

She smiled. "I've never considered reading that way. I read when I'm not memorizing lines or learning a script. Are you getting hungry?"

He grinned. "Anytime you're ready. I'll have whatever you're having."

She looked over at Sheila. "What about my other new friend?"

"I feed her inexpensive roasts, usually beef. I fed her this morning, and I'll probably feed her again tomorrow morning, but she can get by just eating three or four times a week."

Alex picked up the room phone's receiver and pressed a button. "Hi, this is room 208. We'd like to have two prime rib dinners, medium rare, with baked potatoes, fruit salads, apple pie for dessert, and plenty of iced tea." She paused. "That's right, and one more thing. I want you to put one of your biggest steaks, raw, on a separate platter." Again, she paused. "That's right, raw. Furthermore, I need a large, empty salad bowl…. That's it. … How soon? … Great!" She hung up and looked at him. "It'll be about ten minutes. I asked for a large empty salad bowl for water, which we'll put out on the balcony floor beside the steak and platter. I've plenty of bottled water in the fridge."

Bill was impressed. "Wow! That's very thoughtful of you, Alex. Thank you. I'm sure Sheila will appreciate it."

She smiled. "I hope so. I'm fond of her already."

Sheila gazed at Alex with her orange eyes and slowly blinked.

When the bellhop brought a rolling table with our food, he stopped at the door when he saw Sheila. "Is it okay to come in?"

Bill nodded. "Sure! She won't hurt you. Come on in!"

When Sheila stood up, Alex went over and put her hand out. Sheila nuzzled her hand and purred. Alex smiled. "I ordered the raw steak for our Sheila, here, and I'd like you to fill that extra salad bowl with bottled water and put it with the raw steak on the floor of the balcony, okay?"

"Yes, ma'am."

"Sheila, let's get away from the patio door so that he can do his work." Alex came and sat on the sofa beside Bill, and Sheila lay down at their feet.

As the bellhop worked, he probably was not aware of the fact that his mouth was hanging open slightly. After Alex wrote on the electronic receipt, the bellhop said thanks and quickly left.

Bill looked at his cat. "Sheila, go get it!" She went out on the patio. "Alex, may we pray first?" He held out his hands, and she took them. "Master, please bless Alex and bless this food to our use, and our lives in your service, keeping in mind the needs of others, for the glory of God, and in the power of Jesus' name. Amen." Bill held Alex's chair for her before sitting down himself.

Alex gazed across the table at me with her famous blue eyes. "That was a wonderful surprise."

"What?"

"That was the first time that a man I've only just met has prayed with me for any reason. I'm a Christian, but I guess I'm not very good at living out my faith in Jesus."

"None of us is good enough to get into heaven without Jesus. If I ever get married again, my bride will have to be Christ-centered. Is your current boyfriend a Christian?"

"He says he is, but in the two years we've been dating, I've not known him to go to church, even for Christmas or Easter. Last Christmas, when I wanted him to go with me to church, he said he had other plans. Do you go to church pretty regularly?"

Bill nodded. "Most of the time. Obviously, I won't be in church this Sunday because Sheila and I will be out here." Hearing her name, my cat came in from the patio. She lay down between the sofa and the patio glass.

"Speaking of her, I want to ask you something, and if you say no, my feelings won't be hurt."

Bill smiled. "Do you want to go with us tomorrow?"

Her eyes got big. "How did you know?"

He put his hand on his chest. "I felt it here. You'll need a backpack and a bed roll. We can go shopping after we eat our pie. Let's not let our pie go to waste."

She smiled. "Of course not!"

At that moment, Bill realized that he was feeling warm around Alex, and his heart was beating a little faster. He had not felt that way since his Jody had gone on to heaven. Was he simply star-struck? He pondered that possibility, and he didn't think so. Somehow, he thought that if Jody had met Alex, they would have hit it off easily. Was God involved in this? He wouldn't be spending time with Alex if it weren't for Sheila.

Winterhaven is not a large community, but they had no difficulty in finding a backpack that she liked and a suitable bedroll to go with it. It was a little after ten when they got back to the hotel. As Bill walked her to her room's door and said good night, she gave him a very nice hug and a kiss on his cheek before going inside.

Bill thought he was walking a little lighter on his feet as he and Sheila went down the hall to his door. Before going to bed, he shaved and took a long and hot shower. Then, after leaving a wake-up call, he turned off the light. For a while, Sheila gazed out through the patio door glass. Then she went to the other bedroom and dozed.

4.
Adventures Begin

When Bill's wake-up call came on Saturday morning, he dressed fast and reheated food he had ordered the night before in his microwave. When he knocked on the door for Suite 8, Alex was ready to go. Just as Bill was, she was wearing her windbreaker for the early-morning chill. Although both were excited about the day ahead, neither of them was talkative at first, as they set out for a short drive upward into the hills. There was a parking lot carved out of the side of a hill next to the trail head. Bill had Sheila's leash in his backpack, but he decided not to use it.

He looked up at the sky. "The sun won't rise for another hour. I don't see any stars. I hope the weather holds." Their hike took them up and down, but mostly up, with Sheila leading without her leash. Whenever they rested, they drank a few sips of water and took pictures. When they came to a small creek, Sheila drank some, but not as much as Bill thought she would. After crossing the creek, they began climbing more and more. The Chocolate Mountains loomed ahead of them.

They had hazy sunshine when they began, but as the morning wore on, the haze became clouded, and the clouds got darker. When they stopped to get their breath, Alex sniffed the air. "I smell rain. I don't see any coming though. What do you think?"

Bill nodded. "I smell rain too. It may be coming from ahead of us, on the other side of this slope." He pointed ahead. "The trail seems to be going near that outcropping of rock. Let's focus on maybe getting some shelter there."

They began hiking more rapidly upward. They were within a few dozen yards of the outcrop of rock when they heard distant thunder. As they crossed a small stream to one side of them, Alex glanced at Bill. "That doesn't sound good! Let's move faster!" They were feeling the first few drops of rain, when they got under the rock. Their "shelter" was about a dozen feet wide and almost as deep. Alex and Bill ducked their heads and went deep into the space, but Sheila stopped just in far enough in to keep out of the rain. She turned, and she gazed out over the rocky terrain below.

They saw a few flashes of lightning in the distance, as the rain's volume increased. Bill knew Sheila was not hungry, but he and Alex broke out energy bars and drank from their canteens. They then got up to join Sheila to watch their environment. The stream they had crossed began to become a torrent on their right, and on their left, another stream began to flow.

Bill pointed. "It looks like there are some animals headed our way. I see a wild burro, ...a desert bighorn sheep, ...and there're a couple of coyotes."

"That wild burro is kind of cute!"

The coyotes started heading directly toward them when Sheila loudly announced her presence. "Rrooowwwllll!" When the coyotes saw her, they turned to bypass them while looking for shelter.

Alex put her arm around Sheila's neck. "Good job, Sheila!"

"Rowwl."

Bill studied the coyotes as they scampered away. "Most of them are the size of a small dog, but in packs they're very dangerous."

Alex nodded and pointed off to their left. "Do you have binoculars? That might be a flash flood!"

He reached into a pocket of his backpack. "They're ten power and stabilized. Just flip the little switch at the center and then turn it off when you're done." He handed them to her.

"Aren't you going to look?"

He nodded. "You go first."

She flipped the little switch and began to look. "This is just enough! Yes! It's a flash flood. I have no idea how to guess the depth, though." She handed them to him.

Bill gazed steadily for a couple of minutes. "I saw a bighorn scrambling to get out of the way." He took the glasses away from his eyes to look at Alex. "Based upon the typical bighorn size, those flash flood waters are about ten or eleven feet deep, at least right now. Their average size of a bighorn is about thirty-five inches high at their shoulder. They can weigh as much as three hundred pounds." He put the glasses back up to his eyes, looked for another minute, and he handed the binoculars back to her. "That flood is getting bigger. Look."

She looked. "Wow! I'm glad your SUV is parked part way up the hill! This is quite a cloudburst!"

They watched through the afternoon. From time to time, an animal might head toward them, but when they would see Sheila, they would detour around them. Later, as the daylight began to fade, Bill lit his alcohol stove he had carried, and he and Alex had dinner. Sheila hardly moved from her post. She remained lowered on her stomach unless other animals approached.

As it got darker, Bill lit an LED headlamp. "Let's lay out our bedrolls while we still have some light." He paused and looked at his pet. "Sheila, protect."

"Rowwl." It wasn't a soft response.

It did not take them long to roll things out and get inside. Alex leaned over close to Bill and kissed his cheek. "I trust Sheila, so I don't think I'll have any trouble getting to sleep, but if my parents could see me now, they'd just shake their heads and smile."

"Where are your parents?"

"They're in Crockett, Texas. My Dad's a pastor. I'm pretty tired, aren't you?"

"I must admit it. I am too! Good night!"

"Good night."

Bill slept soundly. The morning sun rose bright and clear, shining directly into their little shelter area. The air was cool, perfectly still, and smelled fresh. Sheila was still sitting in the same spot, and she looked over at him. "Rowwl."

"Good morning to you too, Sheila." He put his boots back on and stood up. Alex was shading her eyes, smiling, and looking at him. Bill grinned at her. "Good morning!"

"Good morning! And good morning to you too, Sheila!"

Sheila glanced back again at them. "Rowwl."

Bill walked toward Sheila's post. There were tufts of wool scatted just outside their shelter's opening. "It looks like you tangled with a bighorn last night, girl." Sheila walked over, sniffed at one of the tufts of wool, and then she stroked around him. "Good girl!" He gave her neck a hug.

Alex had gotten up and was standing nearby. "I didn't hear a thing! I must have slept through it!"

"I did too. Any fight would not have lasted long. The only animal in the state that might be a partial challenge to Sheila is a brown bear, but even they aren't really a match for her. You saw how the coyotes reacted yesterday to her snarl."

"What about the bighorn that ventured up here?"

Bill shook his head. "Bighorns are fearless. They weigh more than she does. A snarl wouldn't faze them. Evidently, Sheila had to get physical. A bighorn wouldn't stand a chance against her."

"She didn't kill it, did she?"

Bill shook his head. "I only told her to protect us." In the distance, Bill saw a helicopter. "Sheila, hide!"

His cat moved fast and disappeared into the shadows. As the copter got closer, Alex and Bill began waving. A voice called out. "Are you folks okay? Stop waving if everything is okay." They put their hands down. "Okay. For your safety, as soon as possible, make your way back to your car at the trail head." The helicopter flew off.

Bill gave Alex a hug and gazed at her. "If you don't mind rolling up our bedrolls, I'll fire up the alcohol stove and get some breakfast started. I'm sure the ice packs lasted through the night, but when the sun gets higher, it's probably going to be blazing hot out here!"

She reached up and gave him a quick peck on the lips, but he didn't let go. He gave her a long kiss, and then she spoke. "I'll get out the sunscreen too. We didn't need those little umbrellas yesterday, but I think we will today."

He nodded. They broke from their hug, and they went deeper back into their shelter. "Sheila, relax. Sandbox time if you want it."

"Rowwl." She trotted out of our shelter toward the creek.

It didn't take long to start the stove and start heating some water for coffee. "Alex, in my backpack there's a water filter. If you want to, you might go to the creek and filter some water into our canteens."

"Good idea! What's for breakfast?"

"Sausage links, biscuits with jam, coffee, and boxes of juice."

"That sounds simply **wonderful**."

He lit the stove. "How often do you see your parents in Texas?"

"I last saw them two Christmases ago. Crockett is a small town in East Texas, south of Tyler. Growing up, I loved going to the little movie theater. I think I decided I wanted to make movies before I went on my first date." She started toward the creek for water.

Although they were not at a particularly high altitude, they ate their breakfasts as though they hadn't eaten for days.

About a half-hour later, they started back down the trail, with Sheila taking the lead. Going down was somewhat easier and faster than their climb the day before, but they couldn't go too fast without losing their footing. They had been moving for only a few minutes when Alex pointed off to their right. "There are some people moving along that gully toward Winterhaven."

"I wonder if those people are sneaking across the border. They might also be locals." They watched them as they continued to move downward. They seemed to be about a mile away. Suddenly, they heard a gunshot, and a fraction of a second later, there was a ricochet off a nearby rock. "Take cover! Sheila! Hide!" Alex and Bill took shelter behind a boulder, but Sheila was nowhere to be seen. Suddenly, more shots were heard and much closer. Bullets were landing around them. "Sheila! Kill!"

They heard a couple of yells and a snarl. They waited. There was silence. They waited for what seemed like forever, but it was probably not more than two or three minutes. They heard Sheila's purr, and then she appeared nearby. "Rowwl." She came up and nuzzled them both.

"Good girl, Sheila!" Bill hugged her.

Alex then hugged her. "Are you okay, girl?" Sheila continued to purr and licked her cheek.

Bill stood up and looked into the distance. "Those people we saw are coming back together and are moving in the same direction toward Winterhaven."

Alex stood up and put her arms around him while they looked. "The shots probably frightened them, but they are getting back together. There must be about a dozen or so of them."

"Let's keep moving down the trail."

Alex nodded. "I agree. I don't need to see what Sheila did." She started following Sheila down the trail again, and Bill followed. They walked about three-quarters of an hour before they began to hear coyotes howling in the distance. Alex stopped and pointed. "Those howls seem to be coming from the area where we were when we were shot at." She turned and continued moving down the trail.

As Bill followed, he responded intermittently. "Let's not remember too specifically." He took several steps. "Let's remember the area where we ducked for cover when we heard the shots."

"Okay."

"Let's not mention Sheila unless someone reports seeing her, which I hope didn't happen. I don't want her getting notoriety. Even so, we did not see Sheila do anything."

"Agreed."

Bill took several more steps. "We can say that after a few minutes of silence, we decided it was safe and continued down the trail." He took several more steps. "Let's improvise and be creative. Keep the facts the same, but let's tell our stories a little differently if we're formally interviewed."

"Right." She paused to catch her breath. "I'm sure glad we had protection, but that was scary. I love this high desert scenery though. The cacti and lavender are beautiful, and the reds of the mesquite add nice splashes of color."

She stopped to drink from her canteen, and he stopped beside her. "You and me both!" He paused to look into her eyes. "I hope you're not afraid of our protection now."

Alex kissed him on the cheek. "Thank you for asking, but no. If anything, I'm even more fond of her."

Sheila had stopped, and she was looking back at them. She then pivoted, scanning all around them.

As Alex and Bill continued hiking downward, in the distance, they heard a helicopter. It hardly looked like more than a speck in the direction from which they had come. They also saw vultures circling.

They kept moving, stopping occasionally to drink from their canteens. Bill took a small bowl out of his backpack and poured some water into it. Sheila drank it eagerly. It was late morning when they reached the parking lot. There were several other cars, but they saw no other people.

As they put their backpacks in the trunk of Bill's SUV, they heard a car coming up the road. He looked at Sheila. "Hide." His cat would not have fitted under most cars, but his SUV had more clearance, and she quickly disappeared. A California Highway Patrol car appeared and stopped next to them. "Hello! I'm officer Phillips. Are you folks getting started on a hike, or are you returning?" Above one of his pockets was a CHP star, and above his other pocket, his shirt said Phillips.

Bill pointed. "Yesterday morning we left here and went up the trail. When it started raining, we took shelter under a slab of rock protruding from the hillside. A CHP helicopter hovered over us this morning, asked us if we were okay, and told us that we had better go back down. We just got back here a minute or two ago."

"Okay, did you see or hear anything unusual as you came down?" He looked at Alex. "Aren't you with that movie-making group in Winterhaven?"

Alex handled it perfectly. "Yes. Earlier this morning, we heard some shots seemingly rather close by. We took shelter behind a boulder, but after waiting several minutes, we decided to keep on moving down the hill."

Bill nodded. "About an hour later, maybe a little less, we heard coyotes howling, but other than that, nothing."

The officer scribbled in his notebook. "Did you see anyone else as you were coming down?"

Bill nodded. "We saw a small group of people, way down the hill, near the river, moving toward Winterhaven. We haven't seen them for over an hour now."

"Okay, thank you, folks. I need to see some identification for both of you for the record."

They showed them their driver's licenses. Bill then showed some natural curiosity. "Can you tell us anything about the shots we heard?"

Alex nodded. "Yes! We've been talking about it and wondering. Is it hunting season?"

Officer Phillips cocked his head. "We're not sure yet. There're two men's bodies now headed toward the coroner's office. They had rifles and pistols, so they might have been hunters. By the time we reached them, coyotes had already chewed on them some. One of the men had scratches on his face, like he might have tangled with a puma. It's just too soon to say for sure what happened."

Bill nodded. "We can understand that. Thank you." He went around and held Alex's door for her.

She said, "thank you" before she opened the sunroof.

Bill went around to the driver's side and opened the door. He looked down, and he could see Sheila gazing at him. "Wait."

She blinked. He looked toward the CHP car, and he watched as it went back down the road. As soon as it was out of sight, he said "Okay, Sheila."

She rapidly scooted out from under the SUV and got onto the driver's seat. She paused to let Alex stroke her face while she purred, and then the cat went into the back seat and settled down.

Bill started the engine and turned on the a/c. He looked at his beautiful friend. "Alex, I hope neither of us ever have an occasion to tell anyone that I gave Sheila the command to kill."

She leaned over and kissed him. "Is that what you did? My face was buried in your shoulder. I don't remember much of what happened." She smiled.

"Thank you."

She grinned. "Don't mention it!"

As they headed down the steep road, Bill shifted down into second gear. Alex put her hand on top of his. "This has been a truly amazing weekend. Yesterday and today, I have not missed the paparazzi one bit."

He nodded. "I've been surprised at not seeing much of that kind of activity."

"Out here in the desert, there're only a few. They were hanging around Friday afternoon when a friend in the cast named Dietra and I were talking about the weekend with no shooting until Monday. She said she was really looking forward to sleeping in. I told her that it sounded like a great idea. I did not lie and say I was sleeping in. You, Sheila, and I were driving out of the parking lot before dawn's early light. When I'm asked what I did over the weekend, I'll just say I took a hike with a friend. If I'm asked about my friend, I'll simply say he's an architect who rescued me from Interstate 8 when my car broke down. I won't give out your name, but one or two of them may track you down and ask you questions."

"I think I told you that the manager of the motel is a friend of mine. When he learned that I had rescued you, he asked me for my impression of you, and I simply told him that you seemed very nice and let it go at that."

"You've never pestered me with a lot of personal questions."

"I decided that you would tell me what you wanted me to know.""

"I'm glad you've treated me with that respect. I guard my privacy rather closely."

"I can easily cooperate with that. I don't tell everyone about Sheila, so few people beyond my church family are familiar with my private life. Like you, I also keep it separate from my professional life. May I ask where you maintain a home?"

"I have an apartment in Santa Maria. I hope you won't mind, but I wrote down my address and phone number on the back of one of your cards last night while you were sleeping. I left it in your wallet."

Bill glanced over at her smile. "Excellent!"

"I'm starving! How about we get room service again?"

He nodded. "I'm starving, too, but I'm already checked out from my suite. It will have to be your suite again."

"Okay. Now that we're on the outskirts of town, I'll warn you that we'll probably be greeted by the paparazzi."

He grinned at her. "I wonder what would happen if I have Sheila snarl at them?"

Alex laughed. "Yes! Please do! I'd like to see it!"

As they pulled into the motel's parking lot, Sheila stood up and put her head out of the sunroof. After Bill opened Alex's door, they went to the trunk and got their backpacks with bedrolls. Then Bill went to the back door and attached Sheila's leash. The cat knew her routine, so she hopped down and stood between them before he closed the door.

The paparazzi were approaching them, and he said, "Sheila, protect!"

"Rrooowwwllll!" Sheila crouched down as though ready to spring.

The paparazzi scattered, tripping and falling over each other as they ran. Alex and Bill laughed and started walking toward the doors of the main entrance. Sheila was purring. Inside, the air-conditioning was refreshing. Once again, they walked up the stairs with Sheila between them. They went to Alex's suite, as planned.

Even though Bill needed to get on the road back to San Diego, they lingered, relaxing over a good dinner. They talked, sharing a little about everything. Bill was already growing very fond of Alex.

At the door in the late afternoon, they had a lingering kiss. "I know you've got an early call after you review your lines for tomorrow. Leaving now, I'll be back in the city and home easily before midnight, even if I stop along the way to eat again." He looked at his watch.

She smiled. "I don't think either of us will ever forget this weekend. There are so many details I cannot share with others on the crew, but I'll manage. Where do you think you'll stop?"

"I'll probably stop somewhere along the El Centro area."

"I saw a sign for a *Famous Dave's* as I was driving through on Friday."

He nodded. "As chain restaurants go, those are pretty good. El Centro can be warm, even after the sun goes down. If necessary, I'll leave the engine running with the a/c going for Sheila. There're several roadside rests along the interstate. I'll stop at least once to let Sheila stretch her legs. I know a CHP officer in El Centro that I met several years ago. I always think about him and his partner whenever I drive through there. They got married and had to get new partners. I guess I actually know two patrol teams in that area."

"Have you designed any buildings in that vicinity?"

He nodded. "One of my first projects was designing that large truck stop you passed as you were leaving that area on your way to Winterhaven."

She put her arms around him. "I think you'd better get on the road, and I'd better start reviewing my lines for tomorrow morning. I hope to see you again soon!"

They kissed briefly. He stopped to hold her face in his hands. "I can hardly wait! Bye!"

"Bye!"

He and Sheila walked downstairs and into the lobby. Some of the paparazzi were standing on the far side of the area. One of them called out, "What kind of kind of a cat is that?"

Bill and Sheila stopped. "She's half puma and half cheetah."

The paparazzi stayed where they were. "When we approached earlier, that cat's snarl, well, I think it would scare just about anything in this state! How dangerous is it?"

Bill smiled. "She's only dangerous when it is necessary. Do you have any other questions?"

There was silence as they looked at each other. "I guess not, sir."

Bill nodded. "Good." He looked down at Sheila. "Heel."

"Rowwl." It was soft, and she was purring.

Bill and Sheila went through the door, and then out into the heat of Winterhaven. He pressed his remote start button to get the A/C started, and by the time he unlocked his car and loaded his backpack and bedroll, it was starting to cool off.

A few minutes later, they were traveling west at the speed limit on Interstate 8. Sheila curled up on the back seat and began to doze.

5.
Growing Together

El Centro felt like an oven, so he parked at *Famous Dave's* far from other cars in the lot. He left the engine and air conditioning running as he went into the restaurant. He got home well before midnight.

A month later, Bill took Sheila into see Dr. Stan for her "birthday" checkup. Sheila hopped up on the exam table without prompting. The vet smiled. "Good girl, Sheila. You're used to this place now, aren't you?" He listened to her heart and lungs, and then he examined her all over. "Hmmm. It looks like she has a small flesh wound here, but it is all healed over." Bill looked where the vet was touching her. Dr. Mounce said, "This is not an animal bite."

"Dr. Stan, I'll tell you a short story, if you'll promise me that you'll forget I told you as soon as we go out the door."

The vet hesitated. "You didn't do anything illegal did you?"

"I don't think having Sheila defend a friend and me would be considered illegal."

He nodded. "Okay. I promise. Let's hear it."

Bill summarized the weekend, and then he gave him more details.

"So, you didn't witness Sheila actually doing anything. You only heard some sounds. Our San Diego news outlets have not mentioned anything happening like that out in that area. My records will show only that Sheila is healthy at her checkup. I'll forget you gave that command. I wonder if she was responding to your emotions or to your command. There's no way of knowing."

Each of the days of the six weeks that followed, Alex and Bill had video calls between his house in the La Jolla suburb of San Diego and her apartment in Santa Maria. Then Alex had to go to France to play a supporting role in a movie. She was supposed to be there about a month. Bill began to see on the Internet and on newscasts reports of romance between Alex and the male lead in the movie. They continued their video calls after she left, usually on Saturday nights, when it was early evening for Bill and late at night for Alex. Bill remained upbeat, as with all their calls. "According to the gossip rags, you and Paul Peterson are having quite a romance both on and off the set."

She scowled. "Off the set too? I warned you, remember?" She was thoughtful. "Paul and I are scheduled for an interview tomorrow morning, so I won't get to a worship service if it runs long. Paul is happily married, and his wife is on the set part of the time. We'll simply say that if the media want our continued cooperation, they will ignore the trolls, just as we both do."

"I've ignored the trolls for years. Have you found an English-speaking church where you can worship?"

Alex nodded. "I think so. I'll try it the first-time tomorrow if time allows. They're some kind of Evangelical mission church. I talked to the pastor, and he said that typically they had 65-70 there on Sunday mornings. He also said that they have a strategy for dealing with the paparazzi. I hope it works. Those animals are relentless and merciless over here – even more so than in the U.S."

Bill smiled. "I know it's late where you are. I don't want the makeup artist to have to cover up the bags under your eyes tomorrow morning. Sheila wants to say hi." He turned the camera so that Alex could see her.

"Hi Sheila!"

"Rowwl."

"I love your orange eyes, girl, and I love your master's eyes too."

"I love you, Alex, and that surprises me."

Her eyes got big. "I love you too, Bill. It's hard to believe it is true, but it is." A tear rolled down her cheek. "It'll be at least a month before we can say it in person."

"I know. Maybe I'll have to fly over there to Versailles next weekend!"

"Are you serious?"

Bill nodded. "I can give my neighbors, Abby and Ralph, a spare key. They can look in on Sheila each day and keep an eye on things. I trust them."

"Okay. I'll reserve a suite for you and text a flight number and the name of the hotel."

"Great! This is exciting, Alex, but you don't have to pay for the flights. I can handle it. It's been eight years since I've been over there."

"Were you here with Jody?"

Bill nodded. "We toured Paris just before she was diagnosed with her breast cancer. You'd better get some sleep. I'll see you Friday. Bye."

"Bye, my love!"

They ended the call.

On Monday evening, Bill used Duck-Duck-Go to search the Internet for the video interview with Alex and Paul. Most of the interview was about the movie and its plot. At the end of the interview, the Frenchman doing the interview asked them about their relationship. Paul Peterson glanced at Alex before responding. "My wife, Sarah, loves spending time on the set with us. We've also been like the three musketeers, exploring this magical city. If the media want Alex and I to continue to be cooperative with them as we have been with you this morning, they will have to ignore the trolls and their poison."

Alex nodded. "Both of us keep our personal lives separate from our professional lives. We are friends, but we are *not* 'friends with benefits.'"

Paul shook his head. "Sarah would kill both of us if I cheated on her. She says that trolls are simply pathetic creatures who have no quality relationships of their own, so they attack the lives and relationships of others."

The interview ended with that. When they were no longer on camera, Bill turned on the news. Seeing nothing that could interest him after talking with Alex, he turned everything off and headed toward his study to work. Sheila scampered up her pole and stretched out on one of the rafters. She was now larger than the average cheetah or a puma. Her vet recorded her weight at just under two hundred pounds.

In his study, Bill had a project that was developing nicely. Several months earlier, he was asked to design a house for an acreage on the side of a mountain overlooking the Los Angeles basin. On the walls of his study, he had pictures of the property. On a large table, he had survey maps of the property and geological assessments of the underlying land. It was a complicated and challenging project, and the owner had given him a 25% down payment for his work. The owner said that the land was almost paid for.

Before Bill met Alex, he had submitted preliminary drawings after going to the site and taking measurements. In that day's mail a large envelope arrived, with the return address being the current address of the owner. He slit the envelope open and quickly scanned the letter. Then he read it again more carefully. He approved the plans. "*I've got my work cut out for me,*" Bill murmured to himself softly. He began reviewing all his data.

The next morning, there was a text for him from Alex.

♥ ♥ ♥ AA flight leaves Thursday afternoon for Waldorf Astoria Trianon Palace Versailles. See you Friday! Love! ♥ ♥ ♥

Bill was stunned. He told her he could pay his airfare. Was he ready for this? He wasn't sure, but he knew he was falling in love with Alex. There were men in many countries vying for her attention. He needed to go to the church and pray. Was this God's doing?

He continued the work he had begun the night before on the plans for the house on the Angeles Crest Highway. The land alone was worth several million. The completed project would be a landmark. With more than one earthquake fault nearby, he was going to employ some innovations to make the house safe and secure on the mountain side with anchors deeply embedded in the mountain. He went to the church to pray for an hour at noon. He thanked God for the gifts that had been coming his way. After picking up a hamburger to take home, he went back to his project, eating as he worked. He ordered a large pizza for dinner, and he worked well past midnight. When Bill turned off the light, Sheila was stretched out on a rafter in the great room, purring.

It became his routine through Thursday morning. With working furiously fast twenty or more hours a day, Bill printed out his first set of blueprints. Putting them in a large tube, along with electronic copies on a thumb drive, he would mail it to the Los Angeles County Planning Department at the Post Office on his way to the Los Angeles airport.

Bill stopped to see his neighbor, Abby. Handing her his spare key, he smiled and said, "This is simply a short visit with a dear friend. I'll be back on Monday."

Abby nodded. "Ralph and I have watched your house before. Have fun!"

Since he was just going for the weekend, it did not take him long to pack. Alex's manager had booked him on an eleven-hour business-class flight, and he was staying at a very expensive hotel. After saying goodbye to Sheila, he headed to the Los Angeles Airport. The overseas flight was mostly boring, and he slept for nine hours of the flight. After he went through customs in Paris, there was a teenage redhead holding a sign with his name it. He approached her. "I'm Bill Johnson."

"Oui, monsieur. You look just like the pictures on Alex's phone. We have a studio limo waiting. Your entire trip is being paid for by the studio because Alex is asking you to consult with the set designer for a problem we're having." She took his carry-on and started walking. Bill followed. His mouth must have been hanging open when she glanced at him. "Oui, monsieur, she said you would be surprised. Don't worry. Our driver will take us to the set first. You can watch mademoiselle Alex work for a while, and then the two of you have the weekend. The hotel has excellent security, so you two will not be bothered by the..." She hesitated. "Yes! You will not be bothered by the paparazzi. Yes. I must choose my English words carefully. I do not want to offend."

Bill smiled. "You are doing just fine, thank you. What is your name?"

"Oh! Pardon! I did not introduce myself. I am Noël."

"Thank you. It is nice to meet you, Noël."

The ride from the airport was not long. The limo drove past a guard, and a moment later, Alex greeted him. They hugged at least thirty seconds. "I'm so glad you're here! I hope that Noël told you that we have a little problem that maybe you can figure out for us."

Bill grinned at her. "It's a blessing to see you and hear your voice." He kissed her on the forehead, and she gave him a shy grin. "Let's see this problem of yours."

A man approached them, and she introduced him. "Bill, this is Steve Leone, our director."

"Hello, Steve. It's good to meet you. What's this problem I've been hearing about?"

"It's good to meet you too. Our set designer is stumped, and under most circumstances, there's no one better than he is in our industry." They stepped into a mostly dark sound studio. Steve walked towards a set, where several people were talking. "Here he is…. Logan, this is Alex's boyfriend, Bill Johnson, who is an architect. Show him what we're struggling with."

"Sure! It's good to meet you. I hope you can help. Follow me."

"I hope I can help too."

As they walked onto the set, Logan talked rapidly. "It is a matter of synchronizing a trap door with a regular door." I've got a great assortment of latches and releases. I've also got first-rate electronics. The trouble is, it just won't work in a way that is safe for the actor and still works convincingly for the camera. Here."

They came to the problem area. Bill watched and listened carefully as Logan explained what was supposed to happen. Then Logan showed him what was happening instead. He also triggered it twice to demonstrate it. The second time, Bill held up his hand. "Okay, I've got it. You are a brilliant designer, Logan, but you've outfoxed yourself."

"Huh? What do you mean?"

"You've made it more complicated than it needs to be. Is there a carpenter handy?"

"Sure!" He motioned to a woman wearing a utility belt with some tools. "This is Andrea. Tell her what you have in mind."

"Bonjour."

"Bonjour. Andrea, as I just told Logan, he's made it too complicated. Take that latch," Bill pointed, "and mount it here on the back side of the door, with the catch on the jamb like this…." With her doing things while Bill told her, it took them about fifteen minutes to reconfigure it. Bill took some yellow chalk and put an 'x' on the trap door. "Who is the actor who is going through the trap door?"

"I am." It was Paul, the man Bill had seen with Alex on television.

"Hi, Paul, I recognize you from your interview earlier this week with Alex." Bill pointed. "As you walk towards the door that you expect to open automatically, that mark is your target point. When you reach it, the trap door will open at the same time the door does, and you'll land on the cushions down below. Got it?"

"Got it."

Bill turned. "Steve, it is ready."

His eyebrows went up. "Thank you! I thought fixing this might take several days! I think we can get back on schedule by the end of the coming week. The studio is paying for your trip out of the budget for the movie. You'll be listed in the credits as a consultant."

Bill smiled. "Thank you."

The mechanism worked the first time, but they did six takes. Paul seemed to enjoy each take.

Bill watched Alex as she shot two more scenes, and then it was a wrap for the week.

After the limo took them to his hotel, as soon as the bellhop left and closed the door, Alex and Bill had a long and lingering kiss. He looked into her eyes. "Wouldn't it have been embarrassing for you if I had not figured out how to fix that problem?"

She smiled and hugged him again. "Maybe it would have been a little embarrassing, but it eventually would have been fixed, though not so quickly."

He nodded. "Logan seems pretty smart. My body's clock says it is early morning, not evening. I'm hungry. Are you?"

After lingering over dinner at a restaurant in the hotel, they took a tour of the city. The paparazzi did not know that Alex was at his hotel, and there were none to follow them around. They continued to enjoy the city the next day. While they took in the sites, Bill told Alex about the house he had designed. Despite their frequent video calls, they had plenty to talk about.

One taxi driver recognized her and tried to strike up a conversation. When Alex tipped him generously, his eyes grew wider. He thanked her profusely, and the conversation ended abruptly when she said good-bye and closed the door. She winked at Bill.

Worshiping together on Sunday morning was satisfying for both. Alex has a beautiful voice, so Bill enjoyed singing with her as they stood side by side. There were a few paparazzi when they got back to Bill's hotel, but the staff handled them with no problems. Altogether, they made the most of the weekend. They knew that they would not be together again for at least six to seven more weeks.

Flying west on Monday morning, Bill slept for almost nine hours again, but because of the time difference being the reverse of the previous flight, he left at 10:00 AM and arrived at 12:30 PM. He was ready for lunch.

He stopped at his church on his way home and went inside to pray. Before he went into the worship area, Pastor Ewart approached him. "I saw you drive up, Bill. I missed you yesterday."

He smiled. "I was in Paris."

His eyes grew wide. "France?"

He nodded. "Yes. A few months ago, I met a woman while I was taking Sheila to Winterhaven, east of here. Just between you and me, we hit it off, and things are beginning to get serious. She is shooting a movie in France for a few weeks, and she used my skills to help with a problem they were having on the set. It was great to see her in person rather than on a video call."

"So, she is an actress?"

Bill nodded. "Yes. She's playing a supporting role in this movie, which will come out next year. She'll be back in the United States in six or seven weeks."

"Has she met Sheila?"

Bill laughed. "Has she! They met on my weekend trip to Winterhaven. They're great pals."

"Interesting! I'll be even more interested if this develops into something more."

Bill nodded. "I'm beginning to think it might." He paused. "Before I go on home to work, I have been wanting to pray for a while. She and I worshiped together in Paris yesterday morning. I've intentionally not told you her name yet. I'll ask her about that during our next video call."

"So, she's famous?"

He nodded. "Definitely. We had a few interesting encounters with the paparazzi, but I don't think you'll see pictures of us together locally —at least not for a while."

Pastor Ewart and Bill said their farewells, and Bill went in and prayed. *Was Sheila one of God's special gifts? Was Alex?*

When Bill got home, Sheila was excited very attentive as she purred. He talked to her for a while, stroking her, and then he went into his office. She curled up in a nearby corner of the office while he worked.

The next morning, Bill got a call from the Los Angeles County planning office. They said his plans were approved, subject to some minor modifications. He told them he would put the changes in the mail in a few days, and he did so. Little did he know at the time, but trouble was brewing. On Friday, the lawyer of the owner of the mountain side property called him and informed him that his client was declaring bankruptcy. The project could not go forward at that time! Bill was floored!

He called his lawyer, Gloria Houser, and he told her about the call from the owner's lawyer.

"I'm glad you called me. I can get started on it this morning." Then she said something that startled him. "Bill, there's a possibility that this may turn out better for you than if you had completed the project and collected all of your fees."

"Really? How so?"

"We will have to go to bankruptcy court to get justice. We will argue that this project would have established you as a major architect in Los Angeles County and the rest of Southern California. We will point out to the court that your fully approved plans include innovative designs that would have possibly given you national prominence in your field. We can also argue that the bank can easily write off all or part of the mortgage against the property. Even after I get my percentage, you may well come out very happy with this."

Bill felt more than relieved. "Wow! This just might turn out to be even more profitable than I anticipated!"

6.
Growing Closer

Alex's production in France required another five months. They talked every weekend. The Saturday after Bill got back from Paris, he told her about the bankruptcy and what might happen. Whenever they talked, he did so on the video phone so that Sheila could see Alex and hear her voice. As soon as Sheila saw Alex, she started to purr. Bill had no idea what Sheila was thinking when she could see an image of Alex and hear her voice, while she could not smell her or sense her in any way, but evidently, seeing Alex made Sheila happy. She purred steadily whenever she saw Alex.

Two weeks after he returned from France, Bill decided to go up and re-examine the property on Angeles Crest Highway. Deciding to make it a weekend, he put a rooftop sleeping enclosure on his SUV with his bedroll inside. He took Sheila with him, leaving late Friday afternoon, and he drove into Joshua Tree National Park. They arrived after the entrance station was closed for the day. He found a deserted place to camp, built a campfire, and had dinner. When he was ready to go to sleep, he spoke to Sheila. "Hide and protect, girl."

"Rowwl."

They weren't disturbed, and Bill slept soundly. He got up before dawn and drove back out of the park before the entrance station opened. He stopped at a fast-food outlet to have breakfast, leaving Sheila in the SUV with the sunroof open.

It had not reached mid-morning when Bill parked behind and under a tree on the property where he still planned to build – at least for someone.

The tree under which he parked appeared to be a rather old silver maple. Looking up into the branches, he asked, "Sheila, would you like to climb up?"

"Rowwl." She went up over a dozen feet and went out onto a large branch. She made herself comfortable. "Rowwl."

Going to his glove compartment, Bill grabbed his hand-held laser distance measurer. It was his favorite survey tool. He started exploring the property, taking measurements and sending the readings to his cell phone. He had done all of this before, but he wanted to double-check all his measurements. Up the hill on the other side of the road, he could see a few coyotes feeding on something. He pointed his laser tool in that direction, and they were about 65 yards away.

He could see a utilities tower about a quarter of a mile away, down below the property. He decided to bring the electricity, cable, and phone line underground from there to the house. He would email his decision to the county planning department. During the time he was there, cars and a couple of trucks went by, but none of them slowed down or showed any interest. There was no way they could see Sheila up among the leaves and branches of the maple tree.

It was getting close to noon when he decided that he had done enough and went back to his SUV. He opened the back door. "It's time to go, Sheila." She leaped down and landed about ten feet away. Without a sound, she went into the back seat, and Bill closed the door.

As he turned around, he looked again in the direction where he had seen the coyotes. They were gone. Going back south to San Diego, he didn't stop because he wasn't hungry.

After getting home, Bill went into the kitchen. He laid his phone on the counter, and he noticed that he had a text message from Alex.

> ♥ ♥ ♥Just got in. I'm at the Hilton Garden. Casting call tomorrow AM. I will come south to you tomorrow evening. Love, Alex. ♥ ♥ ♥

He saved it.

He smiled while he fixed some dinner. "Sheila, are you hungry?" There was no answer, so he went into the great room and looked up. "Are you hungry?" She blinked.

"Rowwl." She didn't move, so she wasn't hungry. She probably ate on the night they were in Joshua Tree.

In his study later, he checked all his previous measurements of the Angeles Crest property. He added the addition of the distance to the utilities' tower. With Sheila on watch, Bill went up to his bedroom at about 10:00 PM, and he slept soundly.

Bill had no way of knowing what time Alex would get to the house, so he fixed a big breakfast. He had no appointments that

Monday, and he had plenty to do at home. The doorbell rang at about 4:30. When he opened the door, Alex had suitcases in both hands, and cars were pulling up across the street. Paparazzi!

Her eyes were wide. "Please let me in! Quick!"

When Bill saw those vultures chasing her, it made him angry. After closing the door, he turned. She was on her knees, greeting Sheila. Bill's cat was purring and nuzzling her. He relaxed a little. He realized that Alex possibly didn't know that she was being followed. He decided silently, *'Okay. We'll talk about it later.'*

Alex stood up and gazed at him. "I'm so sorry! I didn't realize that anyone was following me. I guess I just didn't think. I'm not sure why." She approached him, and they passionately kissed for a few minutes.

When they broke, he spoke more calmly than he felt. "Sheila and I need to speak to our unwanted guests outside. I can see shadows on the windows by the door." Bill smiled half-heartedly. "I'm going to tell our guests who is in charge." He looked down at Sheila, who was staring at the door. "Sheila."

"Rowwl." She looked at him.

"Heal."

"Rowwl."

When Bill opened the door, Alex had gone to the kitchen. At first, there was a chorus of voices, all talking at once.

Bill touched Sheila's head. "Rrooowwwllll!"

Bill spoke forcefully. "My cat is telling you to **SHUT-UP!** Listen to me carefully, all of you." Someone started to speak. "**SHUT-UP!** As I started to say, my cat is responsible for security. She is licensed, and the police know her capabilities. She is half cheetah. It looks like there's about a dozen of you. **You are nothing** to her. She's so fast and powerful she can make all of you ready to be taken away in ambulances so fast, you would hardly see her moving. If any of you are smart enough to comprehend what I am telling you, just silently nod your head." They all nodded.

"This lady came here for safety and rest. We happen to be friends. We are not friends with benefits. I am going to see to it that she has that safety and that rest. My cat patrols my property. She is faster, stronger, and deadlier if necessary than any other animal you can see in this state outside of a zoo. If you get too close to my house or do anything to trigger her defense training, you will wake up in an ambulance. She doesn't kill unless she is forced to do so. Is that clear?" They nodded. "My friend will be here for as long as she needs to be. You're not going to know anything else right now. I'm ordering you off my property. If you leave quietly, I won't call the police at this time." He turned and went back inside with Sheila.

Alex was smiling. "I think you put the fear of God into them – or at least the fear of Sheila!"

Bill started nodding when Sheila trotted past them toward his study. He shook his head. "I guess someone is trying to get through the gate between my house and Ralph and Abby's." Bill went into the great room. "Sheila?" He opened his patio door. "Protect!"

"Rowwl." She was off in a blur. A moment later, they heard "Rrooowwwllll!"

"Okay! Okay! We're leaving!" The voices sounded genuinely frightened.

A moment later, Alex and Bill heard Ralph talking with them, but could not make out what he was saying. Bill left the door ajar enough so that Sheila could come back in. They went to the front door windows and looked through the curtains. The paparazzi were talking with one another as they went toward their vehicles. In a few minutes, it appeared as though all of them left.

"Rowwl." Bill and Alex turned, and Sheila was coming in the patio door. She went up her pole into the rafters.

They went into the great room and sat on the sofa. "Again, I want to apologize, Bill. I am so sorry! The casting call went well. Afterwards, as I was leaving the building, someone I would rather not name approached me and didn't treat me with the respect that I expect. I decked him."

Bill grinned. "You decked him?"

"Yeah, I don't do that very often. I had some martial arts training a few years ago as prep for a movie." She paused. "Anyway, my mind was on all that had transpired that morning, and I don't think I even checked my rearview mirror as I was driving south on I-5. I promise I won't make that mistake again."

Bill nodded. "Okay. Apology accepted. Are you hungry?"

"Let's relax and catch up first, okay?"

"Okay. Tell me more about the casting call if you want to."

"I want to. The day we met, I told you that the producers were wanting to do a movie franchise based upon *The Gaardian Saga*."

"Right. I remember."

"Well, this casting call was for another pilot or teaser, but based upon another part of the saga."

"Really! I've never seen anything in the news or on the Internet showing what you shot down there at Winterhaven."

"I know. I got paid, though. I've agreed to do this, and this time the shoot will last at least three months, possibly longer, starting next month. I'm glad I'm available. I did not tell you much about that shoot in Winterhaven because our contracts involve stringent non-disclosure specifications. The same restrictions apply this time. This is the seventh project like this that I've done over the last four and a half years."

"Wow!" Bill paused. "I'm going to have to read that book. Maybe I will while you're on this three-month shoot. Where will this one be?"

"Burbank, because it is all going to be done in a huge sound studio with a closed set. I suppose I'll be able to drive down here on weekends."

Bill nodded. "We can do that some of the time, and for others I can drive up there if there's an event we want to go to together. I wasn't in church yesterday because Sheila and I went out on an adventure."

"Really! Where?"

It took him about fifteen minutes to tell her all about the weekend. Then he stopped. "If I call for pizza, it will take about fifteen or twenty minutes. Are you ready to eat?"

"Absolutely. Also, I've got to say something. You're definitely not like other men I've dated since I graduated from Cal-Tech or even from high school."

Bill took out his phone. "Hold that thought, okay? We've not ordered pizza for us before, although I have an account with a place not far from here. What do you like?"

She grinned. "The only thing I don't like on pizza is anchovies. I have liked just about any other pizza I've ever been offered."

Bill touched a listing in his phone directory. "Hi. This is Bill Johnson. Yes, that's right, on Faculty. How busy are you?" He paused. "Thirty minutes? Okay, I want a large pizza-master salad, a large Hawaiian pizza, and a large one with everything but anchovies. We don't need beverages. Put it on my account." He paused as the order was read back to him. "Right. Thank you." He ended the call.

"You were saying that you graduated from Cal-Tech. What field?"

"Mechanical engineering was my focus. It is not on my resume. Only a few people in my industry know I have that background."

"Okay. You were going to tell me why I'm different than others you've dated."

"Yes. We're both Christians, for one thing. How Biblically literate are you?"

Bill's mouth dropped open. "No one has ever asked me that. I read a few chapters of the Bible every morning before I get out of bed. I don't always read it slowly for full comprehension, and if I have a busy day ahead, I may not pray as much as I should. How about you?"

"If I'm not memorizing lines for the coming day, I usually read a couple of chapters. I am asking you because I'm wondering if you're familiar with the first half of Jeremiah 1:5."

"It's a verse I memorized in church school when I was very young. It says, 'Before I formed you in the womb, I knew you, and before you were born, I consecrated you...'"

"Okay. You're the only man I've ever met who seems to have an interest in the Alexandra that God knew before I was conceived."

Suddenly, Bill saw past times with Alex altogether. He saw God at work. He knew for certain at that moment that they were falling in love. Bill looked into her eyes. "Do you think maybe God has prepared us for each other and set us up?"

Her lips parted. "We've a lot to pray about, don't we? When I was stranded that day on Interstate 8, it was my curiosity about

Sheila that drew me toward your car. The first time I touched her fur, I bonded emotionally with her, like falling in love, and she seemed to show affection for me."

"Rowwl." Sheila could be heard purring strongly.

Bill wondered silently: *Did Sheila have insight that he didn't?* Alex and Bill looked up toward the rafters and their mutual friend. "Maybe God has used Sheila as our matchmaker." Alex snuggled closer to him.

It was late when they headed upstairs. He put Alex's suitcase on the bench seat at the dresser in what he had made into a guest room. It was his late-wife Jody's dresser. He had furnished the room with some of Jody's things that he had not been able to discard.

Alex smiled. "Have you been expecting me?"

Bill winked at her. "Maybe subconsciously I have. I have a little present for you." He opened Jody's jewelry box and took out a jeweled cross. "I gave this to my Mom when I was eleven years old. She wore it frequently until they moved north. After I got engaged to Jody, Mom gave it to her. Jody wore it frequently up until she died." He held it out to Alex. "Does it appeal to you?"

Her eyes grew wide. "Does it?!" She took it, put it around her neck, and fastened the clasp. "It's wonderful!" She wrapped her arms around him, and they kissed.

Bill looked over at the guest room bed. "Are those enough pillows for you?"

"Sure!"

He pointed to another doorway. "Your bathroom is through there. This guest room suite is smaller than the master suite, but it does have a wet room with a whirlpool bath. I've already put towels out. Help yourself to any toiletries you need. It's late. My first alarm goes off at five, and that's when I start reading the Bible and praying."

"May I join you?"

Bill smiled. "Sure! If you're going to join me though, let's get dressed first and go down to the great room. We can have coffee or tea as we worship. Actually, I don't have to get up at 5:00. Let's wait until 6:00, if you're going to join me."

"Okay. Good night."

"Good night."

Down in the great room, Sheila was stretched out on one of the rafters. She was purring.

7.
Next Steps

They spent over an hour the next morning reading the Bible, praying, and discussing what they read. Toward the end of that time together, Alex was leaning against the arm of the sofa, with her legs tucked under her, and having a pillow in her lap. "When I was in Paris, we told each other we loved each other. If we were to get married, Bill, there are some things I would have to get used to."

"Are you going to chew me out when I forget to put the toilet seat back down?" He smiled.

She shook her head. "I don't think so. It's just that I now realize that living out my Christian faith in a Biblical way is going to be a challenge."

"It is for everyone."

"I mean, …I understand that in a Christian marriage, the man is supposed to be the leader of the family."

Bill shook his head with a half-smile. "I'm not a dictator."

Alex nodded. "I know, but even if we didn't have children, I would have to think of both of us in my decisions – as a family. I guess you would too, but I don't think it is the same."

He nodded. "In a course I took once, I learned that full-fledged Christian manhood means shunning passivity, accepting responsibility, leading courageously, and looking toward the greater reward." She cocked her head slightly as he went on. "It was all in the context of Jesus saying to each of us to take up our own cross and follow Him first of all."

She nodded. "I understand that, but like I said last night, you're the first man I've known that takes those responsibilities seriously. When those shots were fired in the chocolate mountains, you didn't hesitate to take control of the situation. I think that's when I decided I was willing to spend the rest of my life with you. That was almost as scary as the bullets landing around us."

Bill was then more serious. "So, if we were to get married, how long do you think it would take to put together the wedding you've been planning for since you were a little girl?"

She shook her head vigorously. "Don't assume that! Don't! I'm telling you that I'm seeing the world differently now since meeting you!"

She paused and looked straight into his eyes. "I know this sounds crazy, and it is truly scary, but I'm ready to merge my life with yours and start living our lives together as soon as you're willing."

Bill's mouth dropped open. Above them, Bill heard Sheila softly respond, "Rowwl."

Alex looked up and nodded. "I knew from the beginning that you are not like any of the lust-controlled men I've ever dated. By the time you turned off your LED headlamp in the darkness of our rock shelter, I realized I could not assume anything about you except that you are a brilliant, honorable, and Christ-centered gentleman."

Bill was stunned. "You knew a lot! I'm sorry! I did not know that much about you until we were in Paris."

She shook her head. "You don't need to apologize to me. All you could possibly know is what my publicist puts out. Being a celebrity entertainer, I tend to close myself off to protect myself from getting emotionally and spiritually hurt – if not physically hurt. When we got back to the parking lot after spending the night on the mountain, I made a conscious decision to be open with you and to trust you. I've been working on doing that ever since."

"It seems strange to me also, the fact that it seems like we know one another as well as I knew Jody – perhaps better."

There was another soft "Rowwl" from above.

Alex nodded. "Getting back to what we were talking about a few minutes ago," she gulped. "I'm ready to throw all of my wedding plans out. I'm reading to elope if you are."

Bill was completely floored. He glanced upward into Sheila's orange eyes. Bill's eyes must have been huge at that moment. He took a deep breath. "I'm ready to elope with you also, but... would you mind if I invite my pastor and his wife over to join us for dinner this evening?"

She smiled. "This is a great idea! Will you let me cook our dinner?"

He grinned. "Do you really want to?"

"Yes! I want to show you that your future bride can cook! We've always eaten out or ordered in!"

He nodded. "Okay. Let's check the fridge and see if we have what you need, and if not, I'll go shopping."

Little did he know! Alex gave him a shopping list, and rather than call it in and have the groceries delivered, he made a quick trip to the grocery store. He saw two of the paparazzi that he had seen previously, but they kept their distance. Back at his house, Bill gave the groceries to Alex and went to his study to work. Sheila seemed to remain sound asleep in the rafters of the great room. If they had stopped to listen, however, they might have heard her purring.

Amazing aromas began to come from the kitchen. Bill learned later that, when Sheila went into the kitchen, purring, Alex went to the fridge, got a roast, and put it in Sheila's dish. They knew each other.

He answered the doorbell when it rang and greeted the Scotts. "Good evening! I'm glad the two of you were available this evening!"

Rachel sniffed. "Good evening. My nose tells me I should go into the kitchen and see if I can help."

Pastor Ewart and Bill shook hands. "Whatever that aroma is, Bill, it smells wonderful."

Bill smiled. "Alex has been doing her thing for a couple of hours in there. I've been working in my study."

"Rowwl." They looked down, and Sheila was stroking around Pastor Ewart's legs.

"Good evening, Sheila! It's good to see you too!" As they started toward the great room, the pastor continued. "Is this the same Alex that you mentioned a few months ago?"

Bill nodded. 'Yes, it's past time that you and Rachel meet her. Now Rachel has introduced herself to her. You'll meet her in a few minutes."

"This was a last-minute invitation. Need I ask what the occasion is?"

Bill shook my head. "We'll explain it all over dinner to you."

Coming out of the laundry room, Sheila walked towards the treadmill and got on. Immediately, she began running, first at a trot, but then, quicker and faster. Bill had seen her do it countless times, but Pastor Ewart watched, fascinated. "Sheila is amazing, Bill. How often does she do this?"

"She runs two or three times a day. I've not been able to figure out if there is a pattern to her exercise. It seems to be spontaneous on her part, and she seems to enjoy it. Sometimes she runs for just two or three minutes, and other times she'll run for five, six, or even ten minutes."

The cat slowed down, hopped off the treadmill, and scampered up her climbing pole into the rafters. Within a minute, she closed her eyes.

"Come and get it, men!" Alex called out. "Dinner is ready."

They went to the table. "Alex, you've met Rachel. This is Pastor Ewart."

"It's nice to meet you at last, Pastor."

"It's nice to meet you too, Alex. Bill told me about meeting you some time ago, and I'm delighted to meet you finally."

"Thank you. Shall we sit down?"

Pastor Ewart and Bill held the chairs for the ladies. They sat down to salads at each of their places. There were also covered dishes down the center of the table. Alex and Bill held out their hands to hold the hands of the others. "Let's pray. Heavenly father, all praise and glory belong to you. We're grateful for how you bless all of us far more than we deserve. Please bless this food, and strengthen the relationships we have here, we ask in the name of your son, Jesus. Amen."

"Amen!" was the chorus around the table. They began eating.

Rachel looked at him. "Bill, you certainly have a well-equipped kitchen. I think you're the only man I've met that has a walk-in fridge and freezer. Did you pick out these dishes?"

He swallowed and shook his head. "No, this is the fine china that I received from my parents. In Alaska, they don't need it. I did choose the daily dishes, though. I'm glad that Alex found the sterling. I simply turned her loose in the kitchen this afternoon. I've not eaten with these in years. The sterling and china together bring back memories. I'm glad you found them. Jody wanted a big house, and that meant a big kitchen."

Alex looked up from her salad and smiled. "As I was exploring the kitchen, I found the daily ware easily, and when I found the china, I had to search for the sterling because I figured there had to be better silverware to go with the china. Your mom has great taste, doesn't she?"

He nodded. "Yes, she does."

Alex pointed. "If everyone will put their salad plates aside, we'll get to the main course."

Pastor Ewart and Bill lifted the lids. Alex got up, took the lids and put them on the counter. As she sat down, she explained. "This is sweet and zesty pork loin. The recipe is passed down through my mom's side of the family. On that side of my family, my forebears had a plantation in Western Pennsylvania long ago. After the Civil War, the plantation's land was given to launch Bethany College in what is now West Virginia. The family's mansion, graveyard, and meeting house are historical landmarks."

Pastor Ewart nodded. "So, on your mother's side, you're descended from the Campbells."

She nodded. "I'm surprised you know that part of our nation's history – or Bethany College's history."

The pastor swallowed and sipped some water. "I'm Scottish, and the Campbells were Scottish Presbyterian." He paused. "So, what's the occasion of this fantastic dinner?"

Rachel stopped eating and smiled. "Yes, we've been wondering about this last-minute dinner all afternoon."

Bill put his fork down. "Last evening, as we were talking, we decided to get married."

Pastor Ewart paused. "Wonderful!"

Rachel nodded. "Yes! Have you set a date?"

Alex had a shy smile on her face. "Bill asked me when I wanted to have the wedding I've been planning since I was a little girl. Amid a mild argument, it was very clear to me that I was ready to scrap all my plans and merge our lives into a shared family right away. Bill was a bit shocked, I think."

"I think I would prefer to say I was startled."

She nodded. "Okay. Anyway, when I mentioned the possibility of eloping, he suggested that we invite the two of you over for dinner, so the four of us can discuss the pros and cons of eloping. I volunteered to cook dinner. The thing is, trying to work on a full-blown wedding with all the preparations involved could be a nightmare for me. I have a very busy life, where I'm here one week, and gone for a month. I could be here for six months, without a call, and then must leave on a day's notice. Bill's been putting up with that as my boyfriend. Now I want him to come home to, and not just platonically. I don't want to sleep in the guest room when I come home to him."

Bill winked. "I hope not!"

Pastor Ewart nodded. "Alex, I can see Jesus in your face, so I know that you are just as Christ-centered as Bill is. Don't you agree, Rachel?"

His wife nodded. "Definitely. While we were putting the finishing touches on this dinner, she made some observations about Jesus that told me a lot about her."

The pastor nodded. "I'm not surprised. I think the two of you would regret it for the rest of your life if you did not have a worship-based wedding." He paused, thoughtful. "The State of California requires blood work before you can get a marriage license. Once you get the blood work done, Judge Andrew Parker is a member of the congregation. He can issue a marriage license without your having to go down publicly to the license bureau."

Alex looked at the Pastor. "This Judge Parker, he has done something like this before?"

The pastor nodded. "Five years ago, a wealthy member of our congregation wanted to get married quietly and without fanfare. If it had been public, more than a thousand people probably would have been there. We had less than fifty."

Rachel nodded. "Alex, could you ask some friends and family to join you in church on a Sunday, say, for a couple of guest speakers that they will recognize, saying that it is not being advertised, and to keep it quiet?"

Alex smiled. "My Mom can get the family together without giving away anything. I also have a few friends I can trust and want to be there, but I won't ask them. I'll just have my Mom and Dad bring the family. How about you, Bill?"

He nodded. "When you say 'family,' how many are you talking about?"

"No more than twenty, Bill."

"Apart from the church family, I can limit my family members to about fifteen. Pastor Ewart, can you invite the Elders and their wives without telling them why?"

He nodded. "Sure. If we invite the deacons in the same way, they can serve as ushers."

Alex was smiling. "This sounds perfect!"

They continued discussing it for the rest of the evening. Pastor Ewart talked to Alex and Bill about Christian marriage, its challenges, and its blessings. They talked about how a thriving marriage must be both exclusive and inclusive, sharing and merging their lives. Rachel and Alex went upstairs because Alex wanted to show Rachel some of Jody's things that were there. They also had what Alex told Bill later was "girl talk."

Later, as they were leaving, Pastor Ewart was curious. "Rachel and I have seen most of this main level of your house, and Rachel has now been upstairs. I understand that you also have a basement. Our three-bedroom and two-bath parsonage is just over two thousand square feet. Just how big is this house, anyway?"

Bill smiled. "If the basement is included, it includes just over seven thousand square feet."

Rachel's eyes grew wide. They were both stunned. Alex gave both hugs as they said their good nights while Sheila was sitting in the kitchen doorway, purring.

Because Alex had to be on the set in less than a month, preparations were rushed. A little over two weeks later, their little 'surprise' wedding came off on Sunday afternoon without a hitch. Their families were a little surprised, but they seemed delighted. As it turned out, part of the "girl talk" between Alex and Rachel two weeks earlier was Alex giving Rachel a generous check made out to the church for the wear and tear on the church and for whatever kind of reception Rachel could organize.

After the bride and groom said their vows and Pastor Ewart preached a brief wedding meditation, Alex's father offered the final prayer. After he said, "Amen," Pastor Ewart presented them to those gathered there in the sanctuary, and there was a reception in the general-purpose hall.

In addition to everything else, it was another surprise to everyone, that Kaitlynn Fellowes of the Los Angeles Opera showed up with her accompanist, and she sang popular music from Broadway productions during the entire reception.

Later, leaving the church in a limo, they turned south. Alex's arm in Bill's, she squeezed it. "Where is she taking us?"

Bill smiled. "You'll see. I have made some special arrangements. You did pack clothing that is casual, comfortable, and warm, didn't you?"

She nodded, "Yes." A few minutes later, the limo turned toward a naval security station, where they were waved in after a brief stop. "Why are we turning in here at the Naval Base?"

"Rear Admiral Jenson is a member of the church. A friend of his is loaning us his Gulfstream III and pilot for the week. We can board this plane without the hassles of the San Diego commercial airport terminal. Also, the paparazzi can't get past the government's security."

Just over an hour later, they landed in Fresno. The pilot told them she had relatives there and would stay with them. Two hours after that, Bill drove their rented Subaru SUV up to the entrance of the Ahwahnee Hotel. Bill had talked to Alex's manager, Charlie, and she had arranged for a suite with a sitting room for them, and there were already dinner reservations made for them in the private dining area at the north end of the dining room.

Before holding her chair, Bill kissed her and asked, "When you were previously in Yosemite, I'm curious as to what you remember of it."

Before she could answer, he sat down, and he reached across their table. "Let's pray." She took his hands. "Father, I've been talking with you about this for days. Please help us throughout our stay and bless our food and us. In the power of Jesus' name, I pray. Amen. What I've been discussing with the Lord is about our not being disturbed during our stay. So long as we don't want to be recognized, we won't be. You know how, when I tell Sheila to hide, she doesn't disappear, but she seems to become part of the background or the environment. You're a fine actress. You can do the same thing."

Alex nodded. "I'll be wearing a minimum of makeup, casual clothing, nothing that accentuates my figure, and a floppy hat. With God's help, we can do this."

The waiter returned, and they placed their orders. While they were eating, they talked about what had been going on apart from preparations for the wedding. "My lawyer is going into court tomorrow morning into bankruptcy court."

That got her attention. "What do you think will happen?"

"I think we'll come out way ahead, owning the property."

Alex nodded. "That sounds excellent. In two weeks, I'll be starting another so-called 'teaser' like the others. This time I'm being paid more because I am playing one of the leads. Just between you and me, I've got a hunch."

"What's that?"

"I think I can share this with you confidentially now as my husband." They smiled at one another. "I think that if these teasers I've done and am doing next are all edited together with a few other scenes, it just might be a whole movie franchise. Do you remember Steve Leone, the director you met in Paris?"

Bill nodded. "He has some major productions in his resume."

"Yes." She took another bite and a sip of tea. "He's directing this segment, and privately he hinted to me that this current production will bring to completion something larger. I believe what he said because I'm going to be on a closed set for the next three months. You and I will only be together on weekends." Alex saw the waiter coming and said she'd like Pecan pie for dessert.

Their waiter arrived, and he and a busboy cleared away their dishes. Bill looked up at their waiter before he could ask. "We're both going to have slices of Texas Pecan Pie a la mode."

"Very good, sir. I'll heat the pie before scooping the ice cream. Will that be acceptable?"

Bill nodded. "Certainly," and the waiter left. "Assuming we get what we want from the court, if you weren't working, you'd be bored silly watching me supervise construction."

"How long do you think it will take to complete the house?"

"If we don't run into any unforeseen problems, I hope we'll have it ready for occupancy in six months. By the way, I've set up a standing reservation for a suite at the Peninsula of Beverly Hills for weekends over the next six months."

Alex nodded. "That's great. I know some of the staff there."

The waiter brought their pie a la mode. They both said thank you as the pie was put in front of them. The waiter again left. Bill lowered his voice slightly. "As soon as we finish our pie, we can go upstairs and sit by a fire in the sitting room before we take a shower together."

She grinned. "I like the way you put that. It was subtle, and it had finesse. ... I've definitely married the right guy."

"What I want to know is, how is it that a little-known architect like me is now married to one of the women who *People* magazine lists among the ten most beautiful women in the world? I love you so much!"

"I love you, too! I have a feeling that word of our marriage has now spread. I guess we'll deal with it as it comes. When we leave, I don't want to go to the hotel next weekend."

"We're here through Sunday noon."

She nodded. "I want to go to our house in San Diego. Sheila's probably searching and watching for us every day, although I'm sure Abby is taking good care of her."

"Okay." Bill motioned to the waiter and signed the check. Arm in arm, they walked out of the dining room and toward the elevator. Upstairs, going to their room, he picked up the house phone. "Hello. Yes. May we have someone come and build a fire in the fireplace, please? Thank you."

They walked to the window, and they looked out over the landscape where the pink light of sunset was rapidly dwindling. They simply stood there, enjoying what they saw and each other.

There was a knock on the door, and he answered it. "Good evening, sir, we'll build a fire for you, and we've brought some extra wood in case you want it." The two women worked rapidly and were quickly gone after making sure that the fire was steadily burning.

Bill and Alex sat down on the love seat, facing the fire. She leaned over and took off her shoes. Then, kneeling on the carpet, she turned toward him and took off his shoes. "Let's be comfortable, shall we?"

Sitting in front of the fire, they wiggled their toes. He smiled. "This feels good, doesn't it?"

They started making out.

Later, having used all the wood that had been brought to them, they were simply enjoying each other while staring at the embers. A thought came to him. "Kaitlynn Fellowes' singing at our reception was a total surprise. Do you know her?"

Alex shook her head slowly. "Before today, I met her once or twice, but that is all. My maid of honor, Dietra, knows Kaitlynn really well, and she set it up."

He nodded. "Talking with Dietra briefly before our wedding, I realized why she has so many fans. She has remarkable inner beauty, almost as much as you do."

Alex nodded. "She's been a friend for a long time. I made it a point to thank Kaitlynn personally. I also spoke to Charlie, my manager, and told her to put a generous check in the mail to Kaitlynn."

"Good. I'm glad that Rachel put our parents together at one table. They seemed to enjoy one another, don't you think?"

"Definitely. Your Dad's a doctor, and mine is a pastor – both professionals. I'm glad my Dad was part of our wedding with Pastor Ewart. Your Mom is his nurse, isn't she?"

He nodded. "When I was much younger, my family used to come here to camp every spring. Sometimes we took our tents up into the high country. If we go to the Visitor Center here in the valley, I 'll be happy to show you a bass relief map of the park, and we can decide together where we want to hike. If we spend too much time on the shuttle buses, there's a greater chance of your being recognized."

"Right." She looked at him. "I'm ready for us to take a shower and head to bed, aren't you?"

"How can I argue with that?" He smiled, winked, stood, took her hands, and drew her into his arms. They did not get much sleep that night.

Monday morning, they ordered more food than they needed brought to their room so that they could explore the menu items. They did not leave the hotel until nearly 10:00 and looked like typical tourists. Bill had a small knapsack for his camera, lenses, and snacks. Alex wore bottles of water hanging from her belt. No one looked twice at them, even when they got on the shuttle.

At the Visitors Center, Alex was fascinated by the large bass relief map. They decided to hike the valley floor that first day in order to get used to the altitude. Tuesday, they hiked to the top of Yosemite Falls in the early morning. After having a snack and taking more pictures of each other as well as the scenery, they went on to Eagle Peak. The sun was setting after a long June's day when they got back to the hotel.

On Wednesday, they rode the shuttle most of the day, getting off at every stop to explore and take pictures. As Alex and Bill explored the valley, they began to realize that they had even more in common than their mutual love for one another. They had similar tastes in the things they liked. As they explored the valley together, they seemed to notice the same things at the same time. They both wanted to do the same things together. God really did prepare them for one another and set them up. Over dinner that night, Bill asked her, "Do you think God used Sheila to set us up for each other?"

She nodded with raised eyebrows. "I wouldn't be surprised."

The most exhausting day for them was Thursday. They hiked up the Four-Mile Trail to Glacier Point. After gorging themselves on hot dogs and chips for lunch, topped off with ice cream bars for dessert, they hiked down the eight and a half-mile panorama trail. Bill filled another memory card with video clips and images just that day alone. As the sun was setting, they took the shuttle to the Mountain Room at the Lodge and ate like they hadn't eaten for days.

Friday morning began with a thunderstorm. They sat in the Great Room of the hotel and enjoyed God's sound and light show. Bill started reading a paperback copy of *The Gaardian Saga*, as he had told Alex he would do eventually. Alex snuggled up next to him and read over his shoulder. He did not get much of it read, however. After lunch, they spent the afternoon napping in their room and playing some games.

Saturday night, Alex surprised him. "Bill, after dinner, let's go over to the Yosemite Theater."

He was startled. "Really? What's going on?"

"I read in the newspaper we got when we came into the park that there's a historical drama being put on this evening. I think it just might be fun to see."

"Okay."

It was a short shuttle ride to the theater near the Visitor Center, and they both became totally engrossed in the production. Vignettes were acted out telling stories of Yosemite's early years. Afterward, Alex and Bill talked with the lead character just like typical fans. The actor didn't seem to recognize Alex.

As they were riding the shuttle back to the hotel, Alex spoke quietly. "I was afraid he might recognize me. If he did, I'm glad he did not say so. Tonight was a treat, Bill. That was a fine performance, don't you think?"

Bill nodded. "I thoroughly enjoyed it too. It was a nice finale to our honeymoon. After worship tomorrow morning, we must get back to Fresno, of course. I'll call our pilot when we get back to our room."

"Right."

8.
Growing Fame

After worshiping in the Yosemite Chapel on Sunday morning, Alex and Bill drove their rented SUV back to Fresno, as planned. Alex enjoyed driving it this time, giving him a break. She told him several times how much she enjoyed the car. Security at the Fresno terminal did not present them with any difficulties. After boarding and sitting down in their plane, Bill took out his phone, touched a button, and turned on the speaker. "Hello, Pastor Ewart! How was church this morning?

"We had a good crowd. Where are you?"

"We've just boarded our plane, and we'll be back in San Diego in a little over an hour. I'm sure the paparazzi have been hanging around."

Alex leaned closer. "Hi, Pastor!"

"Hi, Alex. The paparazzi have not been too troublesome. I've reminded a few of them that freedom of religion has equal rights with freedom of the press. They've been pretty respectful. I think, Alex, your professional photographer, Peter Duvall, did a wonderful job for your wedding. I was very impressed with him. You'll probably love both the pictures and videos. I'm sure." He paused. "Do you remember when those men broke in, Sheila subdued them, and Lieutenant Garvin arrested them? He knows you're coming home today."

Both smiled. "He's become a good friend." "Would you give him a call and let him know we'll be getting home in about 90 minutes? I don't have his number on my cell."

"Sure. I saw him this morning at the first service. He told me that the police are prepared to keep the paparazzi away from your house until you get home."

"Fantastic. We'll probably drop by the church tomorrow morning."

"Rachel and I won't be there. We are going up to Hollywood for the premiere of the remake of 'Heaven Knows Mr. Allison' and spend the night."

Alex nodded and smiled. "Good! Enjoy yourselves! I know almost everyone in the cast. We'll see you when we see you! Bye!"

"Bye, you two!"

Bill put away his phone. "When we get home, we'll have a lot of catching up to do. The police are being helpful, and we'll probably need their assistance from time to time."

She smiled. "Let's donate to the Police Pension fund."

"Good idea. Let's do it a couple of times a year."

The flight back to San Diego was smooth. They both dozed off some of the time. Back on the base, the Admiral supplied a large SUV to drive them back to their house. Near the bottom of their hill, they saw some television vans, but no one followed them as they went up the hill. As they drove into their driveway, Abby and Ralph came out to greet them.

Ralph shook Bill's hand. "We think Sheila's been lonely without you. How was your honeymoon?"

Abby hugged Alex. "Yes! How was your honeymoon? Thank you for inviting us to your wedding!"

"We had a wonderful honeymoon in Yosemite. We'll be home most of this week, so we'll tell you two all about it and show you some of our pictures and video clips."

They went inside. Sheila was there to greet them, and she purred loudly as she enthusiastically nuzzled them. Bill looked into her face. "Sheila, we've had lots of fun this week. Now we're home, and we'll spend some time with you. Are you hungry?"

"Rowwl."

He started for the kitchen, and Sheila followed. Abby had two roasts thawing in the fridge for Sheila, He unwrapped one of them and put it in Sheila's dish. She purred loudly as she ate.

Abby came into the kitchen. "Bill, it was a good thing you installed that electric latch and opener on your patio door. When you gave the remote control to Ralph and me, I did not think we'd ever use it, but we did."

Bill smiled. "Really! What happened?"

"We saw two photographers sneaking into your yard. Ralph pressed the button. I think Sheila anticipated us. When the guys started to run, Sheila got in front of them. She did the same in whatever direction they ran. When they started to run in two different directions, she tripped one of them and got in front of the other. Meanwhile, Ralph went outside and on through the gate between our yards. Ralph simply told them they might as well give up, because they were Sheila's prisoners temporarily.

They sat down on your lawn, and Sheila sat down near them, staring at them and purring."

Bill started laughing as Alex walked in. "What's so funny?"

Abby turned to her. "Sheila held a couple of photographers at bay while Ralph explained your house rules to them. I hadn't got to that part yet. After Ralph gave them a tongue-lashing, they left peaceably, and after Sheila went back inside, Ralph re-set the door."

By the time Abby finished, Alex was grinning. "I'm glad that you and Ralph are our neighbors!"

Abby nodded. "We're glad you're *our* neighbors, too. The way we look at it, if someone tries to break into our house, all we must do is press the remote and call for Sheila. She and Beau are becoming friends."

Bill raised his eyebrows. "Who is Beau?"

Abby smiled. "Last Monday, we got a border collie from the shelter, and we named him Beau. On Tuesday, when I was letting Sheila stretch her legs in your yard, Beau heard her, and crossed into your yard through Sheila's doggie door in the fence. It didn't take long for them to get acquainted after Sheila licked his back and face, and now they're friends. Beau goes in and out of our house through his doggie door, but he doesn't go into your yard unless he hears Sheila." Abby looked at her watch. "I've got to get dinner started. Maybe I'll see you tomorrow." After giving Alex a hug, she waved at them and was soon gone.

Alex looked at Bill. "I'm in the mood for a smoothie. Shall we have a couple of chocolate-apple smoothies?"

Bill nodded. "Sure! I'll start looking through the mail to see if there's anything important. It looks like we've got a pile."

While Alex started making their smoothies, he went into the great room. The first-class mail was in a wicker basket. A few magazines were stacked in a pile, and the rest was in a casual heap. Before Alex and Bill got married, he used to go through the junk mail once a week and throw most of it away. Now he was (they were) going to have to tackle the pile more often.

Alex put his smoothie next to him on the end table. "As people begin to discover this to be my new home address, we may have to hire a mail processing service."

Bill pointed at the Chippendale grandfather clock. "There's a little package on the floor there by the clock. I haven't looked to see who it is for."

She went over and picked it up. "It's from Gold Art Designers. It's addressed to me." She looked at him. "Did you do something before our wedding without telling me?"

He smiled. "Open it."

As Alex began tearing away the brown paper, Sheila hopped down from the rafters to watch. When Alex exposed the outside of the trademarked box, she slowed down and opened it slowly. Inside was a dark-green velvet-covered jewelry case. As she opened the inner case, she stared, and her mouth hung open slightly. Tears were in her eyes when she looked up at him. "Oh, Bill! What an incredible necklace!" She practically jumped into his arms and kissed him. "A kiss will have to '*do*' for now. I'll have to think of something better to do for you later!"

They made out briefly, and then they got into tackling their pile of mail. They phoned for pizza delivery, and it was late when we went upstairs to bed. During the night, Bill got up once, and Sheila was sitting on the cedar chest, looking out the window through the sheer curtains. He scratched her head before getting back into bed. She purred.

Bill was watching Alex sleep at shortly after 8:00 AM when she opened her eyes. "How long have you been awake?"

He leaned over and kissed her. "Only a couple of minutes. Do you want to dive right into our scripture readings, or do you need to clear away the fog with a newscast?"

"I'm clear, but my mouth tastes like an army walked through it."

"Okay. You brush while I get relief, and then we can switch."

They got back into bed a couple of minutes later and snuggled. He looked up. "Begin scheduled scriptures, English Standard Version." The screen on the ceiling lit up showing Genesis 24. "Do you want to read the first one?"

"Sure."

After reading the scriptures and praying together, Bill headed downstairs to start breakfast while Alex got dressed. In the kitchen, he laid out slices of bacon on a broiler pan and put it in the oven. He then made coffee and squeezed oranges, and as he was getting out bread to make toast, Alex walked in. "The bacon's aroma is filling the whole house! Are you baking it?"

He nodded. "I like baking it when I have the time. It comes out better, I think. I was going to fix toast, but if you want to fix some pancakes, I'll run upstairs and get dressed."

She smiled. "Good! I'm hungry too! Shall I scramble some eggs?"

He nodded. "Sure! I could put away a couple of eggs with my pancakes." He looked at his watch. "The bacon should be done in about three or four more minutes. I'll go get dressed."

She put her hand on his arm. "That first New Testament reading that we read this morning, -- I had never before encountered that passage where Jesus cursed the fig tree and talked about it with His disciples. Let's talk about it over lunch this afternoon, okay?"

"Okay." He gave her a light kiss before walking quickly toward the stairs.

After lingering over their big breakfast while talking about their honeymoon, she did some personal projects she had been putting off, and he did some work and made some phone calls in his study. The rest of the morning was spent catching up on things undone while they were gone. Shortly after lunch, her phone rang. It was the director, Steve. "Hi Alex. How was your honeymoon?"

"We had a wonderful time in Yosemite. What's up?"

"I need to have you at Studio Four on Thursday afternoon."

"I figured I might have to go back to work before the end of this week. I'll see you then."

"Tell your husband that, if he signs a non-disclosure agreement like the one you did, he'll be welcome on the set."

"I'll tell him. See you Thursday."

Alex spent most of the afternoon reading her lines for the first scheduled shoot she was in, while Bill made modifications to the blueprints for the mountain house that had been requested by the Los Angeles County Planning Department.

Upstairs that night, they had lots of pillow talk. "Peter Duvall, our wedding photographer, will be here tomorrow morning at 11:00. That was the call sent to voice mail while I was in the shower." She paused. "Before that, however, the moving truck will be here with my dresser and a bunch of portable wardrobes."

Bill nodded. "I remember that you mentioned it during our flight home. The garage is weather tight, and we're only using two of the five spaces. Other than bringing your dresser up here with the essentials of your wardrobe, would you consider storing the rest downstairs in the unused garage space until we have our new home up north ready?"

She moved closer and kissed him on the cheek. "This is another thing I love about you, Bill. You anticipate and plan ahead. You and Jody would never have had five cars, but you anticipated a need for more space somehow. This amazing master-bedroom suite has two huge walk-in closets. You told me that Jody was not a clothes horse, and she used less than a third of her closet space. I'm convinced God gave you input when you were designing this house."

"I can't argue with that. Furthermore, I'm convinced from my personal prayer time that Gloria Houser is going to win a big deal for us in my client's bankruptcy court proceedings. I expect it to be all over this week. She was in court while we were in Yosemite."

"I hope so. Let's play for a while before we go to sleep." Bill didn't argue.

The next morning, the moving crew rang their doorbell at 9:00 AM. They only had time for blueberry smoothies and coffee. Before opening the front door, Bill told Sheila to hide.

Although Alex's double dresser was large, they had made enough room for it. Amazingly, both of their dressers were solid natural cherry, and they looked like they went together as if designed for a couple.

When it came to the rest of her wardrobe, Alex had it organized in her mind amazingly well. By the time the moving crew left, her bedroom closet was almost completely full, and a few portable wardrobes in the garage area were organized just the way she wanted them.

Sheila reappeared as soon as the moving crew left. They had just put their lunch dishes in the dishwasher when Peter Duvall rang their doorbell. Bill told Sheila to hide before Alex opened the door. "Peter!" They hugged. "It is good to see you. Our pastor was very impressed with you." Bill shook Peter's hand. They walked into the great room.

As they sat down, Peter was smiling. "I was impressed with Pastor Scott as well. The day before your wedding, he gave me a sheet listing what would and would not be allowed during the worship and ceremony. He showed me where I could mount my remote-controlled cameras, and he also gave me excellent suggestions for settings for supplemental pictures." Peter took out a tablet computer. "If your video screen is on, I can feed it all to it."

Bill nodded. "It's already on."

For the next two and a half hours, they discussed all the pictures and video clips. They were even better than Bill had hoped for, but Alex seemed to take it all in stride. She handed Peter a sheet from a yellow notepad she had been scribbling on. "Bill's attitude on this," she glanced at me, "is that the wedding day is the bride's day, so I get to choose what pictures and clips we use and how they're distributed."

Bill held up a finger. "I want to request one addition. I think the best portrait of the two of us is number sixty-three, and I want an 11x14 print that I will frame to put above my dresser. Furthermore, Peter, I have a request. Do you have a good camera with you today?"

The photographer grinned. "A professional photographer always has at least one decent camera with him, along with a few accessories."

Bill pointed out toward the patio. "We have some beautiful foliage in our back yard, and there's a number of perennials in bloom. If you'll go and get your camera and whatever else you need, I'd like you to make a portrait of Alex and me with our pet cat, Sheila."

"Sure, I can do that. Where's your cat?"

Alex smiled. "This is a great idea, Bill." She looked at her friend. "Peter, Sheila is a cat big enough to be normally associated with a zoo. First, get a grip on yourself so that you won't be frightened."

Peter's eyes got a little bigger. "Okay."

Alex pointed toward the rafters. "She's up there."

The photographer looked upward, and it took him a moment to see her.

Bill spoke. "Sheila, show yourself."

"Rowwl."

Peter gulped. "Holy crap! She's huge."

Bill nodded. "If you like, I will ask her to come down and greet you. Will that be okay?"

Unconsciously, he gulped again. "Sure."

"Sheila, come on down."

Sheila leaped and landed on the other side of the coffee table. Bill put his hand on Peter's shoulder. "Sheila, come and greet our friend." She approached them fairly slowly, and she was purring. "Peter, she is not growling. That is her purr. You can pet her if you want to."

He nodded and reached out. Sheila nuzzled him, purring. Peter seemed to be in awe. "Her fur is so soft! She's beautiful!" Their cat nuzzled him a second time before strolling toward the kitchen.

"Peter, why don't you come outside with us, and we'll pick a spot to make a portrait."

He nodded, and the three of them went out, across the patio, and into the yard. Peter pointed. "If you two are standing, I would guess that your cat is only a little shorter than your hips. If the two of you stoop either side of her, with her sitting on her haunches, you'll be closer to the same height."

Bill looked at Alex. "What do you think?"

She was thoughtful. "I think we should kneel beside her near the rose garden on the brick platform."

Bill nodded. "I like that idea. Peter, you go and get what you need. As soon as you are out the front door, Alex and I will call Sheila to join us."

As Peter walked toward the house, Bill touched Alex's arm. "I'll check over the fence this way, and you check that way. I don't want any Paparazzi around."

She nodded. "Right." A moment later, she came back. "All clear."

Bill nodded. "Sheila!" The cat bounded toward them. "Sheila, relax. We're going to get our picture taken." Bill looked at Alex and winked. "I took pictures when she was younger, but this will be her first portrait. I've lots of pictures of you, but this will be a family portrait."

They held hands as they walked toward the brick platform. Then they knelt down. "Sheila," Bill patted the bricks. "Come and relax." She came over and sat on her haunches. "Good girl, Sheila."

Coming from his car, it only took Peter a few minutes to set up his equipment. For about a half hour, Peter made images in various poses. With Sheila on her haunches, as Bill and Alex knelt, the cat's head was even with their shoulders. Finally, Peter nodded. "I think we have enough. I'll send the images and video via email."

Bill was surprised. "You made video?"

He nodded. "While I made separate portraits, the other camera was making a 4K video continuously. The digital images from main camera are big enough to make up to a 30 x 40 print, just like your wedding pictures. I won't charge you for this portrait sitting, Alex, except for any prints you want. It has been my pleasure. She has markings like that of a cheetah, doesn't she?" They nodded. "Did you meet Sheila when you met Bill?"

Alex smiled. "I met Sheila just moments after I met Bill. She's half cheetah and half puma."

Bill nodded. "It's been great working with you, Peter." He shook his hand. "When Alex and I move into the Burbank area, perhaps our paths will cross again." Alex gave him a hug. Sheila ran ahead of them into the house. By the time they got there, Sheila was up in the rafters again, dozing.

9.
Expanding Blessings

After Peter Duvall left, Alex and Bill sat at the kitchen counter and had a few cookies. After a sip of coffee, Alex looked at him. "I'm so glad you thought of getting a family portrait while Peter was here. That had not even occurred to me."

Bill nodded. "It just came to me out of the blue, praise God." He bit into a cookie. "Sheila was so cooperative. I think maybe she decided she liked Peter."

Alex smiled. "Maybe."

His cell rang. He looked at the screen. "It's Gloria Houser, our attorney." He turned on the speaker. "Good afternoon, Gloria, how did things go?"

"We got even more than we expected. You've got responsibility for roughly a fourth of the original mortgage on three acres. There's more, however. The Los Angeles County Planning Department filed an *Amicus Curiae* or 'friend-of-the-court' brief. They urged the court to include mineral rights to our property because you are having geothermal heating and cooling, and because of your anchoring the house into the hillside. That also clears your electrical contractor of any complications of hooking up to power at the bottom of the valley. The court granted mineral rights to all of your three acres, along with access for drilling into the hillside under the roadbed to increase the stability of the house's foundation on the hill. Geologically you'll be as solid as you choose to be."

Alex was nodding at Bill and smiling as he spoke. "That's great, Gloria. Is all of this effective immediately?"

"That's right, Bill. It's a done deal. I'll send you a bill for my services, along with all the paperwork, this weekend. It's been good working with you again."

Alex squeezed his arm. "Gloria, now that Bill and I are married, I want you to be my personal lawyer as well. I have a law firm on retainer for my show business issues."

"I'll be more than happy to take you on as another client along with Bill."

He nodded at Alex. "Thank you so very much, Gloria. It's been good working with you as well. Goodbye."

"Good-bye, Bill. Good-bye, Alex." They ended the call.

Alex turned and hugged him. "This is great, Bill! This will become our home!"

"I'll say! It's an incredible blessing, thank God!"

"Yes! Thank God!"

He looked at her. "Next week, when we look at the mortgage, we'll have to decide whether to make the specified payments and take them off of our taxes, or simply to liquidate some investments to pay it off."

"Do you have a tax attorney here in San Diego?"

Bill nodded. "Yes. His name is David Underwood. There's something else we need to talk about, though."

She also nodded, solemnly. "What you'll be doing while I'm on the sound stage most of the time for the next few months."

"Right. Unless you've got a better plan, I remember telling you that I've got us a suite at the Peninsula of Beverly Hills for the weekends of the next six months anyway. Now that the property is settled, we can say good-bye to our friends and neighbors here, and we can put almost everything in this house into storage. We can then live in the hotel."

Alex shook her head. "When I'm working five to six days a week on a set, I need to be able to get away from the area when I'm not working. Let's make this move more gradually. We can rent a motor home and park it on the property. It can be your sleeping quarters and an on-site office as you work. Part of the time, you can have Sheila with you up there, and part of the time she can stay down here. You and I can also commute some of the weekends, and sometimes I'll just come up there and sleep with you there on the property on weekends. At least, I'd be getting out of most of the smog."

Bill nodded. "That sounds much better for you. I agree. Crain Contractors, our general contractor, will have a trailer on the site. It might be better for Sheila as well, to hold onto this house for a while. After all, her vet is down here."

Alex's cell rang. She looked at the screen. "It's Steve, my director. "Hi, Steve, this is a surprise."

"Hi, Alex, I know it is."

"Thank you. I'm expecting to be on the set on Thursday afternoon. Has anything changed?"

"Oh, no. I'm calling to see if your husband can be available as a consultant for the next six to seven months."

He got closer to her phone. "This is Bill, Steve. Hi."

"Hi, Bill. Did you hear my question?"

"Yes, Steve. I could possibly be on call for you, but I won't be able to be there every day. I'm building a house above La Cañada, on the Angeles Crest Highway. As the architect, I want to be there much of the time to supervise in conjunction with the contractors."

"If I limit my use of your expertise to ten hours a week, could you handle that?"

Bill paused. "Steve, I'll have Alex give you my answer on Thursday afternoon, when she sees you. You won't need me this week, will you?"

"No, I don't think so. Why your hesitation?"

"Steve, Alex and I pray about everything. Our marriage is inclusive as well as exclusive. Between now and Thursday, I'll be praying both *with* her and *for* her. I'll make my decision before she leaves on Thursday morning."

"Okay, Bill, I hope to see you soon. I'll see you on Thursday, Alex."

"Okay, Steve." He hung up.

Alex had a sly grin. "It looks like you're going to be one very busy man this year!"

Bill nodded. "Amen to that! We need to spend more time in prayer tonight and tomorrow morning. Meanwhile, I've written to four different companies that custom-build motor homes. I'm sending proposed floor plans for a class-C hybrid-powered van conversion, based upon others I've seen and studied. I'm hoping that one of them can do it for us, so we can buy instead of rent. Maybe there will be times when we can park it near where you're doing some location work. Now that we're married, having it available will make it possible for us to not be apart for long stretches."

Alex got off her stool and took him by the hand. They went into the great room, and they sat down on the reclining love seat. "This sounds like it would be a really good thing for us, Bill. How big will it be?"

He shook his head. "It's not a done deal, yet. If I can work things out with one of these companies, I think it will be in the thirty-foot or less range. When the top is not up, it will fit into one or two of the three spaces in the insulated garage of the house we're building. Moreover, if it is completed quickly, we'll start having it on the property and not use the hotel suite."

"Even if we get it right away, I think we should still have the hotel suite available. It's almost 6:00. Let's order Chinese delivered for dinner and watch a movie, shall we?"

He nodded. "Good idea. You go ahead and order whatever you want for us. I think I've got a few movies in my library that you've never seen." As she took out her cell phone, he went to the shelves near their video screen.

He was debating with himself between two possible choices when Alex came over and looped her arm through his. "What have you got in mind?"

"Do you know who Tony Randall was?"

She nodded. "He died before I got my first role with more than a couple of lines. He did mostly comedic work, I think. Didn't he have a May-December marriage?"

"Right. That was his second marriage after his first wife died. His second wife was 25 and he was 75 when they got married. They had two kids, and he was 84 when he died. Have you seen any of his movies?"

She shook her head. "No, have you got one?"

I smiled and nodded. "Actually, I have several, but the one I think you'll especially enjoy is a fantasy with rather primitive special effects by current standards." He took the disk off the shelf. "It's called '*The Seven Faces of Dr. Lao.*'"

Alex loved the old movie and laughed even more than Bill did. After the movie, they played games for a while. It was well after midnight after they had gone upstairs, prayed, and went to sleep.

Although they thought they could sleep in a little on Wednesday morning, his cell woke them at 8:20. He rubbed his eyes and looked at the screen. It was Ken Crain of Crain Contractors. "Good morning, Ken. I wasn't expecting to see or hear from you until Monday morning."

"I know, Bill, but this is important. We've started excavating for the basement and foundations, and we've made an unexpected discovery. I've just got off the phone with the Bolton Hall Museum. Their curator will be here in less than a half hour."

"I've never heard of the Bolton Hall Museum. What is this about?"

"It's a museum of local history. Evidently, after Pearl Harbor was attacked in 1941, the Army built some underground buildings in your property's area. After the war, they remained abandoned until Eisenhower became president. President Eisenhower ordered them stripped and demolished. Evidently, they missed one, and it's under your property. I've sent the excavating crew home until at least next week."

"Okay, Ken, this coming weekend, my wife and I are going to be staying at the Peninsula of Beverly Hills. We can meet you there on Sunday afternoon, or I can meet you on the property on Monday morning. What's better for you?"

There was a pause. "There are probably others that we'll have to involve in this. Let's wait until Monday morning."

"Okay, Ken, I'll see you on Monday."

Alex turned on the light on her nightstand. "What's up?"

Bill kissed her lightly. He rubbed his face, scratched his head vigorously, and stretched. "That was strange news. It seems there's an army barracks building left over from World War II underneath our property."

"What?!"

He nodded. "My guess is that, in the aftermath of Pearl Harbor, the military considered scenarios wherein the Japanese would come on across the Pacific and attack the West Coast. Maybe this was part of those preparations. There's someone from a museum of local history coming this morning to look things over."

"Dear Lord!"

"Yep!" He got back under the covers. "When we pray, this will have to be part of it. Since we're both awake, shall we go ahead and read the scriptures?"

She nodded. About forty minutes later, they got up, took a shower, dressed, and headed downstairs. It did not take long for them to put together some Spam and frozen waffles, and then convection-bake them while they got other things on the table. Alex started pouring their juice.

"I just had a thought." Bill took out his cell and pushed a speed dial button. "Good morning, Pastor Ewart."

"Good morning, Bill. How are things going?"

He turned on the speaker. "Alex and I are just sitting down to a late breakfast. I've suddenly remembered that we haven't talked with you since we got back in town. We were hoping to see you and Rachel this Sunday, but now that won't happen."

Alex raised a finger, and he nodded as she spoke. "I'm going to be on a sound stage in Burbank for most of the next seven or eight months, Pastor Ewart, and Bill is starting to build our new house up there. He got some surprising news this morning."

"What's that, Bill?"

"We hope to see you on another weekend this month and give you all the details, but in brief, our contractor has discovered an army building, left over from World War II, buried under our new property."

"Whoa! That's interesting!"

"Whoa is right! We won't be in church this Sunday again, but we hope to see you again soon."

"Okay, Bill, keep Rachel and I posted. Enjoy your breakfast."

"Thanks, pastor Ewart."

Alex nodded. "Thanks pastor Ewart."

"Bye, you two."

As the call ended, Alex and Bill started eating. They had eaten less than half of their breakfast when Alex's phone rang. Wanting to keep eating, she put her cell on the table and pressed the speaker button. "Hello?"

"Hi, Alex, this is Steve again. Isn't your new property on Angeles Crest Highway?"

"Hi, Steve, yes, it is. Why?"

"If you turn on KTLA, you'll see their news crew on what I think is your property. I'm at the studio if you want to call me back later." There was a click as he hung up.

They both picked up their plates and coffee, and they went into the great room. They ate the rest of their breakfast silently as they watched. When KTLA took a commercial break, they went back to the kitchen. "Alex, if you want to, we can both drive up there and see what's going on. Afterwards, we can check into the hotel a day early."

She nodded. "Thank you. If you hadn't suggested it, I would. I want to see this thing with you if I can."

"Good. I'll call Abby and tell her our plans have changed."

A little over a half-hour later, they said goodbye to Sheila and went to the garage with their luggage. As usual, when they were both taking their cars to go somewhere, Bill stood by the garage door, letting Abby go first. Her car wouldn't start. She stuck her head out of her window. "What shall we do now?"

He thought a moment. "Put your luggage in my car with mine. We'll both go in my car, and I'll deal with your car next week somehow."

"Okay."

With relatively moderate traffic, it was about two and a half hours later that they reached La Cañada, got off the I-210 freeway, and started up the mountain. A few minutes later, as they pulled onto their property, Bill recognized the man standing by the contractor's trailer. "That's Ken Crain, Alex. He's a rugged dude, but he's easy to work with." He pointed at the glove box. "Alex, will you please grab my handheld laser distance measurer, please? The tool may come in handy." He got out, went around, and opened her door. As she got out and handed him the measurer, the contractor was approaching them. "Ken, this is my wife, Alex. Ken Crain, Alex."

She shook his hand. "It's nice to meet you, Ken."

"It's a pleasure to meet you, Mrs. Johnson."

"Alex."

"Okay, Alex. I assume the two of you came up to see what we've discovered." He looked down at their feet. "In those shoes, I think you'll do okay getting down the hill." He looked at him. "Bill, I think it was a bunkhouse. There're a dozen bunks, a latrine, a small galley, and a dining area. Over the years, all the vents were closed off with debris, so it's pretty stuffy in there, but being below ground, it's relatively cool." He pointed at Bill's laser tool. "I see you're ready to measure things."

He nodded. "I want to see if any of it can be utilized and adapted. I doubt it, but I'm curious."

They started down the hill, which was fairly steep, so Alex and Bill held hands to steady each other. They only had to climb down a short distance before they reached where the structure had been exposed. It had a well-designed steel door with seals that were in surprisingly good shape for their age. Pulling the door open, Ken led the way inside. The two men turned on handheld LED flood lanterns Ken had placed just inside.

Bill set his flood on the ground and surveyed the room. "This is larger than I imagined."

Ken pointed to their right. "The latrine is over there, and the galley and dining area are straight ahead of us."

As Alex picked up one of the floods and started walking toward the galley, Bill turned on his laser tool and began recording readings and sending them to his cell phone. Ken stayed with him in the latrine area and continued to stay with him as Bill then followed Alex into the dining area. Bill recorded more readings there.

Alex looked all around. "The seals on this thing must have been really tight. I'm surprised that there's not more dust accumulated on the tables and chairs."

"Yeah. There's no telling how long the vents have been closed. I'm curious about the galley." Bill walked through the doorway. "That's the biggest alcohol stove I think I've ever seen."

Ken and Alex came in, and he touched the stove. "Did you say this is an alcohol stove?"

Bill nodded. "I would have to examine it more carefully in better light, but the design parallels other alcohol stoves I've seen. Alex, have you seen enough?"

"Yeah. This is all so incredible. Until the crew uncovered this, there's probably been nobody here for well over a half century." She started walking toward the entrance, and the men followed her.

As they stepped outside into the fresh air, Bill turned to Ken. "Did someone come from the local history museum?"

Ken nodded. "That was why KTLA showed up. I told the news anchor, Courtney Sams, that this was private property as well as a construction site, and I asked her to share her video with other stations that asked for it. There was no point in having more people taking the risk of going up and down the hill. She agreed."

Alex shaded her eyes, looking down the hillside. "Who came from the museum?"

"His name is Rod Tanger. He's going to be back here on Monday morning to meet you, Bill. He called someone he knew at the Pentagon, and as far as the Army is concerned, all of this is simply debris from long ago. Demolition crews were supposed to have stripped and destroyed all these buildings in 1954. The Army has no interest in what's left. Bill, did you say you might want to utilize and adapt some of this?"

Bill turned to look at him. "I wouldn't want you to do it officially. This structure is near the west end of the foundations, right?"

Ken nodded. "If we re-survey and shift everything eastward about eighteen inches, the inspectors would never know the difference."

Bill may have smiled a little bigger than he intended when Ken said that. "Ken, that's my thinking, more or less. I'll draw up plans that will be just for you and me. I'll pay the difference in cash. Are you willing to do that?"

Ken nodded. "It has to all fit code requirements, even if it doesn't officially exist. I won't have any liability that way, and it will be both off the books and legally safe."

"Excellent." Bill glanced over at Alex, and she winked. As with virtually everything since they had met, they thought alike. He turned back to Ken. "When we re-bury it, we'll want everything up to code in terms of plumbing and electrical, with modern lighting, a modern kitchen, and a modern bathroom. The latrine is so big, I'll probably design a laundry room to use part of the space. I'll have to figure out how to hide new venting and divide the larger space."

Ken nodded again. "You design it, and I'll make it happen. I have a suggestion."

"What's that?"

"Obviously, you're going to have to re-do the layout of the walkways, stairs, and lower walkways. Have you considered pavers instead of bricks outside?"

Alex cocked her head. "What are pavers?"

"They're like cast concrete stones in various sizes, shapes, and colors." Bill was thoughtful. "You know, you may be right, Ken. In this environment, the right pavers would possibly look more natural here. We'll consider it. I'll be back here about 9:00 on Monday morning unless you call me." Bill turned to Alex. "We missed getting lunch. If we go to the Black Angus in Burbank for an early dinner, there won't be a crowd to bug us."

She nodded. "Good. I'm starving, aren't you?"

Bill nodded. They started climbing back up the hill. "Ken, I can use my laptop to make these private plans of ours, and you can get them printed out here in Burbank. I'll email them to you."

They went back to the level area next to Ken's trailer. Bill continued. "On Monday, Ken, after we meet with Rod Tanger from the museum and the others that may get involved, I'll probably head back south to San Diego for a few days and deal with a problem Alex is having with her car. I'll come back up to the hotel Friday evening. I'm working on getting a class-C diesel-hybrid or gas-hybrid van-conversion motor home. Once I have it, it will be here on site much of the time. We'll probably park it there," he pointed, "near your trailer. That won't be a problem, will it?"

Ken shook his head. That wouldn't be a problem most of the time. If you like, however, we can go ahead and pave your guest parking area on the west side, and then you can park under the trees and have shade most of the day."

Bill nodded. "That's a good idea, but I don't want to interfere with your planned schedule of doing things."

"After the excavators finish cutting the hillside for your foundation, the soil will be available for leveling that area anyway while they are here. It might even save us a little on the bottom line."

Bill nodded. "I'll leave such decisions to you, Ken. You have a sterling reputation, and I trust you." He reached into his pocket and took out a transmitter. Pressing a button, Bill's car's engine started. "Alex, let's wait a couple of minutes until the a/c takes the edge off of the heat inside the car."

She smiled. "That's fine. I was just thinking. While we're waiting for our car to cool a little, I've never seen the revised drawings of how the house will look when it's done."

Ken nodded. "Come on over to my trailer. The a/c in there is going all the time." In the trailer, they went up a short stairway and on inside. It was much cooler. Ken pointed to a wall. "This is the last set of drawings you've sent me, Bill." He pointed to the lower-left corner of the up-the-hill view. "Even with our off-the-books modifications, this area will look the same. There's a new version of perennial grass that's now available in Southern California. Your landscape contractor was telling me about the new grass last week."

"Okay, Ken, thank you. I will see you on Monday." Bill shook Ken's hand.

Alex also shook his hand. "It was good to meet you."

"The pleasure was mine, Mrs. ... Alex."

10.
Construction Begins

When Bill drove up to the site on Monday morning, the contractor, Ken Crain, was there and introduced the museum director and another man. "This is Rod Tanger from the museum and Phil Willets from Platinum Pawn in Burbank. Gentlemen, this is Bill Johnson, the architect for this project and the owner." They all shook hands.

Bill pointed downhill. "Have you men seen what's in the structure?"

They both nodded. The pawn shop owner spoke first. "Everything in there has at least some historical value, if nothing else, including the toilets and basins in the latrine, the bunks and blankets in the largest room, and the kitchen equipment in the galley. Rod and I have known each other for years. Whatever you don't give to the museum, I'll bid for it."

Rod Tanger smiled. "The museum does not have the space for much of it, and a donor has donated $10,000 to buy as much as I can. However, how much of it would you be willing to donate, sir?"

Bill nodded. "This is going to be easier than you might have thought. I have not yet talked to a demolition contractor, but I can confidently tell you that within ten days from now, there will be nothing left down there that is sellable. In 1954, the Army was supposed to strip that thing of anything useable, set explosives, and essentially buried the rest. I will do this, Mr. Tanger. I will donate to your museum anything inside the structure that can be easily removed, so long as you take it away by this coming Friday. You can put it all temporarily in a warehouse of your choosing, and then auction off what you are not going to use. Mr. Willets, it is up to Mr. Tanger as to whether you are the only bidder or one of many. That's up to Mr. Tanger. That's my offer."

The museum's curator shook his head. "Don't you want any reimbursement at all?"

Bill smiled. "That's correct. It's all yours so long as you can get it out of there by the end of the day on Friday." Bill turned. "That works for you, Ken, doesn't it?"

He nodded. "They will all have to wear hard hats because of the heavy equipment that will be here. That crew can stop temporarily to let your people carry things away, but they will continue working. Understood?"

The two men nodded. The pawn dealer was smiling. "Rod, between the two of us, we have enough men to get all of that out of there in a couple of hours. I can't make it happen tomorrow, but would Wednesday be good for you?"

The curator shook his head. "Thursday would be better."

The pawn dealer nodded. "Thursday it is, then. Mr. Johnson, it has been good meeting you. Your view from here is great when there's no smog, like today. I'll have to come up here and see what you've built when it is finished."

The curator was effervescent. "Thank you very much! You're being very generous!"

Bill smiled. "Not really! I never knew it was part of the property when I bought it. You're welcome to it all." Bill shook their hands, and a few minutes later the two men were gone. "Well, Ken, I told them the truth. They did not need to know anything else, right?"

"Right! This won't slow things down at all. It will take about two weeks to get the foundation in, once we drill into the hillside and downward to set the anchors and sink the pilings."

Bill nodded. "Excellent! I'll see you later in the week"

"Later."

Just moments later, Bill was going down the hill, and then he turned onto the I-210 loop. He had driven this route often enough that it had become automatic. He touched a button on his steering wheel. "Call Pastor Ewart Scott."

"Calling Pastor Ewart Scott."

"Hello?"

"Hey, Pastor, it's Bill Johnson."

"Hi, Bill, how are you doing?"

"I'm fine. I'm driving south on the I-5, and I'll be home in a couple of hours. Alex is at work in Burbank. When we were leaving on Wednesday, Alex's car wouldn't start. It has a lot of miles on it. On our honeymoon, we drove a rented Subaru SUV that she loved. Isn't there a man who owns a Subaru dealership in the congregation?"

"Randy Footman used to, but he's retired. He does keep his dealer's license up to date, though. I'll give him a call and have him call you. You'll be home this evening?"

"Yeah. I'm not going back north until Thursday."

"Okay. What's the story about the discovery under your property?"

Bill told the story to his pastor as he drove south on I-5, not telling him about keeping the building. He did tell him about donating all the furnishings to the museum. "As you can well understand, Pastor Ewart, this has been a most interesting weekend and a most interesting day."

"I'll say. Our church women's fellowship group is having their monthly luncheon tomorrow. If Alex were in town, she would be invited. Rachel and I will be there. Why don't you join us?"

Bill paused for only a moment. "That sounds great, Pastor Ewart. I'll see you there."

"I will see you tomorrow." He touched the button on his steering wheel again.

That evening he spent a lot of time playing with Sheila, which he had not done for several months. He decided it was time to teach Alex the next weekend about the kind of fun they could have with their cat. Tuesday morning, Bill went into the church well before the luncheon so that he could go into the quiet of the sanctuary and pray.

The luncheon was excellent, as always. He previously told Alex more than once that the women of the church coach one another in cooking and baking, and the results are invariably excellent. One of the women is the chef for the best restaurant in La Jolla. Jill, the chef, loves taking a day off once a month to join the ladies at the church. Jill doesn't make any effort to teach them unless they ask. She told Bill once that two of her restaurant's menu dishes she discovered at the church, and she learned to fix those dishes from the ladies.

On Wednesday, the retired car dealer introduced Bill to the general manager of a dealer who had the model of Subaru Bill was looking for on behalf of Alex. It had all the options he knew Alex wanted, and it was the same color as the one they had rented on their honeymoon. The dealer followed Bill to his home with a tow truck as well as the new Subaru. Ralph came over with Abby, and they helped Bill transfer all of Alex's personal items into the newer model.

As the dealer towed the old one away, Ralph muttered, "Good riddance, Bill. I don't understand why she kept it so long."

Bill looked at him. "Why do you hang on to that old Jeep of yours?"

Ralph nodded. "That's a good point. I guess any of us can get too attached to a car."

"We can get attached to anything." Abby turned toward him. "Are you still going back north tomorrow?"

Bill smiled. "Definitely. I can't be apart from Alex too long! When she's not here, a part of me is not here." He paused. "The next time Alex comes south with me for a weekend, we'll likely take Sheila back with us when we go back up north. I've paid a security deposit on a hotel suite up north, so that Sheila can have the second bedroom. Are there still enough roasts for her in my freezer?"

Abby nodded. "Sheila seems more subdued and quieter when you're not here. I think she misses you."

"I miss her too, and I'm sure Alex does as well. I'll be leaving early in the morning. I don't know about next week, yet, but I'm sure we'll call you over the weekend."

When Bill was driving back north to Burbank, there was a massive pile-up of cars in Orange County, and traffic came to a stop for almost an hour before it began moving slowly again. It was late when Bill got to the hotel. There was a message at the desk for him to call Alex. As soon as he got into their suite, first he called room service, and then he called her. "Hi!"

"Hi! It's so good to hear your voice!"

"I love you passionately too, girl!"

"About an hour ago, Steve finally called it a wrap for the day and asked me to find you. Part of a set collapsed, and personally, I think he's calling for you to come mainly to do something different. It's been a frustrating week. He's told everyone not to come back until Monday. I don't know why. I heard about the pile-up and hoped your car wasn't part of it."

"It wasn't, but the traffic has been a nightmare. If Steve has called it a weekend, shall I come and get you?"

"Actually, the limo will drop me off there in a few minutes. How late is room service available, do you know?"

"Here? It's always available, 24/7."

"We're pulling in out front! I'll see you in a few."

He stood in the doorway to the hall, watching the elevators. When the elevator doors opened, she ran into his arms, and they simply held each other for a while. Finally, we broke and started inside. "How hungry are you?"

"I've hardly eaten anything since breakfast! Let's get a couple of those dinner samplers that we like so much."

He kissed her lightly. "I had a feeling that's what you would want, so I took a chance. Do you want to take a shower first? There might be enough for a quick one. We usually wait about fifteen minutes for the food to get to our suite."

"Will you take a shower with me?"

"I'd love to, but our food might get cold! You go get started, and I'll clue in Room Service that you're here and to deliver in thirty minutes." He called and told them to put their food on the balcony, but with the dishes covered. He then followed Alex. A half hour passed before they went out on their balcony in their bathrobes and started eating.

"How's my car?" she asked between bites.

"I don't want to talk about your car yet. Custom RVs of San Diego sent the plans I drew to a factory in Michigan. It will be delivered in two weeks. The factory sent me a certified letter. They want to buy the plans from me so that they can offer my version to the public as a new model available the model-year after next."

She put her fork down. "You're kidding! What are you going to tell them?"

Bill smiled at his beloved wife. "I thought I would talk it over with you first."

"Me? Why?"

"I've said this before in another way, I suppose, but for us, Alex, our marriage is not simply about being in an exclusive relationship. It's also about being in an *inclusive* relationship. Everything we say and do is inclusive of one another. I think we should always share big decisions with each other. After we talk it over, then we will call our lawyer, Gloria Houser."

"What did they offer you?"

"They offered a million dollars plus the prototype as our own motor home."

Alex stared straight ahead. She made little motions in the air with her finger. She did the same again. Then she looked at Bill. "Ask Ms. Houser – Gloria – what she thinks of this counteroffer: Up front, our own motor home – the prototype that they are offering. Additionally, parts and labor on everything except for fuel and filters. Then, we want ten percent of the gross sales of the factory price out the door."

Bill grinned. "I love the way your mind works! Maybe by Monday, when I call Gloria, we can come up with a fallback position so that we don't sound too greedy."

She took a swallow of iced tea. "That's a good idea too. How's Sheila?"

"She's okay, but Abby says she thinks Sheila misses us."

Alex smiled. "I miss her too."

Bill's cell chimed, and he took it out and looked at the screen. "It's Steve." He touched the speaker button. "Hi, Steve, we're almost finished with dinner."

"That's good. I haven't eaten yet. Is there any chance you can come to the studio tomorrow morning and look at the situation?"

Bill looked across the table, and Alex was smiling and nodding. "Sure, Steve, what time?"

"How about 8:00?"

"8:00 it is. We'll see you then." They ended the call. "Why were you smiling and nodding?"

"Tomorrow's Friday. If you can instruct our carpenters and other workers so that they can get started, we'll have the weekend to drive down and spend it at home."

The next morning, after having breakfast food they ordered the night before, they drove to the studio, where the guard at the gate was expecting them and pointed the way. Inside the sound studio, Alex led the way to a mess. Steve saw them coming and greeted them. "Good morning! I'm glad you could come this morning! I think it looks even worse now than it did yesterday." Bill and Steve shook hands, and then Bill began looking carefully at the setup as Steve showed him drawings of what had been there before the collapse.

After he had looked the mess over carefully, he stopped and looked at the director. "Steve, how many people were on that second level when it collapsed?"

He pointed at the drawings as he spoke. "Three... two... eleven here... two here... and five more here. It was more than I had originally planned for, but they all needed to be in place. Did I overload it?"

Bill nodded. "Massively! Was anyone hurt?"

"No one was hurt seriously, but paramedics checked them all out."

"Good. You've got two choices. If your workers re-build it the way it was, your load limit for that entire area will be about six hundred pounds, or five people spread out. Your other choice is for me to re-design the supports, which I can do at my office at home in a day or two, and I can send the plans to you by messenger. It will then take your workers two or three days to have the set camera-ready again."

Steve gestured to one of his assistants, standing nearby, and he spoke loudly. "Tell the crew, they're off until Wednesday, and tell the cast members they're on call, but that it might be a week before we get back at it." The assistant nodded and took out his cell.

Bill took the plans from him. "I can work from your original plans, so I don't have to take measurements. Alex and I will head south, and after lunch down there, I may get started on it. We've things planned for the weekend, but I'll get right back to working on it first thing Monday morning. Unless I run into some snags, you should have the replacement plans in your hands by either late Tuesday or early Wednesday." Bill put a rubber band around the plans and handed them to Alex. "We'll be back at the hotel a week from Sunday evening. As it stands now, I'll be back at our construction site a week from Monday." He looked at Alex and winked. "Let's go, gorgeous!"

She reached up and pecked him on the cheek. "Amen to that!"

The drive home from the studio took almost three hours, with "rush-hour" traffic. As they started up Faculty Avenue,

Alex took out her cell and ordered pizza. As they pulled into the driveway, Bill looked over at her. "Before we go inside, there's something you need to see." He opened the garage doors for both his SUV and her car. As Alex's new car came into view, he watched her face.

Her mouth dropped open, and her eyes got huge. "Bill!" She screamed. "Bill! It's just like the one we rented for our honeymoon! I... I don't know what to say!" She threw her arms around him, and they kissed. "I love it!" She walked into the shade of the garage, opened the driver's-side door, and got in.

He pointed. "Your dark glasses are in that holder. Just press that little red stripe. Ralph, Abby, and I transferred all of your stuff from the other car into this one." He handed her a fob. "Put this on your key ring. It's your digital key."

Alex got out and closed her door. They heard a horn beep, and they saw the pizza delivery car approaching. She gave him another quick kiss. "I'll go inside and get our drinks ready."

A kid not more than seventeen handed him their pizzas, and Bill gave him a generous tip. As he went inside, Alex was on her knees, and Sheila was licking her face. Bill put the pizzas on the entry table, knelt beside Alex, and gave Sheila a hug, who was purring loudly.

Later, as they were finishing lunch, Alex snuggled up closely. "That car is a total surprise! I guess I thought I was going to drive that old heap forever."

"I could have had it repaired, and I could even have had it restored, but as Ralph said, any of us can get too attached to a car."

Alex nodded. "I had that old thing since I got my first paycheck for doing a commercial. I had done some things to pay for my tuition and books in college, but that commercial that I did during my last semester got me a sizeable check, and I celebrated by buying that car, paying cash. That was... nine years ago." Sheila walked past us and scampered up her pole to the rafters. "Shall we take Sheila back with us next week?"

He nodded. "That's probably a good idea."

11.
New Vet

On Thursday, their lawyer came to the house while Alex was upstairs studying her script. After Gloria sat down, she began immediately discussing business. "I don't think that first offer from the motor home factory was serious, Bill. That was just to get negotiations started. Of course, they had no way of knowing that they were going to have to deal with me. By the way, I understand that you have a big cat for a pet. Can I see her?"

Bill didn't take his eyes off his lawyer. "I won't ask you how you know. Do you want to see her only at a distance, or would you like a chance to pet her?"

"You're serious?"

He nodded. "Completely. She's only dangerous if she has to be."

Gloria had a slight smile. "That's the way we lawyers sometimes answer questions. Okay. Let me meet her."

Still not taking his eyes off of Gloria, Bill said, "Sheila, come say hello to our friendly lawyer."

Sheila leaped from the rafters above them, and she landed between the fireplace and where they were sitting. "Rowwl." She padded toward them, purring.

"Gloria, this is Sheila. If you put out your hand, face down, she will nuzzle it."

The lawyer hardly breathed as she slowly extended her hand. "Hello, Sheila." His cat nuzzled her and got closer. She let our lawyer stroke her down her neck and back. "Sheila, you are amazing."

"Sheila, Gloria and I have business to discuss. Why don't you run on your treadmill for a while?"

They watched as Sheila approached the machine. As she stepped on and triggered the first sensor, the treadmill began moving. Within a few seconds, her legs and feet and legs were a blur.

"She'll run for five minutes or more."

Their lawyer turned back toward him. "Is she as fast as a cheetah?"

Bill shook his head. "Actually, she's faster. She's half puma, so she has much more stamina than a cheetah, but, like a cheetah, she's not normally aggressive toward humans."

Nodding, she spoke. "As I said, the factory was simply offering to negotiate. If that had been a serious offer, I think it would have been a more generous offer. Motor homes are a big business. My initial counteroffer was like the one Alex suggested, but I asked for thirty percent of the manufacturer's price, along with an annual free replacement of your unit. By the way, your cat's door through the floor under the bed is going to be promoted as a fire escape, as you suggested."

Bill nodded. "So, what's the final deal that you got for us?"

Alex came down the stairs. "Hi, Gloria, I thought I heard your voice."

"Hi Alex. The final deal is twenty percent of the manufacturer's selling price, and my fee will be one of the units that you designed. My husband and I have been wanting a motor home." She reached into her briefcase. "Since I have your durable power of attorney, all you must do is approve the deal, signing the contract they've already approved, and I'll take care of the rest. They want to deliver your motor home this Saturday morning as they announce the new model's availability next year. They've decided to put it into production immediately."

Bill stood up. "Alex, let's go into the kitchen and confer."

She nodded. "Gloria, we'll be back in a few minutes."

Sheila was still running on the treadmill as Alex and Bill went to the kitchen. He held out his hands, and Alex took them as he spoke softly. "Let's pray silently, and then I want to hear what you think." They prayed for a few minutes. When Alex softly squeezed his hands, he opened his eyes. "So, what do you think?"

"When I heard Gloria arrive, I put down my script and began praying. I think this will be a steady source of income for us when we have slow times. I'm sure that God is watching over us."

He nodded. "Agreed. Let's go tell her."

They signed the contract, and Gloria Houser left a few minutes later. Their remaining break-time together passed quickly. On Saturday morning, their new motor home was delivered, and Alex started furnishing it with some clothing and other necessities. While she was doing that, Bill made one small modification. The "fire escape" was designed as exit-only, and Bill added an electronically controlled latch so that Sheila could get back in due to the electronic identification chip that was embedded under the skin of her neck. It was put there years earlier by Dr. Stan. Sheila was soon going in and out of the van conversion with no problems. As Bill had planned, it could be parked diagonally across two of the five spaces in their garage.

Sunday morning, they went to church in Alex's new SUV, and after worship, they lingered over lunch with Ewart and Rachel Scott. They were not going to see the clergy couple much over the next several months, so it was good to spend time with their friends.

Alex was supposed to be in the makeup artist's chair at 5:00 AM on Monday morning. After saying their good-byes to Pastor Ewart and Rachel, they went back home. Sheila seemed restless as they made their final preparations to go north. She was purring when they invited her to join them in the van. As they backed out of the driveway, Sheila deftly jumped into the sleeping space above the driving pit. Alex had removed the mattress, and Sheila was soon content to ride above them while watching out the one-way glass windows up there. It became her mobile lair.

When they parked in the hotel's parking garage, Sheila was again purring as Alex put the harness on their cat. Previously, Bill had had an extended conversation with members of the hotel staff that had been assembled by the manager, talking to them about Sheila and her needs, and telling them not to try to "handle" her.

As they walked through the hotel's lobby, they were just another celebrity couple, only with their unusual pet. No one said a word. Upstairs in their suite, there were still no sheets, blankets, or pillows in the second bedroom. Seemingly by instinct, Sheila "owned" this second bedroom as her local lair. There was even a child's sandbox in one corner loaded with kitty litter.

Since this suite was their "home" away from home, they continued to be comfortable there. The hotel often catered to celebrities, so their needs were different, but not exceptional in most ways. Bill had arranged for a supply of roasts for Sheila through a wholesale meat market and paid for that meat separately. The hotel supposedly did not charge for delivery of Sheila's meals, but their monthly hotel bill was substantial anyway.

Monday morning, the studio limo was waiting for Alex at 4:45 AM. After Bill kissed her good-bye, he and Sheila went to the garage to get the motor home. As they drove toward the mountain property, Sheila sat in the seat where Alex had been the day before, but when they left the freeway and started up the Angeles Crest Highway, she hopped up into her lair above Bill. Driving onto the property, he drove just past the contractor's trailer and parked under the large pine tree there. "Sheila?"

"Rowwl."

"Watch."

She hopped down and went out of her door in the floor under the bed. Soon she was up in the pine tree, almost entirely hidden. Bill flipped a switch, and automatic jacks leveled and steadied the converted van. Since its total length was twenty-four feet, he had a hard time thinking of it as a van. Back in San Diego, when he had rolled out the side extensions, Alex had said, "Wow! This hardly looks like a van this way!" While working here at the site, Bill would probably not be putting out the extensions unless Alex came up there to spend the night. So long as Alex's work continued to be in the Los Angeles Metroplex area, and until this house was completed, they would be spending their nights in the hotel suite.

Not long after sunrise, Ken Crain drove up and parked next to his trailer. As he got out, he grinned. "Good morning! I see you have your new van conversion!"

They shook hands. "Yes, we got it Saturday. Alex and I will probably spend most nights in our hotel suite. As I told you previously, just because I'm here or around here doesn't mean I'll be under foot as construction proceeds. I'm only here if you want me."

Ken nodded. "Did you bring your cat with you?"

Bill nodded. "She's here, but she won't be seen unless I call for her."

"Where is she? Is she in the van?"

Bill shook his head. "I've told her to watch. She's probably asleep or dozing in that large pine tree there, next to the van. So long as I'm around, she's kind of like an ultimate guard dog. You won't see her unless she wants you to, and as I've told you, she's not aggressive toward humans, and she's not dangerous unless it is absolutely necessary. Not too many months ago, three armed men attempted a home invasion while Alex and I were there with our pastor and his wife. One of them pulled a gun, and I simply said 'protect.' In just a few seconds, two of them flew through the air, and one of them simply got on his knees with his hands behind his head. Sheila sat on the man who had been armed until I told her to back off and watch."

Ken shook his head, grinning. "I assume that no one in their right mind would actually want to tangle with her."

Smiling, Bill continued. "When Alex came home to San Diego one weekend, some paparazzi followed her. Sheila scared them into backing off. Right now, I've got a phone call to make, and then I'll be doing some work on my laptop. I'll be around, at least for a while."

Ken went to work, and Bill went inside. He turned the driver's bucket seat around to face the rear and sat down. He took out his cell and called a number he previously programmed.

A male voice answered. "This is the Los Angeles Zoo and Botanical Gardens. How may I direct your call?"

"Good morning. My name is Bill Johnson. I have a large cat — a cross between a cheetah and a puma. Is there a staff veterinarian whom I can speak with?"

"Our vets keep pretty busy. May I have one of our veterinarians call you at the number from which you are now calling?"

"Yes, please. I will be available all day."

"Our chief vet's name is Debra Sue Donovan. She will probably call you back when she takes her lunch break."

"That will be fine. I'll look forward to her call. Goodbye." As he put his cell in his pocket, he heard Sheila's door open. "Hey, Sheila, I'm looking for a new doctor for you."

"Rowwl." She walked toward the rear, and into the shower stall. Bill could hear her drinking.

Bill's cell phone rang. The display said it was the zoo. "Hello?"

"Mr. Johnson, this is Dr. Debra Sue Donovan from the Los Angeles Zoo. I understand you have a cheetah-puma hybrid as a pet. Is that correct?"

"That's right. I've had her since she was a kitten. She's registered in San Diego county and has an identification chip under her skin."

"Really! This is fascinating! What can I do for you, Mr. Johnson?"

"All of Sheila's life, her vet in San Diego has been Stanly Mounce, but he is getting near retirement, and my wife and I are building a home up here on Angeles Crest Highway. I'm looking for a recommendation for a vet here in the Los Angeles area."

"Let me think for a moment," She paused. "I gather that 'Sheila' is your cat's name. If you understand that my obligations are first for the zoo's animals, I'm willing to take Sheila on when I'm not on duty here at the zoo."

"That would probably be okay, Dr. Donovan. During Sheila's first year, she saw Dr. Stan every month, but since then she's only seen him once a year."

"There was a Stanley Mounce that made a presentation at a veterinary convention a few years ago. If it is the same one, I've met him. I would need you to have Sheila's records forwarded to my laptop."

"That's not a problem. He can send it to you by secured and encrypted mail to the zoo's email address."

"Good. Tell him to use the pass phrase Sheila Johnson."

"I'd rather we use 'Ewart Scott' if you don't mind." Bill spelled it. "That way, the pass phrase is not directly connected to either me or to my wife."

"Okay. Is Sheila with you?"

"Yes, but I don't have the time to go to the zoo today."

The vet asked several more questions, and then Dr. Donovan said, "I can visit with you and Sheila there where you are this afternoon."

"That's great." Bill gave her directions.

Before the vet arrived, he started searching the Internet for web sites selling custom furniture. He established several links so that he and Alex could begin working on their interior-design ideas for their new home. He also made a weekend appointment for him and Alex to get to know an interior designer in San Diego, and he called Dr. Stan and arranged to have Sheila's file emailed to Dr. Donovan.

It was shortly after Bill had finished lunch when there was a knock on his door. He opened it to see a woman in a denim outfit wearing a backpack. "Mr. Johnson? I'm Debra Sue Donovan."

He smiled. "Good afternoon, Dr. Donovan, please come in."

As she came up the steps, she said, "We don't stand on formality at the zoo. Everyone calls me Debby."

Bill nodded. "You can call me Bill." He pointed to the other bucket seat, already turned around. "Please have a seat."

"Is Sheila here in the van with you?"

He pointed up. "When she's in the van, that's her lair where she likes to be most of the time. Right now, she's on watch."

"On watch?? Do you mean that she's trained?"

Bill nodded. "Certainly. It is one of the mysteries that make Sheila behave as Sheila. If you have your laptop in your backpack, Sheila's file should be there. Sheila can probably hear us discussing her, because when you arrived, she was hidden in the pine tree's branches above us. She's probably on her way down."

Bill heard the soft click of Sheila's door. "That's Sheila coming in now."

Sheila appeared at the doorway between their area and the rear quarters and settled down on her stomach. "Rowwl."

"Sheila, come and greet your new doctor." Sheila started forward.

Debby's mouth was slightly agape. "Wow! She's not exactly what I expected, and yet she sort-of is. She's bigger and beautiful! Her markings are a cheetah's, but they're a bit fainter." Debby held out her hand, and Sheila nuzzled it. "Her fur is much softer than I expected. May I examine her?"

Bill smiled. "Ask her."

"May I examine you, Sheila?"

"Rowwl." It was Sheila's friendly and calm greeting.

Bill nodded, "Relax, Sheila."

She went down onto her belly again and began to purr softly.

Debby took a stethoscope out of her backpack, and over the next several minutes, she examined Sheila thoroughly. "It appears you're pretty healthy, Sheila. You're much larger than I expected. Maybe you're about 190 pounds?" The vet looked at Bill, and he nodded. Debby put away her stethoscope. "Okay, Sheila, I'm all done with you for today."

Bill looked at his cat. "Inside or outside?" In a blur, Sheila was in her lair above them. "Relax, Sheila."

"Rowwl." She closed her eyes and continued to purr softly.

"Remarkable." Debby took out her laptop, and soon she was reading Sheila's file. "Where's her treadmill that I'm reading about?"

"It's at our home in San Diego. When this house is completed, it will be here. We drove up a few nights ago, and we'll take her back down there this coming weekend. We have neighbors who watch her for us."

Debby continued to read the file. "If I'm understanding all of these notes Dr. Mounce has made is correct, Sheila's understanding of voice commands is nothing short of miraculous."

Bill nodded. "You might say that." His cell phone rang with Alex's ring. "Hi, beautiful. Sheila's new vet is here and has examined her. Sheila's fine."

"Good. "There's still work being done, but I'm through for the day. I'll see you back at the hotel, okay?"

"Okay. I'll see you later." He put his phone away. "That was my wife. They're still shooting at the sound studio, but she's done for the day."

"Your wife's an actress?"

He took his phone out again and pressed a button. "Her name is Alexandra." He showed the vet the screen.

"She's your wife?" Bill nodded as he put his phone away again.

"I met her several years ago when some scenes from 'Some Women Like It Cold' were shot at the zoo. I liked her. She seemed super-smart as well as gentle and compassionate. She's quite a woman!"

Bill grinned. "I think so." He paused. "Would you like me to pay direct to your phone?" She nodded, and Bill paid her.

12.
Two Pregnancies

As an architect, Bill sometimes says it is thrilling to see something that you have imagined and drawn to take on substance. He decided that he wanted to stay on the site until the house was sealed to the weather. Although he saw things happening day by day, Alex only got to see things develop weekend by weekend. After the workers left each evening, Bill would play "fetch" with Sheila, with her running up and down the hill. She seemed to like it. Then they would get in the RV and drive to the hotel.

Each evening, when Alex and Bill talked over dinner in their hotel suite, he tried as best he could to describe what was happening. Even though he had pictures and videos to show her, it wasn't the same. They seldom watched videos, except on the weekends.

Bill got called to the studio typically about once a week – sometimes twice. Being available on their home's construction site, he could solve minor problems as they occurred. Crain Contractors began to get ahead of the original schedule. Bill talked to either Ralph or Abby regularly. They helped him filter the mail that was coming to the La Jolla house. A couple of times, Bill asked them to open something.

A certified letter came from a development company in Arizona. They were going to build a town from scratch to provide housing and business support services for a new high-tech factory just over the northern border of the state. The factory would be in Utah, and the town would be in Arizona. Bill was intrigued, but he put them off.

Meanwhile, one balmy Thursday evening Alex and Bill were having their dinner on the hotel suite's patio. Bill had good news. "Guess what?" Alex paused with a forkful of food and looked at him. "Tomorrow, our new home will be weather-tight. Things are going to move ahead faster."

"That's great! This morning I got nauseous again. The studio doctor tested my urine, and I'm pregnant."

Bill dropped his fork. He had to shout. "Wow! This is great! How will this fit in with the production schedule?"

She shook her head. "We'll be done shooting in three weeks. Then all that's left will be dubbing and post-production work. Furthermore, this coming week is a short week, so I can take Monday off. I've cleared it with Steve. I'm not in many scenes on this next week's schedule anyway. Let's go home tomorrow night. I want to get away from the pressure cooker for the weekend and go to church and hear Pastor Ewart."

"When we get back up here, we're going to have to find new doctors for both of us. Sheila's already got her new doctor. Doesn't she look like she might be putting on a little weight?"

Alex nodded and took another bite. "Sheila's nipples seem to be larger and harder, so she may be as pregnant as I am. Maybe she has gotten together with one of the pumas in the mountains. I'll ask around for doctor recommendations for you and me at the studio. My hair stylist is a great-great-grandniece of Cecil B. Demille. I like her. She and her family have lived in the area since the silent movie days. She talks about dozens of her shirttail relatives who are, in one way or another, involved in the entertainment industry. She has recommendations for everything in this city."

Bill nodded, wondering if Sheila was pregnant. "I'll take Sheila to see Dr. Stan on Monday and have him pass on what he sees to Dr. Donovan. Meanwhile, we'll spend a quiet weekend at home together. Shall we have Ralph and Abby over tomorrow?"

Alex nodded. "We're seeing our interior designers on Monday morning, so hopefully Dr. Mounce can see Sheila in the afternoon. Tomorrow night, let's broil rib eye steaks for Ralph and Abby. We owe them at least a nice dinner for taking care of Sheila so much of the time."

Bill nodded. "I've got a set of drawings already printed out for the interior designers."

Driving South on Friday evening, the traffic was heavy. Sheila slept in her lair, hardly making a move or a sound. They got home late. After letting out Alex and Sheila, Bill backed the van into the garage and shut the door.

On Saturday morning, they slept in. Their breakfast was closer to a brunch, so they made it a bigger meal. Bill was putting things in the dishwasher while Alex cut some flowers in the back yard, and his cell rang. The display simply indicated Naval Base San Diego. "Hello?"

"Hi, Bill, I was hoping you would be home. This is Admiral Jenson."

"Hi, Admiral. Alex and I are down here for a few days. What can I do for you?"

"I'm glad Alex is home too. I want to ask her a favor, and I only have your number."

Bill looked toward the patio and saw Alex coming in with some roses. "Sure! She's been outside picking some roses. I'll get her. I'll put you on hold just for a moment or two." Bill beckoned to her, and she came into the kitchen.

"What's up?"

"Admiral Jenson wants to ask you a favor. He's on hold."

She nodded briefly, putting the roses on the counter. "Put him on the speaker." Bill pressed the button. "Admiral Jenson! Thank you so much for helping us make our honeymoon connections."

"You're welcome! I was just telling your husband that I'm glad you're in town this weekend. I want to ask you a last-minute favor."

"If I can, sure. What do you need?"

"Our U.S.O. is showing one of your movies tonight at 8:00. I was wondering if you could be here at 7:30 to greet the audience and answer a few questions. Of course, you might get asked about just about anything."

Alex began smiling broadly. "This will be my first U.S.O. gig. Which movie is being shown?"

"It's '*Some Women Like It Cold.*'"

"Sure! I'd be happy to do it. I have a suggestion, though."

"What's that?"

"If it starts at 8:00, it will be over at about 9:40. I could answer questions about the movie itself. Furthermore, part of it was shot at the Los Angeles Zoo, where I'm among some cheetahs. Bill and I have a pet cat that's a cross between a cheetah and a puma. We can bring her along to add color to the evening."

They could hear the Admiral chuckling. "I've heard about Sheila from Pastor Scott. Can she handle being around a crowd?"

Bill spoke up. "Sure, Admiral, she's very well behaved. It will be no problem."

There was a moment of silence. "Since this might turn out to be a longer evening than planned, I'll tell the U.S.O. to move up the movie's start time to 6:30 due to special guests who will answer questions after the movie. I won't name names. Is that okay with you?"

Alex and Bill looked at each other, and they nodded together. She raised a finger. "Admiral, we'll get to the base's gate at 7:30 then. We won't come as show-business personalities. We'll just be friends of the Navy and the Marines. We'll need to have an area for Bill and Sheila to wait while I sign autographs."

"I'll take care of it. I'll see you later." He ended the call.

Alex focused her beautiful eyes on Bill. "This is the first time, Bill, that you're entering my world. We need to plan."

Bill nodded. "I agree. I will use the harness and leash with her."

"Right. Let's ask the Admiral to order the men not to cheer or yell."

Bill was thoughtful. "I hadn't thought of that. Sheila has never been around a loud crowd before."

"When the closing credits are done, the admiral can introduce us."

"This will be about you, so I don't expect to do much of the talking."

"You can help me tell the story of the time when paparazzi followed me south."

He smiled. "It's a nice memory now, but at first I was mad at you. You apologized profusely, and I could not remain mad at you very long."

"I was glad for that. Then, when you and Sheila go to the secure area offstage, I'll take questions about the movie. Finally, I will sign autographs and pose for pictures."

The rest of their Saturday went quickly. For dinner, they shared a porterhouse steak, and they gave Sheila one of the larger roasts they had thawed out.

At the base's security gate, they only paused briefly because the admiral had cleared them. They were escorted to a lounge next to the theater at the USO. Sheila was purring when the admiral offered his hand to her, and she nuzzled it. Bill told the admiral that he should have the audience tone down the cheers and shouts, and he agreed. Alex and Bill were given body mikes, and the Admiral simply carried one out to the front.

There was silence as he went to the middle of the stage. "Good evening. As was announced previously, we have some special guests with us tonight. The actress whom everyone simply calls Alex attends the same church that I do in La Jolla. She is here with her husband, Bill Johnson, and they have brought their pet cat with them. Their cat, named Sheila, weighs a little shy of two hundred pounds." There was some quiet murmuring. "At ease! There must be no further cheering or yelling for the rest of the evening. That's an order. Sheila is a cross between a cheetah and a puma. Sheila has never faced a large and noisy crowd before, so that's why I'm ordering all of you to hold down the noise." He turned toward the doorway. "Alex, Bill, Sheila, please join us."

As they walked to the center of the stage, there was silence, and the Admiral walked away.

Alex took the lead. "Good evening! I'm glad we're here this evening with all of you. Bill, Sheila, and I live less than ten miles from here. This is my first opportunity to do a USO show. Before I answer questions about the movie, Bill and I will tell you a little about our beginnings. Later, I'll sign autographs, and I can pose for pictures with a few of you." She paused. "Bill?"

Bill told the troops about seeing Alex's car on I-8. Alex told how Sheila was their matchmaker. When telling about the Paparazzi, Bill gave the troops a sample of Sheila's snarl. As Alex offered to answer questions about the movie, Sheila and Bill went to the lounge where they had previously waited.

Alex was infinitely patient with signing autographs and posing for pictures. Admiral Jenson stood nearby. All Alex had to do was look up at him, and he would have ended the autographs and pictures session. Alex focused on the troops, spending nearly two hours with them. Later that evening at home, they soaked in their whirlpool tub before calling it a night. Sheila stretched out on one of the rafters, purring.

Sunday morning, both Alex and Bill felt energized after spending time with the troops. They felt a real intimacy with God as they worshiped. The sermon was the first in a series on love, beginning with "Love Is Patient." The night before in their whirlpool tub, Alex and Bill had talked about how much they loved being with the troops. Bill pointed out how patient Alex had been in signing autographs. They both noticed how Sheila was totally peaceful during the entire evening.

After church, most of the questions they were asked revolved around their wedding and their honeymoon. Rachel was very curious about Alex's response to Yosemite's environment. "Didn't you work in Yosemite on one of your movie projects?"

Alex nodded. "It was not nearly as romantic as you might imagine. When we found time to sleep, we had minimal housing, but we often worked at night while sleeping during the day. We had no time for sightseeing. My honeymoon with Bill was entirely different."

Pastor Ewart nodded. "I've seen pictures of that hotel. I doubt that it is something Rachel and I could afford."

"Pastor Ewart, anytime you and Rachel would like to spend a week in Yosemite, Bill and I will pay all of your expenses."

He shook his head. "We couldn't."

Alex smiled sweetly. "But we can, and we will. Just figure out when you want to go. May through September has the biggest crowds. Bill tells me that each season has its own charms, however."

Bill nodded. "Winter can be absolutely enchanting, though cold. In the Spring the waterfalls and river are full. In the Fall, some of the colors are spectacular."

Later, as they pulled out of the church parking lot, Alex pointed toward downtown San Diego. "We haven't had a really good seafood dinner in a long time. What's your favorite here in San Diego, Bill?"

"The best I can think of is The Ocean Air Seafood Landing."

"Let's gorge ourselves on seafood for lunch. Does Sheila like seafood?"

"I don't know, but I would be worried about her getting small bones in her system. Pumas will eat fish, but cheetahs are not known to do so. There's a fish market down that way. Maybe we can pick up some filets and see how she likes them."

They had a wonderful and filling lunch, and then they picked up ten pounds of halibut filets to try with Sheila. At home in the kitchen, Bill took out one filet and put the rest in the freezer. He put the one fresh filet in Sheila's dish, and she approached it tentatively, sniffing it. After taking a small bite, she wolfed the rest down. For the next ten minutes, she was purring and nuzzling them.

Bill left a message with Stan Mounce's answering service that he wanted to bring in Sheila for a checkup on Monday afternoon. He did it just before going upstairs with Alex. Before going to sleep, they talked more about their USO visit in addition to talking about their morning at church. Sheila laid down at the foot of their bed, purring, as Bill turned out the lights.

13.
Interior Design

As expected, their doorbell rang at 9:00 AM Monday morning. Bill opened the door. "Good morning! Are you the McGuires?"

The man nodded. "Good morning! Yes, I'm Roger, and this is my wife, Mary Ann."

"I'm Bill Johnson. Come in."

Alex came into the entry hall from the kitchen. "Good morning! I'm Bill's wife, Alex. Instead of having you sit down in our great room, we'll start by giving you a tour of our current home." Both nodded, and Alex led them into the kitchen. She continued. "Bill was the architect of both this home and our new one up north. We have a walk-in refrigerator there," she pointed, "and inside and beyond it is a walk-in freezer. As you will see later, our new home will also have a very modern kitchen."

They went into the great room. Roger pointed up toward the beams, and Mary Ann nodded. Then she froze. "What – or who is that?"

Bill grinned. "That's Sheila. She's our 190-pound house cat. She's half puma and half cheetah. She gets a lot of her necessary exercise on that treadmill by the window." He pointed. "Would you like to meet her? She is not dangerous unless it is necessary." They looked at one another and then shook their heads. Bill nodded. "That's okay. That's fine. Different people react in different ways." Bill looked up. "Sheila, relax." She closed her eyes.

Alex touched Mary Ann's arm. "Sheila was our matchmaker. She brought us together." She pointed down. "We have a basement in both this house and in the new one, but we don't need your expertise for that, I don't think." The door beyond the stairs that you see goes to our laundry room. The other door next to the stairs, " she pointed, "leads to a half bath. The door closest to the front simply goes into the garage."

Bill nodded. "In our new home, the great room, kitchen, and dining area are on the entrance level, just as it is here."

Roger slowly turned, scanning all that was in view from where he was standing. "Will you be putting this house up for sale?"

"We will, as soon as we have moved into our new home. This door," Bill pointed to the one next to the fireplace, "leads to my study. We might as well go in there next, as I have sketches of our new home displayed on the walls there. After that, we'll go upstairs to the bed and bath suites."

When they went into Bill's study, Alex and Bill stood back as Roger and Mary Ann studied Bill's sketches one by one. They made notes on their tablets. Bill gave them a mailing tube with copies of all the sketches displayed in the study. Upstairs, they made generous compliments regarding the walk-in closets and bath suites. They were there most of the morning.

Finally, the interior designers were ready to leave. Alex and Bill stood with them in the entry hall. Mary Ann was enthusiastic. "You haven't told us why you chose us, but we're glad you did. So, do you think you'll have the inside mostly completed by late summer?"

Bill nodded. "If everything stays on schedule, I anticipate mid-August as the time to move in."

Roger nodded. "We'll have some suggestions ready for you to look at in early June. That will be preliminary. Mary Ann and I will have to go up there and see the inside, even in a rough state, before we can sit down with you and discuss everything we will propose to you."

Alex nodded. "When we have that final discussion, it will have to be on a weekend. I'll be in a sound studio most weekdays. Bill and I share in all of this and in all of our important decisions."

Mary Ann smiled. "I understand. It's been nice to meet you in person."

Roger also smiled. "Yes! It's been great meeting you."

Alex closed the door behind them, and Bill looked at his watch. "We have an appointment with Dr. Stan in a little over an hour."

"How about I fix us some smoothies?"

"Good idea. Can I help?"

"Sure."

They were drinking their smoothies at the counter a few minutes later. Alex looked at Bill. "What were you smirking about earlier, Bill?"

He put his glass down. "I think Roger and Mary Ann have a good marriage, but I hope she did not notice how Roger sometimes looked at you."

"She noticed. She mentioned it when we were going through my closet. Mary Ann asked if it bothers me when men leer at me. I told her that it was part of being in show business. Like I told you a long time ago, Bill, if men don't leer at me occasionally, I become a bit self-conscious about my makeup or wonder if there's something wrong with what I'm wearing. I also told her that one of the things I noticed about you from the beginning, Bill, is that you have always been transparent and very real to me, caring about the real me – and not merely how I look."

"How did she respond?"

"Mary Ann simply nodded. By the way, I've never met Dr. Mounce. I'd like to go along."

"Okay. This visit will be different than usual because previously, I've always gone in the early morning before other animals are in the waiting room that could get upset." He looked up. "Sheila, let's go see Dr. Mounce. He's waiting for us."

"Rowwl." She leaped down. The three of them headed into the garage.

As they drove into Dr. Mounce's parking lot a few minutes later, it was full of cars. Bill touched a button on his steering wheel. "Call Stanly Mounce DVM."

"Stanley Mounce veterinary services, Sally speaking."

"Hi, Sally, this is Bill Johnson. We've just pulled into the parking lot. I'm wondering if we should come in the front door as usual, or is there another entrance?"

"Our waiting room is packed. Hold on a moment." It did not take long. "On the east side of the building, there's a door with a sign that says 'private.'"

"Okay, Sally."

Bill got out, went around, and opened Alex's door. After she got out, Sheila hopped down next to her, and Alex fastened on Sheila's leash. They walked rapidly up an alley next to the building, and Sally was standing in the doorway, holding the door open. When she saw Alex, Sally's mouth dropped open in surprise, and her eyes got big. Inside, Alex extended a hand. "You must be Sally. I'm Bill's wife, Alex."

"I'd recognize you anywhere! It's very nice to meet you!"

Alex nodded. "It's nice to meet you too, Sally. Where shall we go?"

"This way." She led them to an examination room that Sheila and Bill had seen many times. The cat hopped up on the table and settled down. "Dr. Mounce should be here in less than five minutes."

Bill nodded. "Okay, Sally, thank you." She closed the door behind her. He scratched Sheila's head. "Well, girl, we'll find out soon enough if you're preggers."

"Rowwl."

A few moments later, Dr. Mounce walked in. "Good morning!" He looked at my wife and nodded. "And you are Alex!" He extended a hand, and she took it. "My wife and I are fans. You select your scripts very carefully, don't you?"

Alex nodded. "I do, but why do you say so?"

"I'm 83 years old, and my wife and I like movies with clean dialog and good story lines. Your movies never have a lot of violence or gore." He paused and looked down at their cat. "Hi, Sheila!"

"Rowwl." She began to purr softly.

He scratched her head. "What brings you in here at the last minute like this?"

Alex smiled. "We think maybe she's pregnant."

"Really! Okay, Sheila, it's examination time." Their cat flopped over onto her side as her doctor pressed and probed, and he listened with his stethoscope. "Yes, Sheila, you are definitely pregnant." He turned to Bill. "Gestation time for either a puma or a cheetah is about three months, so I wouldn't expect Sheila to be any different. This is only a guess, but she appears to be about in her second month. She probably won't slow down or get lethargic until about a week before she gives birth."

Bill nodded. "The other day, we gave her a halibut steak, and she really seemed to like it."

"Pumas eat fish and almost any meat protein. In Africa, cheetahs prey upon small mammals. Fish should be okay. I think fish should be a periodic diet variation rather than on her regular diet. She'll give birth to a litter in 5-7 weeks. I'm retiring at the end of the month. I will send my findings from today to both Debby Donovan up near your new home and to Dr. Miles Soto at the zoo here in town. I've discussed Sheila with him. He's a good man, and you can trust him as you do me."

Alex looked at him. "So, do you and your wife have plans for your retirement?"

He grinned. "She has plans, and I'm going along for the ride. We've always wanted to visit Israel and Greece. She has us booked on a cruise." He looked down at their cat. "Sheila, this may well be the last time I see you. You have spiced up my patient list these last several years!" He scratched behind her ears one more time as the cat nuzzled him and purred.

As they drove out of the parking lot a few minutes later, Bill looked over at Alex. "I'll have to spend the rest of today and most of tomorrow working on those revised plans for Steve. I told him I would try to have them finished and in his email by tomorrow night, remember?"

Alex nodded. "I've got to talk to our current doctors and specialists here in San Diego about referrals for up north. As you've noticed, I have morning sickness nearly every morning now. By the way, there's a church dinner tomorrow night. I'd like to go, but what about you?"

"If my work isn't done by then, I guess I can go to the church dinner to take a break. Come to think of it, why don't you call Rachel, and see if she can get some of the doctors in the congregation to sit with us at the dinner, so we can get their input?"

"That's a great idea! Los Angeles is so huge; we'll probably get a dozen or so suggestions."

Bill worked throughout the day. The plans he created were the same outward design as the original set, but the structure beneath the set was such that, if he thought it necessary, Steve would be able to put more than fifty people on the set. Bill did not even think about taking a break for lunch, and time flew by before Alex walked in. "We need to get ready to go. The church dinner starts in less than an hour."

He looked at his watch. "Good! This is a good time to stop. I've probably got less than an hour's work left to do, and I can email everything to Steve before we go to bed tonight."

A short time later, they pulled into the church's parking lot. After filling their plates in the serving line, Rachel pointed out a table where she wanted them to sit. A couple sitting there looked vaguely familiar to Bill, but Alex recognized them immediately! "Niña! It's great to see you! We haven't seen you in a long time." They hugged, and Bill shook hands with her husband. When Alex spoke to Niña, Bill remembered their names and who they were. Niña and Paul Eddy both attended the church almost every Sunday. She was head of the residency program at the medical school, and he taught diagnostic imaging.

Alex and Bill sat down, and Bill turned to Niña's husband. "Paul, I'm glad that Rachel has directed us to your table this evening. Alex and I are building a home in the La Cañada Flintridge area, and we're looking for medical recommendations. We've got a vet for Sheila already, and Sheila's preggers, but Alex is pregnant too, so we're hoping you and your wife can make some suggestions."

Niña nodded. "Sure. When Rachel told us about your moving up north and what you needed, I made some calls. Paul and I wanted to visit with you first before we make recommendations via email in a day or two."

Their dinner conversations were interesting, and the food was every bit as good as they expected. As they were eating their desserts, the Christian Youth Fellowship put on a skit about Joseph and his eleven brothers who had everyone laughing in several places. Alex and Bill got home at a little after 9:00. He sent the set plans to Steve via email before they went to bed.

Wednesday morning as they were finishing breakfast, Bill's cell rang. The caller ID said the Los Angeles Zoo. He put it on the speaker. "Hello?"

"Good morning, Bill, this is Debby. I received Stanley Mounce's notes on Sheila yesterday, and this is my first chance to call you. I want to see Sheila as soon as we can arrange it in order to monitor her pregnancy. Where are you right now?"

"Good morning. We're at our home in La Jolla today. What is your schedule like this week?"

"I could drive up to your construction site this morning, but that's out. The rest of this week I'm booked solid here at the zoo. What about this coming weekend?"

"We have a standing reservation for a suite at the Peninsula of Beverly Hills for the weekends over the next six months. Would you like to make a house call there?"

"How about Sunday afternoon? What time may I meet you there?"

Alex held up a finger, and when Bill nodded, she spoke.

"Debby, this is Alex. We're going to go to church Sunday morning here in La Jolla, but if we leave right after church, there should be no problem meeting you at the hotel in our suite in the late afternoon. How about 4:00 o'clock?

"That sounds fine. I'll be there at 4:00." There was a quiet click as she hung up."

Alex was nodding. "This works out fine for all of us. After church, you and Sheila go in the van, and I'll follow in my Subaru. I'll keep my car up there from this day forwards in the hotel parking garage."

"Good. Eventually, we'll park the motor home in our new home's garage, and I'll be using my car when you're at work. I think I'll have Roger and Mary Ann McGuire meet us at the new house this coming week, now that it is closed to the weather. They said they wanted to see it even in its rough state. Let's make a reservation for them at the hotel for a night or two."

"Right."

Other than a thank you phone call from Steve on Friday afternoon, Thursday, Friday, and Saturday were a mini vacation for them. They took Ralph and Abby out to dinner on Friday night to express their appreciation for all the times they had watched the house and taken care of Sheila.

Sunday morning, they had a surprise. Many months earlier, Bill drew up plans for some simple ways to expand the seating capacity of the worship area. During the announcements, Pastor Ewart acknowledged Bill's donation of the plans, and then it was announced that a contractor had been secured to do the work over the summer. An anonymous donor was covering the expenses of the expansion. (It was Alex, by way of a foundation that was established with Gloria's assistance.)

While they were having lunch, Bill gave Sheila a roast to eat. They were on their way north in the motor home before 1:00 PM. The Sunday afternoon traffic was very light. When they got to the hotel, Alex and Sheila went to the suite while Bill went to the front desk.

The manager was on duty. "Good afternoon, Mr. Johnson. How may we assist you?"

"Good afternoon, Mr. Thompson. We have secured the services of a veterinarian from the Los Angeles Zoo to be Sheila's doctor. Her name is Dr. Debra Sue Donovan. I understand that she has been here previously once or twice."

He nodded. "That is correct. Will she be making a house call this afternoon?"

"Yes, she is due to be here at 4:00 PM. Please have someone escort her to our suite as soon as she gets here."

Again, he nodded. "I'll see that it is done, Mr. Johnson. Will there be anything else?"

Bill shook his head. "No, thank you, that will be all." Bill went to the suite. Inside, Sheila was asleep in her lair, and Alex was seeming to take a nap in one of the recliners.

She opened her eyes when Bill came in the door. "Is everything set?"

"Yep." He looked at his watch. "Dr. Donovan should be here in about a half hour. I'm thirsty. Can I get you something from the fridge?"

She raised the recliner and got up. "I'm not sure what I want, so let's look together."

They watched a newscast while they slaked their thirsts and waited for the vet. At 4:35, there was a knock on their door, and Alex answered. "Good afternoon, Debby, it's good to see you again."

The vet smiled broadly. "Hi, Alex, I'm surprised that you remember me! It has been what, three years?"

Alex nodded. "We wrapped that production three and a half years ago next month. Bill and I recently were at the Naval Base in San Diego when the U.S.O. showed that movie, and after I introduced Bill and Sheila, I signed autographs and posed for pictures. It was a great experience."

Bill was smiling at the vet. "Hi, Debby. It's good to see you. Sheila probably woke up when she heard your voice."

Alex nodded. "Come on, I take you to Sheila's local lair." They went into the second bedroom of the suite.

"Hi, Sheila!" Debby reached out and scratched the cat's head. "I'm here to see about you and your future litter, okay?"

"Rowwl." Sheila rolled over on her side as the vet opened her satchel bag and took out her stethoscope.

Debby's expertise was fluid and swift. After about ten minutes, she put away her stethoscope and closed her bag. "My best estimate is that Sheila will give birth to four kittens in about five weeks, maybe a few days more. She will probably start slowing down and being more sluggish in the last week or so. Her appetite will increase, and she won't be inclined to do much running. She'll probably still be moving around right up until an hour or two before she starts to give birth. Give me a call about once a week. I don't charge for phone calls." She smiled.

14.
Coming Deliveries

Unlocking the front door on Monday morning, Bill let decorators Roger and Mary Ann go in first. He had left Sheila in the suite at the hotel. "This is the mud room. There needs to be places for people to sit down, take off their shoes, and put them on a shelf or a rack. There also needs to be a rack for house-supplied washable slippers for those who want to wear them over their stockings. The door on the far right goes to the garage and workshop. This door here on the left leads into the great room."

Mary Ann took in the little room. "We're familiar with how popular it is in the Mid-west to have so-called mud rooms as a buffer between the outside and the interior. Roger, the lighting is warm, so we'll need to create coziness."

He nodded. "The setting and the architecture are both rustic, so we must ensure a natural coziness."

"You've got the idea." Bill gestured. "This way." They stepped into the great room.

Roger whistled. "Wow. Your sketches don't do this justice. This is the most spacious log home I've ever seen. I can see how your using logs just for the posts and beams help you keep things well insulated."

Mary Ann nodded and pointed. "Where was that log staircase made?"

"The factory is called Custom Stairs Inc., and it is between Riverton and Casper in Wyoming. As you know, the stairs lead to the bedrooms and baths upstairs and down into the basement. On this level, the extra-large half-bath is next to the kitchen. You might like to check that out first."

Most of the day, Bill just watched and listened as Roger and Mary Ann took pictures and made measurements. They were so immersed in their work that they did not stop for lunch, although Ken Crain supplied them with some iced tea and bags of trail mix he brought over from his trailer. Bill went into his van and fixed a light lunch.

Late in the afternoon, Alex arrived. "Hello Roger! Mary Ann! I'm surprised you're still here!" She gave Bill a hug and a brief kiss.

Roger shook his head. "Mary Ann and I want to come back tomorrow morning. I'm glad you've arranged for a night in a hotel. We've seen the upstairs level, but Mary Ann and I still need to discuss the possibilities up there. Your husband was not sure our expertise was needed down below in the basement, but Mary Ann and I have taken some pictures down there, and we'll give you some suggestions in a couple of weeks."

She nodded. "We're excited about the possibilities here on the main level. On this beautiful clear day with the Santa Ana winds blowing, being able to see Catalina Island in the distance, beyond the Los Angeles basin, is wonderful."

Alex turned to Mary Ann. "I'm interested in your ideas for the basement. Let's go downstairs. I want to hear some of those ideas."

As the women headed for the stairs, Roger and Bill walked toward the kitchen. He showed the same enthusiasm as Mary Ann. "I love the way you designed both of your houses. When you and Alex are ready to sell your house in La Jolla, let us know. We want to bid. Mary Ann says that when she saw your walk-in fridge down there, that was the clincher for her."

"I understand that you and Mary Ann are vegan. Alex and I are going to take you two to dinner at a place called Union in Pasadena that has excellent vegan fare."

The sun was low in the sky when they left the house and went down the hill to dinner in Pasadena before going on to the hotel. Sheila was happily purring when she greeted Alex and Bill. He picked up the house phone. "This is Bill Johnson. What kinds of pie do you have for desserts today?"

"In addition to cherry and apple, we have Texas pecan and our seasonal special, strawberry."

Bill looked at his beloved wife. "They have strawberry pie." She nodded with a smile. "My wife and I will have slices of strawberry pie with plenty of whipped cream. Furthermore, send over a large roast for Sheila."

"Two slices of strawberry. Would you like coffee?"

"Make it decaf Earl Gray instead of coffee."

"Okay, Earl Gray... and a roast for your cat."

"Correct."

"It will be about ten minutes, Mr. Johnson."

"Thank you." Bill hung up.

Alex put her arms around him. "We've not had Earl Gray in months! After we eat our dessert, let's get a shower and head for prayers and sleep."

He kissed her. "I agree."

Alex had an early call to the makeup chair, so Tuesday morning they had only a light breakfast before she left in the studio limo-van. Sheila started to purr louder when she and Bill started for the parking garage and the motor home. When they got to the home site, Sheila got out with him. She stayed by his side as he went into the house. Quickly going up the stairs, she leaped across to a nearby rafter, and soon she was stretched out and fast asleep.

The previous days' time with Roger and Mary Ann was on his mind as he strolled about and made notes on his tablet. He also stood for a long time by the main windows of the great room, gazing out and studying the fog that had come in during the night. In the distance, he could see Signal Hill standing above the fog.

He was standing there when Ken Crain walked in at shortly after 8:00. "Good morning, Bill. Is Sheila with you?"

Bill pointed upward. "I hope she won't spook any of those working today. Our interior decorating team will be here shortly."

He shook his head. "I doubt Sheila will bother anyone. They all know that she is around, and most of them have gotten at least a glimpse of her. Besides, plumbers are finishing up the old barracks, and nothing seems to bother the electricians."

"Okay, Ken. Yesterday, when the decorators were here, they made some remarks I want to discuss with you, maybe this afternoon."

"Sure."

"Also, aren't the landscapers coming this week?"

He nodded. "Tomorrow."

"Good. I've got a friend named Will Sullenberger, who is an ecologist. I'm going to ask him to join us first thing tomorrow morning to talk about landscaping fire buffers. I want both Alex and I to feel as secure as possible when the brush fire season comes along."

"Okay."

"Sheila and I will be here most of the day if you need me. I'll see you around."

As Ken walked toward the kitchen, Bill went to the wall of windows and sat down on the floor, leaning against one of the log beams. The house was beginning to feel like a home. He put in his phone call to Will Sullenberger, and Roger McGuire called to say they decided they had enough information and would have a presentation ready for the following weekend.

That evening, when Bill and Sheila walked into the hotel suite, Alex was already there and greeted him. "Hi, handsome!"

"Hey, gorgeous! How was your day?" They hugged and shared a lingering kiss.

She looked down. "Hi, Sheila!" She scratched their cat's head.

Alex was relaxed. "Unless we have to re-shoot a scene, the camera work was a wrap this afternoon. In the weeks ahead, it's all dubbing and post-production work. How's our house coming? Are we on schedule?"

"Actually, Ken indicated to me this afternoon that we're a little ahead of schedule. I've called Will Sullenberger, an ecologist friend of mine, who is coming in tomorrow morning to consult with us and with the landscape people. I want us to do all we can to protect our property from brush fires."

They sat down and snuggled together. "You've talked about that several times. We're having an outdoor sprinkling system. Won't that be enough?"

Bill shook his head. "Even with a hundred gallons a minute being pumped over our acreage, we have to have fire-resistant foliage zones around the house. Meanwhile, Mary Ann and Roger plan to have a presentation ready for us next weekend, and you and I will have decisions to make. What time do you think you can get away from this area on Friday?"

"I'll talk to Steve about it tomorrow. Maybe we can get away as early as Friday at noon."

"Good!" It looks like neither of us is sleepy. Shall we watch a video?"

"Sure. A while back, you mentioned a Disney movie I had never heard of, and during our lunch break today, Dietra mentioned the same movie."

"Which one?"

"*Something Wicked This Way Comes.*"

"Let's see if it is on the hotel's movie list." Bill picked up the remote control for the entertainment center. He scrolled down the list. "There it is!"

Bill enjoyed seeing it again, and Alex had mixed feelings. "I've read the book, and I don't think the screenplay was a good reflection of it." They had a lively debate. An hour and a half later, they turned off the lounge area lights and went to their bedroom. Sheila remained in her bedroom lair.

The remainder of the week went quickly, and Alex got away from the sound studio after lunch on Friday. She decided to leave her car in the new house's garage so that she could drive Bill's car north after the weekend. Driving south in the motor home van, Sheila stretched out on the floor near the rear of the van. Her pregnancy had slowed her down slightly, and she no longer leapt into her lair above the driving compartment.

Saturday morning, Roger and Mary Ann McGuire rang their doorbell promptly at 9:00 AM. Alex and Bill had finished their breakfast and had put the dishes in the dishwasher. Mary Ann was full of energy as they went into the great room. "We've worked up this presentation more quickly than we do usually for clients because we're both so excited about this project."

Roger opened a laptop and sent a signal to Alex and Bill's video display. "We were talking about your new house all the way back here to San Diego as we drove. We think your house may become a showplace, so we want everything to be just as perfect as we can make it."

Alex nodded. "We picked you two because you were recommended by several families at our church."

Mary Ann looked at her. "What church is that?"

"We are part of Torrey Pines Evangel Church."

Mary Ann's eyes grew wider. "Oh! That is such a beautiful complex, and the worship area is magnificent!"

Roger started with the basement. "You told us about wanting your library to be along the long wall on the right facing toward the windows. We are recommending that the lower thirty inches be enclosed cabinets with a countertop like this." Their display showed a sketch.

Bill glanced at Alex. "Alex and I have talked frequently about this. We would like a forty-inch wide cabinet on each end of the wall that is separated by a slight gap from the bookcases like you've sketched there. The cabinets at each end should have shelves spaced much wider – maybe eighteen to twenty inches – to display art pieces and awards."

Bill told this to Roger and Mary Ann because the hidden door into the secret space has a door that is forty inches wide. That's the one in the front near the windows. The door was temporarily hidden by sheet rock. A safe was going to be installed in the wall behind the case at the hillside end.

Roger continued. "That's an easy adjustment to make, Bill. We recommend that your basement be carpeted with sixty-ounce ultra-plush Herculon except for three feet of tile close to the windows."

The presentation lasted almost all morning. Bill and Alex were particularly happy with the bedroom furniture they had selected because the wood was a carryover from the post and beam construction of their new home. They designed three conversation pits for the great room, allowing for the video screen for one of them. The fireplace was the center of the second pit. The third conversation area was around a table near the kitchen. The table could quickly be enlarged and raised for a meal, with seating for twelve. Within the tiled kitchen area, Alex and Bill agreed on a smaller table in addition to the counter space.

As Alex closed the door behind them shortly before noon, she turned, and they hugged. "Bill, this is going to be incredible! I'm so glad that our current bedroom dressers will fit into the new décor. It's ingenious how they've designed a space for Sheila's treadmill."

Bill nodded and smiled. "I was also impressed that they've provided industrial-grade carpeting for that one narrow wall in the great room. Sheila will love climbing that to get to the log beams."

They walked into the great room and sat down together on the sofa. Alex spoke more softly. "Will you bolt that one cabinet to the door of the World War II bunkhouse?"

Bill nodded. "We'll have a fully equipped workshop next to the garage. Whenever I need to build or adapt something, I'll have all the tools I need. Ken has already ordered everything for it. By the time we move the stuff we're keeping from this house into the new one, Ken will see to it that everything else is in place. Some of this furniture will go into the hidden apartment next to the basement, so we're not giving away very much. Let's rent a storage unit to save the rest for the church's next yard sale."

Alex nodded. "That sounds fine. Let's see if Abby and George would like to come over this evening for dinner. We might not have another opportunity."

That decision turned out to be important. The finishing touches on their new house would take less than a month, and the next morning, they worshiped for the last time with their church friends at Torrey Pines.

The whole month of July was a blur of memories to be treasured in years to come. On the fifth of July, Phil Willets from Platinum Pawn in Burbank drove up to see how the house was coming along. As he pulled into the now-concrete parking area in front of their garage, Ken Crain and Bill were talking. Bill waved.

Phil Willets got out of his car. "Wow! This place has come a long way! I hardly recognize this area. How soon will you and your wife move in?"

Bill smiled. "Good morning, Phil. This is Ken Crain, our contractor." They shook hands. "It will probably be early next month when we move in. Would you like to look inside? It's cooler!"

"Sure!"

Bill led the way as he opened the door. "After everything is moved in, this will be the mud room, where people will take off their shoes before going on inside." He led him through the door into the great room and stopped.

Phil let his gaze sweep throughout the room, but he did not spot Sheila gazing down at them from nearly thirty feet up in the beams. "I love it! Maybe I'll have you build a house for my family someday."

Bill nodded. "Just let me know. ... The bedrooms are upstairs. This level includes the kitchen, my office, a workshop, a half bath, and the garage. The laundry is upstairs. The basement includes a family room and library, as well as a half bath."

Phil smiled. "Did you have any problem getting rid of the bunker?"

Bill shook his head. "I didn't see any demolition. I saw them start drilling the anchors into the hillside, and I saw some of the creation of the foundation."

"I'll bet finding that thing was a surprise."

Bill smiled. "It certainly was."

He nodded. "What's left to do?"

"Some custom furnishings will be coming during the next two weeks, such as bookcases for the basement and custom bedroom furnishings for upstairs. Those will fit in with the log home motif. The tools for my workshop are already here. We're almost ready for our final inspection. I'm glad you stopped by. How much of the furnishings from the old bunkhouse have you taken on for sale?" They started moving toward the door.

"I took ten bunk beds, and I've already sold three of them. I got a really nice price for that old alcohol stove, and I gave 75% of the sale to the museum."

They went outside, and Phil left a few minutes later. That evening Bill told Alex about it. Her eyes grew wide. "I guess I should not have worried about how we would handle questions about the bunker."

"I've been expecting to have to call Debby about Sheila almost every day, but she doesn't seem to be particularly sluggish yet."

Alex shook her head. "No, her gestation seems to be taking longer than either vet anticipated." They had similar conversations for the next two weeks.

Sheila was obviously heavier than usual, but otherwise she seemed very normal. She was up on one of the beams in the great room when the custom furnishings arrived. Bill installed an electronic lighting control in the great room so that when the sun was particularly bright in the afternoons, the voltage to the electronic shading would change. The changes were so gradual they were hardly noticed.

On the second Thursday in August, they had their final inspection and approval. The next day, the furniture from La Jolla arrived. Alex was at the studio, and Bill had the movers store the "extra" furniture, the things that would go into the secret apartment conversion of the army barracks, at the rear of the basement. After the movers left, Ken Crain and two of his brothers moved that furniture into the secret apartment. They worked together to get the one shelving cabinet mounted to the bunker door so that the shelving lined up with the other units. Ken also helped Bill fasten a hidden connecting latch for the door in the cabinet, which was anchored to it.

Leaving Sheila to watch things, Alex and Bill drove down the hill and got some tacos. They then stopped at Mel's Supermarket. Bill handed a clerk a list he had made, and Alex added several things to the list after signing a few autographs. Going back up the hill, their motor home and Alex's car were already in the garage, and Bill parked next to Alex's Subaru.

Alex and Bill were in their new home at last.

15.
Litter Arrival

Bill slept like a rock. Alex was still sound asleep when he slowly and quietly got up and went into the bathroom. He was almost to the door when Alex spoke. "Good morning!"

"Good morning!" He turned, went back to the bed, and knelt beside her on her side. "It's good to wake up here rather than in the hotel, isn't it?" He kissed her, and she put her arms around his neck. When they broke for air Bill said, "I still have to go where I was going, but I'll be back."

"Only if you must!"

They spent more than an hour that morning singing, praying, and reading the Bible. As they got dressed, Bill called out, "Sheila?" He put on his shoes. "Strange! I wonder what Sheila's up to?"

"Normally, she's with us and purring by the time we start dressing." Alex headed toward the door into the hall and stairs. "Sheila?"

They went downstairs and looked around. She wasn't on any of the beams. Bill touched Alex's hand. "You check the other bedrooms upstairs, and I'll check the basement."

"Right!" She started back up as he started down.

Downstairs, Bill looked in both the main area and the bathroom, but no Sheila. He took the stairs upward two steps at a time past the great room and on upstairs. When he got into the hall, he saw Alex at the far opposite end from the master suite near the window, with her index finger over her lips.

Bill strode rapidly, and when he reached Alex, she was smiling, and she took his hand. Leading him past the bedroom, they went into the bathroom. Sheila was in the oversized bathtub. With her were four nursing kittens. Bill was thrilled. "Good morning, Sheila!"

"Rowwl."

Alex knelt by the tub and scratched her head. "Your timing is perfect, girl. Bill and I got moved in yesterday, and now, here's your family."

Bill knelt beside Alex and scratched beneath Sheila's chin. "Debby was right. You have a litter of four." He took out his cell, hit a speed dial button, turned on the speaker, and put the phone on the edge of the tub. "Good morning, Debby, this is Bill Johnson."

"Good morning, Bill. Is Sheila finally slowing down?"

"We are looking at a litter of four kittens. Look." He turned the phone's camera on and turned it toward their new family.

"That's fantastic! That looks like a bathtub. Where are you?"

"Alex and I are in our new home. We moved in yesterday."

"This is great timing for you! I'm not on duty this morning, so I can be there in an hour or so. Would you mind if I bring my husband along, so that he can see them too?"

Alex turned toward the phone. "That's no problem, Debby. We'll see you later."

Bill ended the call and looked at his watch. "Our first grocery order, the one you ordered last evening, is supposed to be delivered in around ten minutes or so. Let's take Sheila's dishes upstairs, so that bedroom will be her lair. We can move her sandbox in there later if necessary."

Alex nodded. "Okay. When the groceries get here, I'll put everything away and make a pot of coffee while you go down the mountain and grab us some breakfast sandwiches. Get two for each of us! I'm starving."

Bill heard a noise outside. "That must be the grocery truck. I'll go and let them in if you'll get Sheila's dishes."

They started moving quickly. After Alex put Sheila's dishes in the guest bathroom, then she went into the garage and into the motor home. There was still a roast there in the fridge that they had taken with them when they left the hotel. She went upstairs and put it in Sheila's dish.

Meanwhile, Mel and his assistant manager of the Mel's Supermarket brought in the groceries. This initial stocking of the pantry, fridge, and freezer was a big order. All pantry items were piled on the counter and breakfast nook table. It was probably at least three times the size of a typical order. After digitally signing the chit, Bill went looking for Alex as the grocers drove away.

She was with Sheila and the kittens. "The grocers are gone, but there's lots of stuff to put away. I'm headed downhill for our breakfasts, so I should be back in twenty or thirty minutes."

Alex nodded. "Okay. I've been talking with Sheila, and we've named the kittens. When I suggested a name, but she didn't respond, I tried other names until Sheila responded." She pointed. "That's Harry." The kitten looked up at Alex. "His markings are almost identical to Sheila's, and amazingly he seems to respond to that name, doesn't he?" She pointed again. "That's Tammie." The little female came over and nuzzled Alex's hand, and when Bill reached down, Tammie also nuzzled his hand. "She doesn't look at all like Sheila, but rather looks just like a normal puma."

Alex pointed again. "That is Krister." He bounded over and started playing with Alex's pointing finger. "As you can see, he physically looks like Tammie in shape and proportions, but he has some of Sheila's markings." Alex pointed toward the other end of the tub. "Finally, that's Cherrie. She's the wildest of the four. She is playfully attacking the others frequently, and Sheila has already swatted her once. She looks a lot like Krister, but she isn't as nice." She stood up. "I'm still starving. If you can, get some side orders of bacon and anything else that looks good." As they started out, Sheila got out of the tub and went to her dish. She quickly disposed of the roast as Alex and Bill were leaving the bedroom. Cherrie started walking past her, but she put the kitten back in the tub.

They started down the stairs, and she spoke quietly. "I'll help get us settled in during the weekends, but for the next few weeks, my days will be filled with sound dubbing. Do you think we should keep all four kittens?"

Until that moment, Bill hadn't given it any thought. "I don't know, but I doubt it. It's one more thing for us to pray about." At the bottom of the staircase, they started toward the kitchen, and his cell beeped. His caller ID said it was the developer from northern Arizona. Bill showed the display to Alex, and she waved as she went on into the kitchen.

Bill headed for the conversation pit near the windows as he answered. "Good morning. This is Bill Johnson."

"Good morning, Mr. Johnson, this is Carlton Weathers of Weathers Developers."

"Yes, Mr. Weathers."

"I'm calling to ask you to re-consider my proposal to design a company town for Northern Arizona."

Bill sat down. "I've just completed building a house in the foothills northeast of Los Angeles, and my wife and I moved in yesterday. In my spare time, I've been looking at two similar projects in Northern California and Southern Oregon. Are you familiar with them?"

"Yes. My partners and I have a development in mind like the one near Yreka, California, except we want our development to pursue a goal of net zero energy consumption."

"I see." Bill paused to think. "You're talking about each building being super-insulated and generating as much electrical energy as it consumes." He paused again. "There would be two major consequences to that approach, Mr. Weathers."

"Call me C-W."

"All right, C-W. You can call me Bill. First, you are talking about a development cost of twenty-five to thirty percent higher than a development cost of a town that does not pursue net zero. If done right, and I would not want to do it any other way, the energy savings would pay off the increased development cost in five to seven years. This is August. It would take six to eight months of long hours of work to get this ready for beginning the construction, which at the earliest couldn't begin before next May." The call ended a few moments later, and Bill headed down the mountain to get their breakfasts.

Alex and Bill had almost finished off all the breakfast goodies he bought when the doorbell rang. He looked at Alex. "That's probably Debby and her husband."

As Alex quickly gathered up their trash and put it in the compacter, Bill went to the door. "Good morning, Debby."

"Good morning, Bill, this is my husband, Walt."

Bill shook his hand. "Good morning, Walt. I'm Bill. Come in. Just leave your shoes on one of the racks. If you want to wear slippers, take your pick, but Alex and I are just in our socks." They sat on the bench and took off their shoes. As they entered the great room, Alex was there to greet them. "Good morning! I overheard the introductions. You must be Walt. Call me Alex." They shook hands.

They looked up and around at the great room. Debby's mouth hung open slightly. "This is an amazing house you've created! I love it!" Walt nodded.

"Thank you." Bill smiled. "Sheila's upstairs. Follow me."

As they went up the spiral staircase, Debby and her husband continued to take in the surroundings. At the top of the stairs, Alex pointed. "All the bedrooms are up here. The guest room, one of the bedrooms, has become Sheila's lair and a nursery. This way."

As they entered, Sheila looked up at Debby and her husband and greeted them. "Rowwl."

After Alex pointed out each kitten by name, Debby let each one smell her hand. The only hostile kitten was Cherrie, as Alex and Bill expected. Sheila reacted with her "Rowwl," and Cherrie calmed down immediately.

The examinations took over an hour. Debby gave each of the kittens a shot. She also used a local anesthetic and put ID implant chips under the skin of their necks. Later, sitting downstairs, the prognosis was good for all of them. Debby was slightly amused. "They all have such amazingly different personalities, even when they're less than a day old. Are you going to keep all of them?"

Alex smiled. "It's too soon to make final decisions, but I suspect that we may have to donate Cherrie to the zoo."

Debby nodded. "You may be right." Alex offered them coffee, but they declined, and they were gone less than thirty minutes after Debby had finished her examinations.

The following Monday morning, Bill received hundreds of photographs of the development area, both at ground level and aerial views. It was a more than fifteen-pound package, delivered by messenger. They also sent Bill the results of surveys that had already been done, along with a proposed budget. Bill's proposed fee would be astronomical. It was a bigger project than anything he had imagined himself doing.

Bill immediately put in a phone call to Gloria Houser, giving her the essential details. She said that she would contact C-W's lawyers and then get back to him. By the time Alex got home late in the afternoon, Bill had started making some sketches.

Later, after Bill and Alex hugged and made out a little, they sat down on a sofa where they could gaze out at the sea of smog with the ocean beyond. "I'm having Gloria talk to the lawyers for the developer. I'm not sure whether it will work out, but my fee stands to be huge."

Alex nodded. "I've got news, too, on two fronts. Today, Steve explained the reason for the closed sets and non-disclosure agreements. The post-production work we are doing now is for the final movie in a seven-movie franchise. The first movie in the series, called *The Gaardian Saga: A Second Life*, will come out during the holidays this December. Furthermore, Dr. Koster says our family is due November 10th, so we've got preparations to make.

Bill was grinning. "Fantastic! We'll turn one of the bedrooms into a nursery."

"It's triplets. Evidently, it is three boys."

His eyes must have grown to overwhelming size. "Whoa!"

"I've decided to stop doing any more movies until after the kids are in school. I talked to Charlie during lunch today." She paused. "After all this time, you've still not met my manager! You have only talked on the phone. We'll have to have her over one day next week. Anyway, I told her I would do commercials or modeling gigs in the Spring, but no more movies for a while."

Bill smiled. "It will be great having you around while I'm working. I know we're not ready to put on any parties here yet, but would you like to try having a party the night of the Los Angeles premiere of the movie?"

"That will be great! We'll have it catered, of course. Meanwhile, Steve wants to bring his wife, Michaela, over for a visit after post-production ends next month. He wants to see what we have built."

Time flew by. For Labor Day weekend, Alex and Bill flew to Arizona. They asked Abby and George to spend the weekend in their new house to watch over Sheila and the kittens.

Flying a chartered flight on Friday afternoon to St. George, Utah, C-W and his wife met them at the airport and gave a tour via helicopter of the area where the town would be built. Bill asked the pilot to set down in several places so that he could make some of his own panoramic images. They got back to St. George in the late afternoon, in time for C-W and his wife to invite them to have an early dinner with them.

Alex and Bill declined with thanks. Alex was very diplomatic. "Because I tend to draw crowds wherever I go, we would not be able to have a relaxing dinner after such a long day. I hope you understand, but please excuse us."

Bill and Alex rented a car and drove to the North Rim of the Grand Canyon. Alex's manager, Charlie, had secured a room for them at North Rim Grand Canyon Lodge. They had a wonderful but late dinner in the dining room there as the last reds and pinks of sunset were fading. After a quick shared shower, they crawled into bed and were quickly fast asleep.

It was a good thing. With the time zone difference, and by going to bed relatively early, they could spend most of the day Saturday exploring the north rim of "the big ditch." Sunday morning, they attended an outdoor worship service, and by mid-morning they were on their way back to St. George, the airport, and on home.

On Labor Day and the day after, Alex and Bill took Abby and George to places in the Los Angeles area that many tourists fail to see. They were continuing to enjoy their friendship. With Alex's baby bump getting so much bigger, they didn't do much walking, however. Additionally, they would do no more flying until after the triplets were born.

Dr. Koster had planned on doing a caesarean section on the tenth of November, but God and the triplets had other plans. On the morning of the eighth, Alex went into labor, and Bill rushed Alex down the hill to the nearest emergency ward. Her water broke as she was being wheeled into the hospital. The ER doctor said that having birth so soon after labor pangs was unusual and having triplets that quickly was almost unheard of.

While Alex was in labor, Bill called Angela, a private duty nurse they had hired, and told her she would be needed sooner. Everything worked out. Angela met them at the hospital two days later, and they took the triplets home.

Up until the second week of December, their household was constantly in a state of flux, with babies and rapidly growing kittens. Bill was in his study most of the day and night. For breaks from work, Bill helped feed the triplets and visited with Sheila.

The kittens grew rapidly, and so did the triplets. Cherrie began to look more and more like Krister, but she didn't learn commands and continued to be mostly wild. Sheila disciplined her frequently, especially when the kitten sneaked outside. Harry quickly learned vocal commands from his mother. He could run just as fast as his mother on the treadmill, and he began to look more and more like Sheila. As Tammie grew, she developed more puma characteristics than her siblings. She could not run as fast as Harry or Sheila, but she quickly learned to respond to voice commands. Finally, Krister also looked mostly like a puma, but unlike Tammie, Krister had some of Sheila's markings. He could also run like his mama, and he learned commands quickly.

Several days before the premiere and party, Bill took Sheila on a tour of the secret apartment that had been the army bunkhouse. He had already put a sandbox in the laundry room and put extra feeding dishes there. He showed Sheila the emergency escape door, and she seemed to enjoy testing it.

On the morning before the premiere, Bill put food in the dishes there, and then he took Sheila and the kittens in there and left the lights on. He knew they would sleep most of the day in there when he closed the door on them, virtually locking them in except for the emergency escape door.

There were at least two hundred people that came and went from the party. Bill and Alex hired a private security company to watch over everything, and the food provided by the caterers was way above average. Alex was very pleased with them, and she and Bill decided that they would use them again when catering was needed. Everyone they knew agreed that the party they put on after the premiere of *A Second Life* was a success. For the next three years, their calendars in June and December had days set aside for premieres of films in the *Gaardian Saga* film franchise.

With the completion of both their house and the self-contained town in Arizona, Bill became almost as famous as Alex. From the beginning, the houses in the new town were generating more electricity than they consumed. Several news outlets featured the development, and Weathers Developers made the most of the publicity.

16.
Big Adjustments

Alex invited Peter Duvall over one weekend, and he took pictures of the kittens, the triplets, and all of them together as a family. The whole session was also recorded as a video. The kittens had very different personalities.

Cherrie was hopelessly wild, often leaping from the rafters to the floor and back. She did not take to commands, and when Sheila would discipline her, she came back for more. Alex talked eye to eye with Sheila. "Sheila, Cherrie cannot stay in the house. She can't stay here, girl. I'm sorry." Sheila licked her hand and walked away. A moment later, Debby fired a tranquilizer dart into Cherrie's flank, and the kitten was taken to the zoo.

Shortly after, Pastor Ewart and Rachel came up north for a visit. Alex was in the kitchen, and she came out and greeted them with hugs. As they took off their shoes in the mud room, Rachel asked, "Where's Bill?"

"He's in our study. He told me this morning that he would come out and spend time with us starting at dinner. He's almost finished with a phase of his current project, and he wants to remain focused. I try not to disturb him because, if one of the triplets goes into his study, he stops whatever he is doing to focus on them. He's a great father for them, and I have him as a great husband at other times. Work is work."

Alex took them into the play area of the basement, and the triplets loved Pastor Ewart and Rachel immediately. Then something unexpected happened. Krister wandered in. While the boys were pulling on his tail and playing with him, he kept his eyes on Pastor Ewart and Rachel. When the boys decided to go outside and play, they tried to take Krister with them, but he wanted to be with Rachel and Pastor Ewart. Purring and stroking around them constantly, Krister evidently adopted them. The pastor and his wife were at the mountain house for most of four days, and when they left, Krister went with them.

On a Monday a month later, their former neighbors, Abby and George, came to spend a week. When they arrived, Alex was fixing a snack for the boys, so Bill greeted their friends. "Hey! You must have had light traffic. You're here earlier than we expected! Alex is in the kitchen. She'll meet us in the great room in a few minutes." After taking off their shoes, they came in and got comfortable. The boys took their snacks downstairs, and Bill joined Alex, Abby, and George.

They started talking about small things, and Tammie wandered in. Alex introduced her. "This is Tammie. She's about half-grown now." She sat and gazed at them with her orange eyes for a moment, and then she scampered up the carpeted wall and began leaping between the rafters. It was entertaining. Suddenly, Tammie leaped the full distance to the carpeted floor, approached them, and began nuzzling Abby and George, who grinned. "Whoa! Aren't you friendly!?"

Abby joined George in petting her. "Aren't you beautiful, Tammie?"

The half-grown kitten acted like a house cat with catnip. The entire week Tammie was playful and affectionate with both George and Abby.

Saturday night, Tammie sat at their feet as they watched an old movie. Bill was amused by the way Tammie was acting. "It looks like Tammie has adopted you. Do you think Tammie and Beau would get along?"

George's eyes got big. "Are you serious, Bill?"

He nodded. "It appears that Tammie has adopted you two. Tammie is not super-fast like her mother, but she takes commands well." He glanced at Alex, and she nodded.

She looked at Abby. "What do you think? Would you like a house cat?"

At first, Abby and George were skeptical, but Tammie was so affectionate, they fell in love with her. When they left after church on Sunday afternoon, Tammie went with them.

Sheila and Harry did not seem to miss the others. The following Monday, the boys started going to Kindergarten. The two cats started spending more time outside during the day. That weekend, Alex and Bill had a Skype call with George and Abby. They showed them a video of Tammie and Beau playing together. It was a good match.

When Bill was almost finished with his third small-town development, he was tired in a different way than he ever had been. One cold January evening, Alex was snuggled against him as they sat in front of a roaring fire in their fireplace, with their cats up in the rafters. The triplets were in bed. "I don't want to do another small-town development, Alex. When this one in northern Minnesota is completed in June, I think it will be the last. This one will easily generate more electricity than it consumes." He paused. "I suppose we could pass the word through Steve and others that I'm now offering set-design services."

Alex kissed him on the cheek. "You've certainly had lots of experience as a consultant."

"True enough." They discussed it into the late evening.

Alex and Bill never anticipated what came next. One Saturday morning the following April, they were eating breakfast, and Bill put his fork down. "Where's Sheila I wonder? We've not seen her at all this morning."

Harry came into the kitchen. Bill scratched the cat's head. "Good morning, Harry. Where's your Mom?"

"Rowwl."

Alex and Bill searched for some sign of Sheila, both inside and outside. They hiked at a mile or more in every direction. They put search notices in the social media and got no responses that were helpful.

Just as Sheila had appeared inexplicably as a kitten on Bill's patio in La Jolla many years earlier, Sheila had suddenly disappeared just as mysteriously. For more than a week, they called out for her. They never saw Sheila again.

Bill called Dr. Mounce, who lived in a Florida retirement village, to let him know. For days, Alex and Bill felt lost, and Harry would stare out the big window in the great room all day.

Bill needed to get back to work. Alex made several calls to Steve and other friends in the entertainment industry. From scratch, Bill designed the sets for three movies. The third one got him an Oscar nomination, but his heart just simply was not in his work.

With Sheila gone, Alex found that she no longer had real enthusiasm for acting or even directing. She started accepting fewer roles and other opportunities. She did not announce that she was leaving show business, but she simply drifted away for nearly a year.

Money was not a problem for Alex and Bill. For years, they had given away about half of their earned income, both from their work and from their investments. During this time, they only took on jobs if they were in the mood to work.

They worked at being good parents to the boys. They supported them and all their school activities. They also tried to be generous participants in community activities. About one dollar in five of their income was given to church work, either locally or for missions.

17.
Family Developments

Since their last name, Johnson, is a very common name, people seldom connected the boys with their famous parents. Alex and Bill did their best to maintain privacy for their sons. They keep them out of the public eye as much as possible. Publicity photographs never included all of them.

While Sheila was still fresh in their memories, it took some time for them to regain their enthusiasm for their work. They focused upon their family life.

While their sons were in grade school, family outings were usually in Alex's Subaru SUV. They explored all kinds of tourist traps in Southern California. Alex always dressed so that she wouldn't be recognized, dressing super-casual and playing down her appearance. She often wore a floppy hat she could tip down over her face and dark glasses.

When the boys were in the fifth grade, their adolescence began, and they physically began to grow very rapidly. Just as quickly, the family became too big for the Subaru.

Their modified van SUV had been plenty for Alex, Sheila, and Bill, but they had outgrown it. Bill designed another van modification layout to both seat and sleep five plus Harry, and he sent the plans to the same company that supplied the previous van-modified motor homes.

The new van conversion was delivered two months later. Bill sent a letter of appreciation with their payment. Once again, it was easier to go out and explore as a family.

The boys were also in the fifth grade when Alex directed her first Oscar-nominated movie in which she did not play an on-screen role. As an actress, she was still simply known as "Alex," but as a director and producer, she listed herself in the credits as Alexandra Johnson. She really enjoyed being a director, and she began to act in fewer movies after that. When people asked for her autograph, many asked why she was no longer making movies. She always handled the question graciously and honestly, saying she liked behind the camera more.

Bill began to become famous back when he built the house on the highway to Mount Wilson. The triplets grew up in that house, which continued to be somewhat of a tourist attraction. With Harry around, they never worried about the house being burglarized or invaded.

They were a close-knit family. Beginning when the boys were in the second grade, they began trying to fool people by switching with each other. Bill warned them repeatedly not to use their identical appearances in ways that offended or upset others. They were never able to fool either of their parents, though they tried a few times. It seemed they could fool just about anyone else in those days. Their teachers sometimes got angry when they stood in for one another, but when the teachers told Alex or Bill, they got disciplined.

The boys became very skilled at acting like each other, but there were significant differences in their personalities. Bill found a diagram on the Internet that explained it. All three inherited some acting abilities from their Mom.

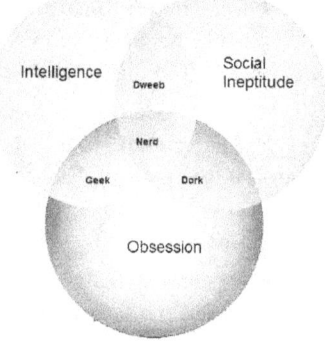

Based upon this diagram, Sandy tended to be a bit of a dweeb. Dick was definitely a geek, and Bob was somewhat of a nerd.

In middle school, Sandy preferred texting and email to talking with people. There was a girl he really wanted to get to know named Paula, but Sandy was introverted and was scared to death to talk with her. One morning before school, Dick pretended to be Sandy and showed an interest in her. After that, Paula started initiating conversations with Sandy, and he was in heaven. They became pretty good friends, at least Alex and Bill thought so.

Dick always could talk with everyone – he was very skilled socially – an extrovert. At school dances, the boys' parents watched as Dick would talk with people and danced with any girl who wanted to. He had lots of friends. Bob was never as skilled socially as Dick, but he did develop some solid friendships while they were in middle school. Some psychologists could identify him as an omnivert.

Dick was a prankster, but since he did not want to get blamed if anything went wrong, he would convince Sandy and Bob to help him. In the middle of November when they were in the fourth grade, there was supposed to be a baseball game on a Saturday at a park about two miles down the mountain road from their house. Alex and Bill let them walk down there.

While talking with other parents, Bill and Alex came to understand that kids seldom realize how much their parents hear when they whisper to each other. In this case, Bill overheard their whispered conversations after they got home.

Back on the baseball field, just as the game started, it started to rain. At first, everyone ignored it, but it began to rain harder. They heard thunder in the distance. Everyone decided to leave. From what Bill could gather later, when they went out the gate to go home, Dick pointed to the far end of the fence. Dick said, "Hey, guys, do you see that drain spewing water and mud?"

Bob nodded. "Yeah, that comes from the drain near the backstop."

Dick smiled, ever the prankster. "That gives me an idea."

He did not say anything else while they hiked up the highway back to the house and went to the workshop next to the garage. Dick was excited and invited his brothers into a conspiracy. "Let's make something to put in the pipe between the drain opening near the backstop and the pipe coming out near the grandstand. We'll make muddy water spray out of the pipe. There's probably a low spot in the pipe where the water won't evaporate for a couple of weeks."

Bob was interested. "It sounds like it might be fun to spray muddy water onto the grandstand. How will we trigger it?"

Sandy smiled. "I can take care of that part."

Alex and Bill heard a lot of their whispered conversations during the days that followed. A week later, there were a couple of Little League teams playing there. The three of them sat at the other end of the bleachers, as far as they could get from the pipe. The game was about to start. Sandy glanced at Dick and Bob. "What do you think?" Dick and Bob nodded. Sandy took out his cell and dialed a number.

The result was both better and worse than they expected. When Sandy pressed the last number, two things happened. First, muddy water spewed over the entire bandstand, drenching everyone, not just drenching those nearby. Everybody started shouting at each other as they left the stands. Then, the chain-link backstop behind the home plate began to lean over the plate. The kids on the field ran to get out from under as the backstop fell almost to the ground.

The boys walked home. Alex was working at a sound studio in Hollywood, and Bill was in his study. He looked up from his desk. "What happened? The game can't be over already."

Dick shook his head. "Just before the game was supposed to start, muddy water came shooting out of a drain and got everyone in the bleachers wet. Then the backstop began to lean over, and the kids ran off the field. It was weird!"

Sandy and Bob nodded. Sandy was very serious. "It was strange!"

Bill did not allow himself to smile. Instead, he looked back and forth between the three of them as solemnly as he could. "Okay, you boys get cleaned up. I've still got work to do before your Mom gets home."

They continued to do pranks from time to time. Bill made sure that they didn't know how much he knew of what they were doing. Since no one got hurt, Bill did not press them for answers. As it turned out, that little device they had put in the drain at the baseball field had damaged the foundation of the backstop, and some major repairs were required.

Bill helped with the repairs without telling anyone what he knew. The boys learned a valuable lesson. They at no time again engaged in a prank that damaged public property. Alex and Bill never let them think that they even suspected that the boys were behind what had happened.

The boys talked about their Mom many times before going to sleep. After listening to others talk about their Moms at school, they gradually came to realize that Alex's intuition was amazing. It often seemed to them as though she could discern what they were doing, even when she was not nearby.

The one thing that was particularly special to the three boys was that their parents prayed both with them and for them every day. They also read the Bible together several times a week.

When one of the boys did something wrong – frequently – their Mom and Dad confronted them and demanded total honesty. The boys learned the importance of always telling the truth. Life at home was mostly fun, but even when it wasn't, their sense of family unity never faltered. When punishment was needed, both parents talked the boys through it, and afterward they saw to it that they knew they were forgiven.

There were times when Alex worked long hours away from the mountain house. Whenever that was the case, Bill made sure he always made time for the boys. Alex was away making a movie one Sunday when Bill took them to church. The boys were in grammar school at the time. After the worship service, Bill wanted to speak to the pastor. Sandy, Dick, and Bob went forward with him. Bob got distracted and wandered off, looking carefully at a large acoustic piano on the stage.

As Bill talked with their pastor, he kept an eye on all three boys. The musician sitting at the keyboards spoke to Bob. (Bill spoke the artist later that afternoon on the phone.) The artist said to Bob, "Hey, what's your name?"

"Bob."

"Well, Bob, do you play the piano or a keyboard?"

Bob shook his head. "I don't have a keyboard, but maybe my Dad can get me one."

"This is an electronic keyboard sitting above the piano's keyboard. Are you interested in both?" Bob shook his head. The musician played a little for him. "The acoustic piano sounds a little different, doesn't it?"

Bob nodded. "I like it. The electronic piano doesn't sound quite the same."

The musician nodded. "That's right. If you want your parents to get you one of these, you had better be ready to take lessons and practice every single day for a long time."

Bill walked up behind Bob without his knowing it. He overheard that last comment. "Listen to the man, Bob. If you want to learn to play the piano, you'll have to promise your Mom and I that you'll take lessons for at least five years and practice every single day."

After Bill talked to the musician later, he told Alex about what had happened when she got home that night. "What do you think?"

She was thoughtful. "Up until now, I had not seen any musical possibilities among them. This is interesting. I think we should leave it to Bob. If he wants a piano, let's get him one, but we'll make sure he understands the implications." Bill concurred.

For almost a month, Bob thought about what his Dad had told him. When Alex got home from a production she had worked on in Italy, Bob told his parents he wanted to take piano lessons. Alex and Bill went shopping after she talked with some professional musician friends. Because the great room was so large, they got a seven-foot grand piano, which was placed near the spiral staircase. Bob ended up taking lessons for almost ten years and sat at the piano virtually every day.

Alex and Bill consistently had an attitude of contentment in their lives and towards the boys. Sandy, for instance, found his peace in reading. As the boys were learning to read in school, one night at dinner Sandy decided that he was going to read all the books in the family library in the basement. Dick said, "You're crazy! There're thousands of books down there!"

Bob nodded. "That'll consume so much of your time!"

Even though his brothers tried to discourage him, Sandy started making his way through the hundreds of books in the bookcase systematically.

As triplets, the boys began to have a nightly boy-talk that seemed to grow important to them. It first started when they were in the second grade, and Alex and Bill listened in. As the triplets grew older, they stopped eavesdropping and let them have privacy. Other kids at their schools did not talk to their brothers and sisters like the triplets did.

After the boy-talk began, their conversations over breakfast became livelier. Subsequent to Sandy announcing his reading project, before they went to sleep each night in their room, Sandy would talk about what he was reading and learning. The boys sometimes reported their boy-talk over breakfast. Dick and Bob learned that Sandy's observations and evaluations of what he was reading were always interesting and accurate. Bob would talk about the music he was learning and often talked about the music's history. Dick would talk about models and other things he was building in the workshop.

As the three of them approached their tenth birthday, the family's daily Bible reading seemed to have deeper meaning for everyone. The boys talked extensively about getting baptized. After the tenth birthday party for them, the following Sunday the three boys got baptized in the ocean.

Bill then began teaching them what it means to be honorable Christian gentlemen. Both Alex and Bill taught them to trust in God, and what that meant, beginning when they were younger. They also taught them that God doesn't want us simply to go to church, but to *be* the church.

About the time of their baptisms, Dick shifted his focus to develop more friendships with other people in their church. Just as Sandy was soaking in all he could from Dad's library, Dick began soaking in what it means to be the church and to have relationships with both Jesus and other Christians. The nightly boy-talks got longer because after Sandy talked about what he was reading, Dick talked about their developing themselves spiritually. That also meant that Sandy shifted to another part of their Dad's library, reading church history and Bible commentaries.

On Monday of their last week of middle school, Bob was helping his Mom fix breakfast. She turned to him. "Bob, your Dad and I think that it's about time you and your brothers went on a date together. We want the three of you to get dates by this Friday, and we'll all go to Knotts Berry Farm together on Saturday."

Bob's eyes must have nearly popped out of his head. "Really?"

His Dad walked into the kitchen as he overheard them. "Yes, Bob, really. You and your brothers get yourselves dates. If Sandy needs help getting a date, Dick will know what to do."

Years later, Dick and Bob couldn't remember the names of the girls they took to Knotts Berry Farm at the end of the eighth grade, but Sandy still did. Sandy almost had absolute recall.

Their triple date to Knotts Berry Farm was a turning point in their lives as triplets, because so much was going on at home. Their nightly boy-talk shifted to talking more about girls. Because the house is on a mountain highway, their nearest neighbors were some at some distance up or down the mountain. Growing up was, for the triplets, a great adventure. Perhaps it was more of an adventure for them than for other kids because they were triplets, and they lived in the mountains.

The boys always had questions. When their Dad was working in his study, if one or more of them came in, Bill would invariably stop what he was doing to talk with them. It came naturally to him.

Their Mom was the same way. After they turned twelve, they felt they could approach Alex about any questions they had about anything, including girls. Alex and Bill were both amused at times because they would ask the same kinds of questions of both. During their pillow talk, Alex and Bill would compare notes.

As Sandy, Dick, and Bob started at La Cañada High School, order began to emerge out of the chaos of their lives. Many of the kids in their classes had not gone to the same middle school. In all their classes, other kids discovered that Sandy could be relied upon for answers to the toughest questions. None of the other kids called him a dweeb though. Their teachers thought that it was because there were three of them, and it was hard to tell who was who.

Sandy began to develop some photography skills, and as he did his shyness began to disappear. Dick still helped him get the dates he wanted during the first two years of high school, though.

As with Sandy, the chaos of Bob's life began to disappear as he began to play the piano in the music room at school for groups of various sizes. Something stirred within him as he coached kids with their singing. The band director was not interested in choral music. Some seemingly crazy ideas for the future began to brew in the back of Bob's mind. Music began to be his source of stability in his life beyond his family.

By the time their high school junior year began, Sandy and Bob started to see Dick as the center of attention with school life. It all began with a conversation Dick had with his Mom when he and his brothers were in the tenth grade. Dick had been listening to Bob practice for several minutes, and then he heard a sound from the kitchen. He went in to investigate. Alex looked up from chopping some veggies. "Dick, you have an instrument you can play if you want to."

He shook his head and scowled. "You know I don't know how to play an instrument, Mom."

"Actually, there's an approach to acting where the actors see their voices and their entire bodies as their instruments. Just as musicians perform with musical instruments, actors perform with their bodies."

Dick thought about that. "Interesting." He continued to think about it while he watched his Mom making preparations for dinner. "I suppose you could say that a chef's instrument are his utensils, pots, and pans."

Alex nodded. "Many say that great cooking is an art form."

After that conversation, Dick began making short videos about life at La Cañada high school. He would create a script to follow, and then create the video and post it on the Internet. He also began to take more interest in everything his Mom was doing. At the same time, during the boys' junior year, Sandy began to be more interested in everything his Dad was doing.

Bob began to toy with ideas about a career in music. He was not at all sure how it would happen. He only knew that music was going to consume his life, and that it would be centered on vocal music. In his self-assigned reading, he read music history.

Bill doesn't know if it had anything to do with their being triplets, but when the boys got into high school, their interests began to shift both at school and at home. Alex and Bill talked about it many times before they went to sleep at night during their pillow talk.

Sometimes, in the early mornings, the three boys would get dressed a little earlier, and they would go into the study before their parents came downstairs. Their Dad always had sketches of the projects he was currently working on pinned to a bulletin board near his desk. All three boys began to be more interested in whatever their Dad was doing. Maybe it was boys wanting to see a man's work. Their Dad never asked them.

In another part of the study was their Mom's desk. She sometimes worked the Internet there, and often she worked on video clips she had made for her own use. While there were a few autographed pictures of entertainment industry celebrities in other parts of the house, pictures of her closest friends were around her desk.

No one has ever been sure why, but Harry had a spot in the study where he liked to doze while Alex and Bill worked in there. Most of the time, Harry's favorite spot in the house was on top of a rafter in the great room, however. Bill once told the boys that Harry's Mom, Sheila, used to hide in the rafters of the great room of the San Diego house. He said that when they moved into the mountain house, Sheila immediately established a favorite place in the rafters of this house too, where she would seem to sleep for hours. Everyone thinks that Harry learned this from his Mom.

Evidently, when Alex or Bill talked about Sheila, they got a far-away look in their eyes. The boys asked about it once, and they told them the story of how Sheila had brought them together when they first met.

18.
Changes & Growth

On a cold day in November of the boys' junior year of high school, it was lightly snowing outside. Below them in the San Gabriel Valley, it was raining steadily. Alex was studying a script in the great room, and the boys were with their Dad in the study. Dick and Bob were texting with their friends, but Sandy was studying his Dad's large computer monitor as he worked. "Dad, I hope you don't mind, but I've been studying the blueprints of some of your past projects."

"I don't mind, so long as you don't make any changes, Sandy. If you started doing that, I would have to take my work computer off our home network."

"No! I would never do that, Dad." He was emphatic. "I've been really interested in your innovations, particularly the super-insulated walls and ceilings for that town in northern Minnesota."

His Dad turned away from his workstation to look at Sandy. Dick and Bob stopped their texting and listened. He was still always ready to make time for the boys, so he shifted his focus from his computer to Sandy. "What about those walls and ceilings, Sandy?"

"First, I noticed that the walls in all the rooms of one of the floor plans were one hundred inches tall. I then checked all sixteen floor plans with their decorative variations. All the rooms have one-hundred-inch ceilings."

His Dad smiled. "That's good detective work, son. What else did you notice?"

Sandy scooted his chair a little closer. "I created a database for the walls of all the floor plans, and I had our computer tabulate the dimensions of the walls. For all the houses, there are forty-two wall sizes, including rooms, closets, and storage spaces."

His Dad was amazed and was grinning. "What have you learned from all of this, Sandy?" Dick and Bob were staring at their brother. Where was this leading?

Sandy's face got a little pink." I'm... I'm not sure, but.... I've got a crazy idea. I know it's crazy, maybe even off-the-wall nuts, but what if...."

He swallowed, and his Dad waited patiently because he could see that this was important to him. Sandy sat up straighter. "What if there was a factory that assembled standardized walls like this? Architects could build houses with standardized components." He slumped back into his chair.

That got his Dad thinking. "That's a brilliant idea, Sandy. In fact," He looked up at the study's ceiling for a moment. "In fact, such a factory could also have computerized units to create custom-sized ceilings for the variety of room sizes. It's like a process used in Japan. I like this idea!" He paused because of an idea forming in his head. "I'll tell you what. I have to keep working on this." He pointed at his monitor. "Next weekend, when all of your homework is done, why don't you try adding to that database by adding such factors as outlets and windows. Don't worry about the floors and plumbing, Sandy. In Japan, houses can be delivered as kits to sites and assembled without technical skills being required. Everything bolts together, and plumbing and electrical connections are made at the joints with instant connections."

Bob was stunned. "Dad, do you mean that Sandy's come up with a workable idea?"

Bill steadily nodded. "Possibly. We might be able to improve upon what is done in Japan. I can foresee several difficult design challenges, and I would want to bring in Gloria Houser, our lawyer, to see about securing patents. We'll take this slowly, Sandy. If we're going to do it, we've got to do it right the first time. The three of you are graduating from high school in a year and a half. While all of you have indicated that you intend to go to college, starting today, I want you boys to consider college or university attendance as merely one alternative future pursuit beyond high school. The three of you have been getting ready to take the SAT. Focus on that, and after you take it, we'll talk about alternatives."

Bill was still processing what he was suddenly seeing in his sons. "Bob, you are showing some significant musical talent. You may want to pursue a degree in music at a university or a music school like Julliard, but as you approach your graduation from La Cañada High School, something may come to you that is entirely different from either of those alternatives."

Bill pointed in the direction of the garage and shifted his focus. "Dick, I've watched you spend hours in the workshop making things for yourself and for friends, but I've also noticed your interest, like Sandy's, in projects I have designed and built. While you might end up pursuing a career in architecture, following a career path like mine, you might also go into one of the trades. For instance, I've noticed that, whenever Ken Crain and his wife, Wanda, have come to visit us, you have asked him many questions about his managing the construction of this house. Additionally, lately you've been asking him endless questions about things he is currently building. Instead of architecture, you might pursue either general contracting like Ken, or you might head for a trade school to learn one or more specialized skills."

Bill turned to Sandy. "Sandy, if this idea of manufacturing standardized housing is going to work out, you are going to have to explore areas of mechanical engineering as well as explore the issues associated with industrial management. This also might just be a temporary interest on your part if something else is going to be the center of your professional life." Bill looked at his watch. "Let's go and see if your Mom has plans for lunch."

Alex was in the kitchen, and after they ate, the family went Christmas shopping online together, talking about what they wanted to buy for each other. They connected their computer network to their largest display in the great room. For more than two hours, they explored Christmas present ideas online.

One thing the boys loved doing was being on their church's praise team on Christmas. Bob always played the piano and sang every Sunday. On Christmas Eve, the family opened their presents after dinner in the great room. Then, they headed down the mountain to the church. Sandy joined the team on bass guitar, and Dick sang harmony with the other singers. Harry went with them but stayed in the van. The worship had a blend of music, including both traditional carols and contemporary music. The church family also shared communion.

When Christmas Eve worship was concluded, they headed to the airport. Their van was shipped out by air freight as soon as they arrived at the airport. They ate snacks in the lounge and enjoyed watching other people go by at the Burbank airport for about an hour. Their chartered plane was getting some extra attention for some reason. Alex had chartered the plane for them, and at last, their plane was ready. They were headed to Mammoth.

As they took off, everyone looked out the windows. Harry stretched out on the floor. They all continued to have the festive Christmas mood from the worship at church. "Your Dad and I have things to talk about with you boys while we're at Mammoth, so let's plan on having family discussion time before we pray together each evening. We'll be here for four full days after today before we return home on Saturday." The boys nodded.

Just before they landed at the Mammoth Yosemite Airport, Bill put the harness on Harry. It had been Sheila's, and it had been adjusted slightly smaller for him.

Their reservations were for the Ansel Adams Lodge and Conference Center, where they had two connecting rooms. As they approached the front desk, a few people approached us to get autographs from Mom. Harry looked at them with his orange eyes, purring, and they backed off.

Everyone except Sandy went skiing all day. Sandy kept his mirrorless camera around his neck, with two extra lenses in cases hanging from his belt. He also had a lightweight tripod. He made hundreds of images and videos. That evening, they tried eating in the dining room, but they were pestered with autograph seekers. They returned to their room and ordered dinner from room service, with a raw steak for Harry.

Later, they joined dozens of others gathered around a large fireplace. Alex signed autographs for about a half-hour before she spoke up. "Listen everyone. I'm here with my family to enjoy Mammoth, just as all of you are. Is anyone here leaving tomorrow?" No one responded. "Good. After I sign this young man's autograph book, it will be the last one for this evening. My family and I will be here through Friday. If you want my autograph, please try to pick a time when there's not a line, okay?" Many of the people nodded.

At night, Harry stayed outside on the balconies. He found it easy to leap from the balcony of one of our rooms to the other. He always seemed to enjoy being outside in the snow. Harry was inside for our family conference and worship in Bill and Alex's room the first night. Alex led off the discussion. "Boys, you may have noticed that I've not taken on any new acting roles at all since last Spring. I started tapering off my acting when Harry's mother died. Next month, I'm going to be directing a film that we'll be shooting mostly in Long Beach. I've also signed contracts to make some commercials over the next few months."

Dick nodded. "So, you're not going to be doing any more acting, Mom?"

She shook her head. "I'm going to do mostly directing and producing from this point on. I'm tired of being constantly in the limelight. Tomorrow evening, your Dad will be telling you about a change he is making in his work."

For about fifteen minutes, they discussed the possible things she would be doing soon. Then, they read the Bible and prayed for a while.

They put Harry out on a balcony, told him to watch, and called it a night. The boys went through the connecting door to their room, where there were two queen beds and a roll-away. During registration, Alex and Bill told the boys to take turns sleeping on the roll-away. All of them mostly followed the routines they each had at home for getting ready for bed.

That night, after the boys turned off the lights, Sandy was the first that night to start their boy-talk. "Guys, I saw someone today over by the gondola lift."

"Who?" Dick and Bob asked together.

"Carole Maddux. She's here with her parents."

Dick spoke intensely, but softly. "She's a babe, Sandy!"

"I know. I was making an image of a young pine tree sprout poking through the snow when she came up behind me and tapped me on the shoulder. She said hi, and at first I was tongue-tied."

Dick chuckled. "Okay, brother, did you swallow your fear and talk with her?"

"When I looked into her eyes, I don't know why, but all my fears vanished. She's been given a full scholarship to a school for professional photography when we graduate. We talked about the equipment we were carrying. Guys, I almost froze up when I took a quick glance at what she was wearing. It was tight and form-fitting, and she has a figure like Mom's." Sandy was speaking in an excited whisper that Dick and Bob had never heard before.

Dick whispered. "Really? I didn't think she had a figure. At school, she always dresses frumpy, in loose-fitting clothes."

Bob was immediately curious. "Are we talking about the Carole that almost lives at our school's library?"

Sandy didn't answer for a moment. "Yeah. She's brilliant. She may be smarter than me. She told me that she was glad she had run into me. We're meeting in the dining room for breakfast tomorrow morning. I'm still on a cloud I think."

All Bob could think of to say was, "Cool!" They went to sleep.

The next morning, Sandy had been gone for almost an hour when Dick and Bob joined their parents for breakfast in their room. Bob told them about Sandy's meeting Carole. They smiled. Their parents told them they were going to try some of the intermediate ski runs they hadn't tried yet. Dick and Bob said they might try one or two of the more advanced runs. That night, after dinner Alex and Bill went back to the fireplace because she felt they should.

The boys didn't join them. Dick and Bob dragged Sandy to the games' room. Dick was almost aggressive with his brother. "So, tell us, did you see her again today?"

They got soft drinks at the counter before Sandy answered. "As I told you last night, we met for breakfast this morning. We both had big appetites."

Bob smiled. "And...."

"We spent the whole day together." His face brightened. "Here she is now!" He stood up and greeted her with a hug. Dick and Bob were stunned.

Carole was dressed in a colorful and very feminine ski outfit. "Hi guys! It's good to see you! I must confess, I can't tell the difference and say which one of you is Dick and which one is Bob, but I know Sandy when I see him, whether in the hall at school or here." She stood on her toes and kissed Sandy on the cheek. "He's the only guy I've ever met who's smarter than me."

Bob's mouth was hanging open when Dick spoke. "Sandy's the smartest of the three of us. I won't be surprised if he aces the SAT."

Carole sat down next to Sandy when all of them sat down. "Listen, guys, my parents told me at dinner that we are leaving tomorrow for Tahoe because my Dad wants to play some poker." She turned to Sandy. "I want to try some night photography. There's not a cloud in the sky, and the moon is less than a quarter full. What do you say? Do you want to try it with me?"

"We'd have to get away from the lights of the resort. I'll ask my Dad if we can borrow the van. I want to bring our cat along."

Her eyes got bigger. "That big one?"

Sandy nodded. "He's pretty big. Harry weighs about 150 or so."

Her mouth hung open slightly. "Okay, I guess. I trust you, Sandy."

"Great!" Sandy grinned as they stood up. "See you later, guys!" They walked, holding hands, towards the main lodge room with the large fireplace.

Dick had a sly grin on his face. "Was that our brother, our dweeb brother, with a girlfriend?"

Bob nodded. "He's getting to be less of a dweeb, isn't he?"

Dick nodded. "Praise God! Maybe I won't have to help him get dates anymore!"

When Dick and Bob went to their room later for family time, Sandy was out. Their Dad anticipated the question on their minds. "Okay, boys, last evening your Mom talked about the changes she's made in her professional life. Tonight, I'm going to tell you about the changes I'm making in my professional life." He paused. "Sandy's with Carole doing night photography. Harry's with them as their bodyguard. You can fill him in later." Dick and Bob nodded.

"I'm still going to be designing custom homes from time to time, but now that the little town in Northern Minnesota is up and running, I'm no longer going to be doing developments like that."

Their Dad drank some coffee. "For the immediate future, I'm going to be designing sets for movies and for television. In the future, Sandy and I may do something different, like home component manufacturing, but right now I'm going to design sets." They discussed it for quite a while. "Boys, tomorrow evening, your Mom and I want to introduce the rest of our family to those who have been with us around the fireplace each evening. We're going to include Harry."

Bob grinned from ear to ear. "This ought to be really interesting!

Dick nodded. "We know that Harry can handle being in a crowd of people, but can they handle being around Harry?"

Their Mom spoke confidently. "I've had a talk with the General Manager of the Lodge. She said she's willing to risk it because it will be great publicity for the Lodge. The County Sheriff will have a couple of extra deputies stationed nearby, but they will stay on the edges of the crowd, unless there's trouble."

Their Dad smiled. "I'll have Harry wearing his harness as he wore when we arrived, and I'll hold the leash."

After they read the Bible and prayed for a while, they went to bed. Bob heard Sandy come in at about 4:00 AM, but Dick didn't wake up.

At breakfast on Thursday, Sandy said he was going to strap his camera to his chest and make some videos going down the beginners' slopes. "I might try one of the intermediate runs if Dick and Bob will go with me."

Bob was intrigued. "Sure! I'll go with you! Dick?" He nodded.

It turned out to be an unforgettable day. Sandy had previously done a little skiing at Snow Summit. They went to Big Bear Lake one weekend in the San Bernardino mountains east of the Los Angeles area. By the time they left Snow Summit, Sandy had gotten to be a pretty good skier. This time, Dick and Bob stayed close to him.

Sandy had to give his brothers instructions. "Unless necessary guys, don't say anything. I'm making these videos with sound." They made two videos on the beginners' slopes.

About 9:00, Sandy said he was ready to try doing something more challenging. "I want to try making a video on an intermediate run. Make sure you guys stay nearby, but behind me a few feet. I don't want either of you or your skis or your shadows to show." Their parents went down behind them the first of those runs.

When the sun was high in the sky, the family headed to a snack bar, and each of them practically inhaled two or three hot dogs. Dick was scanning the mountain. "Bob, there's an advanced run that's steep but not otherwise dangerous over there." He pointed. "Does anyone want to try it with me?"

They all shook our heads. His Dad looked straight at him. "If you break a leg, you'll be stuck in the lodge tomorrow while the rest of us ski."

Dick nodded. "I want to risk it."

Sandy took out a big lens from a holder on his belt. "I'll make a video of you from the benches over there at the bottom of the run. With this zoom telephoto, I should be able to keep up with you from there."

They all went to the nearby lift, and as Dick started up, they sat down on a bench next to the machinery. They have watched that video many times since, and they've shown it to friends. For more than half of the way down, Dick's skiing was spectacular. Suddenly, he lost control. A crowd ran to him with the family, and less than twenty minutes later, Alex and Bill were riding with him in an ambulance to the hospital. The rest of the family followed in the van.

That night, Dick was on the roll-away bed watching videos upstairs, while the rest of us introduced Harry to the other guests. Harry was a big hit and enjoyed the attention. When Bill sensed that Harry needed to get away, he nodded at Alex, and she announced that nature was calling Harry. After they took him outside to do his business, inside, they all took an elevator back to their floor.

When Sandy and Bob went into their room, Dick said, "Even if Harry has done his business, I think we need to let Harry be outside for a while, don't you think?"

Bob nodded and looked at Sandy, who was also nodding. "Okay." When Bob let Harry out, he immediately began chewing on some snow. Just as Bob was going to close the door, Harry's purring stopped, and he crouched down on his belly, peering into the darkness. Then he leapt into the black beyond the hotel's lights.

Dick's back was to the door on the roll-away bed, so he didn't see it happen, but Sandy joined Bob at the door. "What do you think? Has he gone to get himself some dinner?"

Dick was missing out. "Who? Harry? What do you see? What's going on?"

Bob spoke quietly & held a finger to his lips. "After chewing on some snow, his purring stopped. He crouched, and then he leaped into the black of the night."

Sandy shivered. "It's getting cold in here. Let's close the door, but keep the blinds open. When we turn off our room lights, we'll be able to see the balcony clearly. We can stay awake to see when Harry gets back."

They shifted the roll-away bed so that Dick could see outside. Then, Sandy and Bob fell asleep.

The next morning, Dick was already awake when his brothers opened their eyes. "Harry was gone almost two hours last night. He went to the area on the balcony under the overhang," Dick pointed, "and settled down. I doubt that he has moved for the rest of the night. I wonder if he had a good meal?"

Sandy got out of bed. "I'll let Harry in." He slid open the patio door, and Harry stirred. He got up, stretched, and came inside. Good morning, sleepy head! Did you get yourself a good meal last night?"

"Rowwl."

19.

Approaching Graduation

As with others their age, the triplets' final year of high school involved several turning points for them. They continued to have fun by shuffling their identities to confuse people, but they didn't do it as often. Bill and Alex talked frequently about how they were growing up.

Sandy and Carole were inseparable. She took a keen interest in Sandy's vision of manufactured components for homes. Sometimes they brainstormed for hours. When the weather was favorable, they took photographic expeditions together. They both got external storage drives for their computers just to store their images and videos they made.

At the end of October, Dick convinced all of them to celebrate Halloween at La Cañada Flintridge Town Center. The mall was set up so the children could go trick-or-treating in a safe environment. Nearly everyone was in costumes, including first responders, who you could only recognize by their badges or their hats. Dick was of course prepared to pull some pranks on people he knew they might see there.

Niña Yoshpé, the best makeup artist in the entertainment industry according to Alex, brought her costume-designer husband, Randy, to the mountain house for lunch on Halloween. After lunch, they worked on all of them for the rest of the afternoon. Alex and Bill were put in full theatrical makeup and costumes as a witch and her familiar, a hunchback.

The same artistry was used to make the boys into an almost-realistic Hewey (Sandy), Dewey (Dick), and Louie (Bob), the nephews of Donald Duck. As the sun was setting, Carole came over, and she was made up to look like Daisy Duck, Donald's girlfriend.

At the Town Center, Carole and Sandy had a great time as Daisy and her boyfriend's nephew, Hewey. They had been there about an hour when Bob spotted Jess Carlson, a talented soprano he had coached to play the lead in Amahl and the Night Visitors as a sophomore, which was performed just before Christmas that year at the high school. Now she was made up to be a young Jessica Simpson, and she had the face and figure to pull it off. As she approached Bob with only minimal makeup, she looked like the singer's twin, from head to toe. "Happy Halloween, Bob!"

At first, it did not occur to Bob that Jess knew him from his brothers, even with all his makeup. Everything was very natural for them. She and Bob found a place where they could watch everyone going by, and they talked about everything. No one knew it then, but it was the beginning of a lifetime together for them.

Dick was walking past the American Rag store when a girl that he vaguely recognized threw him an apple and called out, "Catch, Dick!"

She recognized him! It wasn't a real apple, and he almost screamed "Whoa!" when he was drenched from head to foot. Dick remembered her name, reached into a pocket, and tossed back to her what appeared also to be an apple. "Catch, Trina!"

As she caught it, it dissolved into half-dozen spring-loaded "snakes." She screamed and sat down on the tile floor, laughing.

Dick sat down beside her, also laughing. "How did you know it was me?" She didn't answer. They remained there, laughing and talking, for more than ten minutes, before he helped her up. He took her hand as they went looking for some cotton candy. Halloween was great fun for the whole family. They talked about it for weeks afterwards.

Alex and Bill were totally unrecognizable and had the time of their lives that Halloween at the Town Center. Alex was thrilled to interact with everyone without being recognized, and Bill shared her fun.

On throughout the boys' senior year, it was one adventure after another. Their SAT scores were emailed to them. Sandy scored a perfect 1600, and he didn't want to talk much about it for some reason. Dick was not surprised with his 620 score in reading, with a 650 in math. Bob got a 780 in reading, with a 680 in math. He wasn't sure what to think about his results.

For Presidents' Day weekend a few months later, Southern California was blessed with warm Santa Ana winds. On Saturday morning, the family was filling up on pancakes, bacon, eggs, and melon with their juice and tea. Sandy looked at his Mom. "These Santa Ana winds can make a great weekend for us. Maybe, my brothers and I can go on a triple date tomorrow to Knotts Berry Farm. This time though, I want us to do it without our parents as chaperones. Sorry Mom. Sorry Dad."

Bill smiled and nodded. "That's okay, Sandy. Your Mom and I can do something tomorrow after church without you."

Dick nodded. "That's good. I told Trina yesterday that I'd think of something for us to do. Knotts sounds great. Bob?"

He also supported the idea. "Jess told me a couple of weeks ago that she hadn't been to Knotts since she was in the fifth grade. Anyway, she and I can have fun almost anywhere." Bob grinned. "Don't you remember when we all went grunion hunting under the full moon at Christmas?" They all smiled.

"Okay," their Dad said, "Tomorrow your Mom and I will go in my car, and you boys take the van. This morning, you boys clean everything upstairs and, in the basement, thoroughly, while your Mom and I take care of this floor. You boys can get your part done in a couple of hours. Then, I want you to spend some time with Harry. You boys haven't played with him much during the cold winter days these last few months."

"While you're working on the basement," their Mom added, "I want you boys to give the hidden apartment area a once-over. If we must use it, none of us will like it if we have to contend with dust and dirt." She looked around. "Anyone still hungry?" The rest of them shook their heads. "Okay, you boys go and get started upstairs. Do a good job!"

The three of them had done this several times. As triplets, they were in some ways connected mentally. They didn't get in one another's way. Their parents thought they did well what they were told to do, and they did it quickly. Even though they had not cleaned the hidden apartment previously, they made quick work of it.

Going back to the basement outside door, the boys nodded to each other, and Bob called out, "Harry! Let's go play!"

A beige blur came running down the staircase. "Rowwl."

Sandy grabbed an extra-large *Kong dog* toy off a nearby shelf. As they went outside, Sandy threw it down the hill. Harry raced after it, and they started hiking down the trail into the canyon. As the three of them moved downward, Harry brought it back several times, and one of the boys would throw it again.

When the trail ended at the creek bed, Harry dropped the toy at Dick's feet, turned, and drank. Suddenly, Harry stood up, stiffened. He looked to the other side of the creek towards a boulder there. "Rowwl." It was a louder than usual snarl.

Dick shaded his eyes, peering in the same direction. "What is it, Harry?"

From high on the boulder, the boys heard a puma. "Roowwl."

Harry answered with an even louder, "Rowwl." He turned left, up towards the creek. Coyotes began coming out of the brush, and Harry crouched. "Rrooowwwllll!" It was the loudest snarl the boys had ever heard from Harry.

One of the coyotes made a mistake or should have known better. He turned his head up and let out a howl.

Suddenly, the boys instinctively knew that a battle was about to be waged. Dick said, "Harry! Protect!"

"Bob said, let's get out of here!"

"I'm way ahead of you!" Sandy was going as fast up the trail as he could.

When they saw Harry racing towards the coyotes, Dick and Bob started scrambling up the trail after Sandy. They had never climbed that hill so fast. Behind them, they heard cries and yelps from time to time. When they got to the basement door, they opened it, stopped, and turned. Where they had been, there was a dust cloud with fighting and a few occasional yelps. "Harry can get back in through the emergency door." Dick started inside, and Sandy and Bob followed. They closed the door, sat down, and waited.

After about ten minutes, the boys heard their Dad's voice as he called them from upstairs. "Boys?"

Dick called back up the stairs. "We're in the basement!"

Their parents came down the staircase and saw their boys at the basement door and looking out. They walked over and sat down with them. Alex looked at Dick. "What's going on?"

Sandy took a deep breath. "At the bottom of the canyon, we encountered a puma, and Harry exchanged greetings with it. Then a pack of coyotes emerged from the brush a little upstream."

Dick nodded. "I told Harry to protect, and the three of us scrambled up the hill as fast as we could."

Sandy nodded. "Now we're waiting for Harry."

As if on cue, they heard Harry softly cry from the hidden apartment. "Rowwl."

Bob went to the display case, grabbed the secret latch, and swung open the door. "Harry?"

He stood there, bleeding in several places. "Rowwl."

As the boys knelt down with Alex to welcome him back, their Dad took out his phone and pushed a speed-dial number. "Debby, this is Bill Johnson. We have an emergency. Are you available?" He pushed the speaker button.

"I've nothing pressing the rest of the day. What's going on?"

"Harry took on a pack of coyotes and possibly a puma in order to protect the boys. He's pretty chewed up."

"From the tone of your voice, it sounds like you'd better get him over here to our zoo's veterinary hospital. He might have to stay a few days."

"Okay. We're on our way, Debby." They ended the call. As Bill put his phone away, Alex was coming out of the secret apartment with a stretcher.

"Your Dad and I kept this relic as a souvenir. Now it'll come in handy. Bob, Dick, help Harry get onto the stretcher. Sandy, run upstairs and get the van out of the garage."

It seemed like an hour, but it was about five minutes later when they started down the mountain. Being a Saturday, traffic was not heavy, and Bill pushed the speed limits all the way. Still, it took what seemed like hours to get there. Along the way, Alex called Debby to ask where they should unload, and there was a security guard holding open a mostly hidden gate for them when they got there.

Zoo staff carried Harry into the veterinary hospital, and the family was shown to an area where they could wait. Finally, Debby came through a door into their waiting area. "Harry is going to be fine. I want to keep him here for observation until Monday. There were a couple of skin tears that I had to stitch, and there were several puncture wounds. I went ahead and sterilized him as we had talked about a few months ago. Harry is sleeping, and we'll keep him sedated for a while – probably until tomorrow morning."

Alex looked at her. "We know that this is not a public animal hospital. Will any of this create a problem for you, Debby?"

The vet shook her head. "I have talked briefly with our Director of Animal Operations. From time to time, there have been emergencies that we are better equipped to handle than anyone else in the county. We cannot charge for our services, but as always, a donation would be welcome."

Alex looked at Bill. "I've got our checkbook in my purse." She leaned over and whispered into his ear because she did not want their sons to know the cost.

Bill nodded. "Based upon previous services from Debby, that seems fair." They both knew they would take the donation off their taxes. She took out the checkbook.

Alex looked at the vet again. "Do I make a check out to the Los Angeles Zoo and Botanical Gardens? We assume that your services here are covered by the zoo, is that correct?" She started writing.

Debby nodded. "That's correct on both counts."

Alex tore out the check from the book and handed it to the vet, whose eyes got a little bigger. "Thank you, very much!" She smiled. "This is more than adequate. While you're here I'll tell you about something interesting."

"What's that?" Alex was putting away her checkbook.

"When Sheila had kittens, you gave us one of them, Cherrie, because she was simply too wild for you, remember?"

Bill nodded. "We remember. What's going on?"

"One of the keepers saw her leap out of a moat into the cheetahs grotto. We increased security around her. A month later, she started acting a little differently than usual, so we checked her out. She had gotten pregnant from one of the cheetahs. It's still too soon to say, but one of the kittens looks remarkably like Sheila, her grandmother."

Several in the family muttered, "Wow!"

Later, they didn't talk much as they drove home. As they started up the mountain highway, Alex called Pizza Heaven, and she ordered pizzas and salads to be delivered to the house. The boys called their girlfriends and were still talking with them when Bill put the van in the garage and went into the house.

Sitting at the kitchen table, Bill spoke. "While you three are at Knotts tomorrow, your Mom and I will probably go over and check on Harry."

Alex took another slice of pizza. "That's right. By the way, boys, what time are you picking up the girls after church? How have you set that up?"

They were all busy chewing pizza, but Sandy spoke up. "Trina and Jess are meeting at Carole's house at Noon for tacos. We're supposed to pick them up at 12:30."

Alex looked at Bill, nodding. "It sounds like our boys don't need us, and we can leave for the zoo directly from church, doesn't it?"

"Yep."

Later, their sons talked for a long time after turning the lights off. As Alex and Bill learned while driving to church, Dick wanted to talk about Harry. "He had to choose his battle. He's the son of Sheila and a puma. Maybe that one was Harry's father. The short interchange between the two cats did not seem hostile. I think the coyotes were after that puma, maybe because he's old."

Bob agreed. "That seems entirely possible. Harry's fur did not stand when he called to the cat on the boulder, although he stiffened at attention."

Sandy concurred. "I also think that God is continuing to deliver us and bless us. That puma did not chase us when we scrambled up the hill. That's also significant." He paused. "I don't know about you two, but I'm beginning to see Carole as a special gift that God has prepared for me. I want to spend the rest of my life with her."

Bob only hesitated for a moment. "I cannot think of a time when Jess and I have not been totally comfortable with each other. When I started giving her singing lessons two years ago, I liked her from the beginning, and up until then, we had never had any classes together. This final year of high school, we have two classes together. After spending so much of my time with her these last few months, it feels like we've known each other forever. I think we might really enjoy marriage and having a big family. Like you, Sandy, it seems like God prepared us for each other."

Dick hesitated, but they waited. Dick spoke quietly. "I'm not sure. I suppose we could make a long list of the things Trina and I both like. I have as much fun with her, more fun than I do with you guys, and that's very unusual. It's really very different. When we get back from Knott's tomorrow night, I think we'll have even more to talk about."

Though the boys did not get a full night's sleep, all of them were wide awake before the alarms went off. The triplets were all excited, looking forward to the day. The girls previously had come over to the mountain house to celebrate New Year's Eve with them and greet the new year. Since then, the boys had all dated separately. They knew that with this triple date, the day would be memorable.

At about 10:30 Sunday morning, Sandy drove the van with his brothers, and Bill drove his car with Alex. They pulled into the church parking lot. Alex and Bill led the way as usual. As they went into the church's foyer, Carole, Trina, and Jess were there to greet them. Bill grinned broadly. "Good morning, beautiful ladies!" He and Alex were expecting to see them, but the boys weren't. She was smiling too, as she and Bill gave each of them a hug.

The triplets stood there with their mouths hanging open, and then they recovered and greeted their girlfriends. The girls took the boy hands, and the eight of them entered as couples, going down the aisle and taking most of a row of chairs. Sandy, Dick, and Bob were silent. They wondered how it had happened. They knew they'd have to wait until later to ask their girlfriends about it.

After about a half-hour of singing God's praises in worship, their pastor, Ernest Ford, read a Bible passage where Jesus calls the twelve men to be his disciples. He made a brilliant case for how our lives are defined by the decisions we make and the relationships we nurture.

After church, Alex and Bill moved rapidly to the rear. After greeting their pastor, they went straight to his car and left, waving to the kids as they drove out of the parking lot. They would learn about the kids' day later.

The six kids got into the van. As they started away from the church, Dick and Trina were in the bucket seats of the driving pit. As expected, Dick spoke up first. "Okay, ladies, what gives? Why did you meet us here at the church this morning?"

Trina put her hand on Dick's shoulder. "We'll tell you all about it while we eat lunch." Dick pulled into a *Taco Bell* a few blocks later. After getting their orders, they pushed three tables together and sat down. Trina swallowed some root beer before she spoke. "Dick, it all started in December, two weeks before Christmas. I called your Mom, and I told her I wanted her opinion. I asked her if she thought you and I would always be great friends, or if she thought there was more in our future."

Dick glanced at her. "What did she say?"

"Maybe I'll tell you sometime. It's not important right now. I called Carole to see what she thought. Carole, Jess, and I had talked in December many times about what we were going to give you three for Christmas and what we wanted to do at your place when we all got together for New Years' Eve."

Carole took over. "All of us have discussed your Mom's instincts and intuition, how she always seems to know what we're thinking before we say anything."

Jess touched her boyfriend's arm. "Bob, you and I have talked several times about how your Dad seems to have solutions ready before we see problems."

Bob nodded. "True. What's all this leading up to?"

Trina took over again. "We're getting to that. Do you remember that incredible computer game that your Dad wrote, compiled, and then brought out on New Years' Eve?"

Dick remembered. "Yeah! That game is powerful and fast! There can be as few as two and as many as twenty playing at once. You girls weren't interested."

Trina touched Dick's arm again. "That's right, my love. We weren't interested in playing the game on that day. Your Mom took us upstairs for a girl-talk.'"

Sandy shook his head. "Girl-talk? Uh-Oh, guys, I think we're in trouble."

"No!" All three girls spoke simultaneously.

"I want to tell this part." Carole spoke intensely as she ate. "Your Mom started telling us about her high school prom, and by the time she finished, we were all laughing so hard we could hardly say anything. Anyway, your Mom took us into her closet. It's huge! She has dozens – maybe over a hundred – dresses in there! She invited us to look at them, to think about what kind of dress we wanted to wear to prom."

Jess spoke more quietly. "We each found one or more dresses that inspired us. She then told us she would get us a day with Wendy Palm, the costume designer for countless movies and a good friend of hers. Mrs. Palm will help us have original dresses for our prom. Isn't that incredible?! After that, we went into your parents' bedroom and sat on their bed. We had a girl-talk for more than an hour while you boys played that game with your Dad. We've had girl-talk, either in conference calls or in person, almost every week since then."

Trina nodded. "While we were waiting for you at the church this morning, each of us decided we think your Mom is like our best friend. We can talk to her about anything. It's particularly important to me, Bob, because... well, you know, my Mom and I don't communicate very well because alcohol gets in the way sometimes."

Carole nodded. "My Mom means well, but she admits that she simply does not understand my world at all. She likes your Mom though, both in movies and in person."

Jess smiled. "I'm with my Mom all the time, but we don't see eye to eye. I'm glad I can turn to your Mom when I need to."

"Last night, after you boys went to bed, your Mom called, and we had a conference-call girl-talk session. Jess, Carole, and I decided that it was time for us to start worshiping with you and your family, at least occasionally. Your Mom liked the idea."

From there until they entered the Knotts parking lot, they talked about that morning's surprise, and they also talked about the music and sermon. Bob told them he wanted to assemble a chorus or two at the church.

That day at Knotts will be one discussed for years to come. They started out together, but each had their own ideas of what they wanted to explore. The triplets saw the park very differently than they had some four years earlier. Their girlfriends helped them see the fun through new eyes.

They decided before the end of the day that they were going to go back to Knotts in the summer to visit Soak City, which is an area separate from the rest of the park. Although Knotts is not as big as Disneyland, the six of them made wonderful memories that day.

As planned, they met at Mrs. Knotts Chicken Dinner Restaurant for dinner. Four of them were shocked when, as they sat down, Carole held up her left hand, and there was a large solitaire on her ring finger. Sandy smiled broadly. "We're not ready to set a date yet, but we're definitely thinking about it." They discussed the engagement until their food came.

As they ate, they were mostly quiet, except for one short exchange started by Dick. "Trina, have you ever tasted Boysenberry Pie à la mode?"

She shook her head, looking at Dick. "I've seen Boysenberry Preserves on grocery shelves, but I've never tasted a Boysenberry. What's a Boysenberry?"

Sandy smiled. "It's an incredibly delicious cross of the European raspberry, European blackberry, American dewberry, and loganberry. I looked it up after our family went to Knotts four years ago."

Dick looked into her eyes. "You've got to try the boysenberry pie. Even if you don't want to order it for yourself, you've at least got to taste some of mine." He looked around the table. "Right, Sandy?" He nodded. "Right, Bob?" He agreed.

After they finished dinner, there were still a few rides that they had not tried, so they all continued to explore the park. Jess and Bob found parts of what was left of the old ghost town. At Jess' insistence, they bought matching candy-stripe shirts with Roaring-twenties-style hats and canes. When she came out of the dressing room wearing her outfit, Bob kissed her. "Jess, we can't limit our use of these to Halloween!"

She nodded. "Right! I've got a couple of other ideas too!"

Shortly before midnight, they all got back to the van, carrying packages. Jess showed off the shirts. Carole made a big deal of some books she had bought for Sandy. Trina had gone back to the restaurant and had bought three boysenberry pies to go. "I'm going to share one of these with my family tomorrow, and I'll freeze the other two for special occasions. I've got vacuum-seal bags that these pies will fit into. I'm in love with boysenberry pie!" (A year later, Dick would tell them during their guy-talk that, when he and Trina shared that pie together, he knew he wanted her to be his wife. Before the wedding, however, the six of them had more adventures awaiting them.

20.

Graduation and Beyond

Just like his mother, Harry healed quickly from his battle with the coyotes. By the Wednesday of the following week, he was starting to use the treadmill again – though not quite as fast as usual. He also scampered up the staircase, leaped onto one of the beams, and stretched out. He was almost back to normal.

Late in the second week after the boys got back from Knotts, Friday morning began with a phone call on Alex's cell when she and Bill were still reading scriptures and praying. Right then, she looked at the display. "It's Steve." She pressed the speaker button. "Good morning, Steve! What's up with you this morning?"

"Michaela and I were just finishing breakfast when she looked out at our beach and came up with a great idea. We are so blessed here in Santa Monica to have our own private stretch of beach, with added security when necessary. My wife pointed out that you and Bill have never been over here. Would you like to bring your boys over tomorrow? Our weather is clear and clean today, and it promises to be just as great tomorrow."

"Steve, we appreciate your invitation, but our boys would not want to spend the weekend away from their girlfriends any more than I enjoy having time away from Bill. One of our sons is already engaged." Alex was emphatic.

"Okay! How about this? We've got plenty of food. If they and their girlfriends think it is too cold to go into the ocean, we've got a heated pool. It will be just our two families with a chef and a couple of waiters. How about it?"

Alex looked at Bill. "We'll talk to the boys at breakfast, but it is probably a go. The girls will be especially thrilled to spend the day with a famous movie director."

"Great! Unless I hear from you otherwise, Alex, we'll see you tomorrow morning about 10:00 or so, okay?"

They nodded together, and Alex responded, "Okay."

They told the boys about it over breakfast. "What do you think?" Bill asked. Suddenly, the house began to shake. Bill pointed towards the great room. "Everybody, go to the staircase and hold on to something!" Stumbling and helping each other from falling, they made it. As the mountain shook and rocked, they hung on. Harry came up from the basement and wrapped his paws around the first step.

"Dad," Sandy asked, "why are we here by the staircase?"

Dick's voice reflected Bob's fear and Sandy's. "Yeah, Dad, why here?"

When there was a slight pause in the quaking, their Dad answered. "The stairs are wrapped around a kind of spine for the house. The rafters are like ribs on the spine. What looks like a wooden beam is a cluster of steel beams wrapped with wood. Inside are utilities lines and pipes. I should have told all of you about it long before now. We've had smaller quakes before this, so I've neglected to tell you." The quaking seemed to pause. "You boys didn't answer my question about going to Santa Monica."

Dick looked at Sandy and Bob, and his voice was now calm. "We'll ask Carole, Trina, and Jess at school, but I'm pretty sure they'll jump at the chance to go." The floor began to move some more. After about a half an hour, the quaking seemed to be over.

Dick was right. All three of the girls were thrilled with the idea. Sandy said it was a great opportunity for him and Carole, but he wouldn't say why.

When they drove to Santa Monica Saturday morning, they were greeted by Steve's wife, Michaela. Until that moment the kids met her, they hadn't made an important connection. That stunningly attractive wife of Steve's had been in three different movies with Alex, and the boys and their girlfriends had not realized that Michaela Leone was Steve Leone's wife. They thought she was amazing. She gave each of them a hug. "Kids, it is so nice to meet all of you! My husband is finishing up some editing work. I'll introduce you to him, and then the day is free to enjoy as you like it." She turned to go into the house. The rest of them followed their hostess.

Michaela led them into a large windowless room with movie and television posters on three of the walls. There were all kinds of equipment scattered around the room. At the far end of the room was a theater-sized screen. Alex's director friend turned from his monitor and stood up to greet each of them.

The girls seemed to be almost in trances as he shook hands with them. "I'm glad all of you could come today. When Michaela and I realized that we had never had Alex and Bill and their boys over here, we decided that now is the perfect time. I'm at a good place to stop for now."

Bob had to say something. "Mr. Leone, our whole family is not here. Harry is home, house sitting.""

The director nodded. "Yes! Harry is an amazing cat. Harry's mother, Sheila, was even more amazing. Michaela and I loved Sheila. I guess you girls never got to know her." They shook their heads, listening intently to every word he said. "Maybe later I'll tell you about the time Sheila saved Michaela's bacon. I've never told your parents." He paused. "Later, maybe. The beach is waiting!" They headed outside, where Alex and Bill headed for the pool's diving board, taking off their outer clothes as they went.

Bob looked at his girlfriend. "The pool or the ocean, Jess?"

"The sun is nice and warm."

Bill dove into the pool and called out, "The pool's warm!"

Jess looked at Bob. "If the ocean's too cold, we can come back. Let's try body surfing, okay?"

Alex and Bill knew Bob was ready to do whatever she wanted to do. "Sure!"

They walked fast and stripped down to their swimsuits. Bob had never seen Jess in a bathing suit before, and it seemed to him like he was in another world. The ocean was very cold, and after about a half an hour, Bob and Jess stretched out on their beach towels to bake in the sun. When they turned over fifteen minutes later, they looked each other up and down and then looked all around. They were by themselves. They were on a steep slope down to the ocean, so they couldn't even see the house behind them. They made out for a while. About an hour later, they could smell barbeque, and they decided to go back to the pool area.

At the top of the incline, they stopped and took in the scene. Smoke was billowing up from the outdoor barbeque. A hundred yards off to their right, they could see Dick and Trina walking towards them together, holding hands. They all waved at each other. They were all headed towards the aromas coming from the patio next to the pool.

Jess spoke out as Dick and Trina got closer and joined them. "Where have you two been?"

Trina glanced at Dick before responding. "I was turned around at first. So was Dick. Because of the curve in the coastline, that" she pointed toward the ocean, "is south. We've been walking and talking. Dick and I went a couple of miles east towards Santa Monica before we turned around. Then we went at least a mile west, beyond the Leone house in the other direction. We went back towards Santa Monica a little farther the second time. Now we're hungry."

Dick nodded. "I guess we've needed to talk like this for a long time." They all walked around the pool and on to the food that had been spread out.

There's one thing that the Johnson family goes for whenever it is available: barbeque spare ribs. What made choosing the ribs difficult that day was that there were also porterhouse steaks ready to be grilled to order, barbequed chicken, and grilled swordfish filets. Their hosts had hired a chef to handle the grill and a couple of others to serve them. There were also a variety of other foods to choose from on a table. For nearly two hours they ate whatever appealed to them. They would eat a plateful, lay out by the pool, have a soft drink, and then start over.

While the chef was fixing a steak for Sandy, Carole approached the director. "Mr. Leone, Sandy and I both have a passion for photography. I've got a photography scholarship to U.C.L.A. I've also been offered a scholarship to the U.S.C. Film School."

Steve Leone smiled. "That's fantastic! The U.S.C. Film School is a great place to start getting into making movies. If you're also interested in the overall art of photography, U.C.L.A. is one of the three best in the country."

By this time, the rest of them were listening in to the conversation. Carole was nodding. "I know. Sandy and I would like to take advantage of you after we eat."

"How so?"

She handed him a thumb drive. "After *The Gaardian Saga* movies started coming out, Sandy and I decided that you're probably the best director in the entertainment industry right now. Would you mind taking a quick look at some of our efforts and give us some feedback? Anything you can share with us can be helpful."

"Absolutely! As soon as we've finished eating, you and Sandy can join me in my workshop. Michaela and I probably owe Alex and Bill a dozen favors between us. It'll be my pleasure."

After eating their fill, when Carole and Sandy went into the house, the other two boys and their girlfriends tagged along. Michaela, Alex, and Bill went into the living room to talk. There, their hostess told them about the time that Sheila had saved her life.

In the workshop, Sandy felt he needed to explain why his brothers and girlfriends were there too. "You've probably heard or read stories about how twins often seem connected to each other in ways that other children are not. For Dick, Bob, and me, as triplets our internal connections are truly powerful. We share almost everything. The others want to be here as a kind of shortcut to later discussions."

The director nodded. "I understand. Since there are so many of us, I'll use the 8K projection monitor to display your files on that wall screen over there." He pointed. "We'll start by putting thumbnails up on the wall screen." After just a few keystrokes, they were seeing thumbnails filling the wall. "These are all from the Mammoth Mountain Resort, aren't they?"

Carole pointed. "All the of the videos and stills are from Mammoth except that one on the lower right. Just for fun, Sandy shot a video of Harry running on the treadmill two weeks ago."

The director double-clicked it. "Wow! Your cat can move as fast as his mother did! Doesn't that display say 92?"

Sandy nodded. "Yes, ninety-two miles per hour. It is a seven-minute clip. It's all the same, so it's kind of boring. Can your software slow him down?"

Steve worked his keyboard, and Harry was seen running at a tenth of normal. "He's beautiful, isn't he? Let's see what else you've brought with you. We'll look at the stills first." As they discussed each image, the director was infinitely patient and supportive, even when he criticized. He was a good teacher.

When they went back to the thumbnails view, Carole seemed unusually shy when she spoke. "Mr. Leone, the video clips are where we need the most improvement. Most of them are four minutes or less."

Steve Leone nodded. "Okay. Let's start by looking at them sequentially. We can skip ahead any time we need to." Just like he did with the stills, he tried to be encouraging with Carole and Sandy as he had been with the stills. Everyone paid extra attention to Dick's skiing accident. By the end of the afternoon, all of them were getting hungry again. "Carole, you and Sandy have the originals of all of these things at home, don't you?"

Carole nodded. "Yes, why?"

"If you don't mind, all except the video clip of Harry on your thumb drive are from the Mammoth Resort. If you'll leave the drive with me, I'll create a Mammoth documentary using your materials. It will give you and Sandy some ideas of how you two can do some more advanced editing."

Sandy grinned. "Wow! That would be fantastic, wouldn't it, Carole?"

She also was smiling broadly. "Absolutely! That would be great!"

The last reds and pinks of Saturday's sunset were fading over the ocean when the eight of them headed home. After taking the girls to their homes, the Johnsons headed up the mountain highway to their house. As late as it was, the boys talked long into the night. At church the next morning, they were more than a little sleepy.

That final semester at La Cañada High School was a fast and busy sequence of classes, special events, and parties for the boys and their girlfriends. Alex and Bill bought the boys tailor-fitted tuxedoes. Alex told Carole, Trina, and Jess that the dresses created by her friend, Wendy Palm would be theirs to keep. Privately, Alex had made it worth the woman's time with a generous check.

Before Prom, however, came Spring vacation. Without telling the boys, Alex and Bill took the parents of their sons' girlfriends out to lunch one Thursday afternoon when all of them could get off from work for a couple of hours. As they ate, they all talked about what it was going to be like after their children's graduation. They agreed that it would be great to spend time with their kids during Spring vacation. Alex and Bill had a plan, and they presented it to them very diplomatically. The rest of them enthusiastically agreed to it.

Friday afternoon before Spring vacation started, Jess, Carole, and Trina brought their families, including two more brothers and three more sisters, over to the mountain house for a pizza feed. Enough pizzas and salads were delivered to feed a small army. After Bill asked a blessing, they all started to eat.

Harry was sitting by the windows, looking out over the canyon. "Rowwl."

Alex looked at him. "What is it Harry?"

Harry turned his head and looked straight at Alex. "Rowwl." He looked back over the canyon.

Alex got up to see what Harry was seeing. "Bill! Come and look!"

All of them got out of their seats. Bill joined her by the window. "The wind is in our favor right now," he said, "but it could shift." All of them could see smoke billowing up from further into the canyon. They could see a line of flames in the distant brush.

Alex looked at her husband. "Bill, what do you think?" She held his gaze, and they looked at each other for what seemed like a minute or more.

Bill knew what she was silently asking. He nodded and spoke loudly. "Okay, everyone. Grab all the food and drinks. We're moving to the basement." Bill picked up a stack of pizza boxes and led the way to the stairs. In the basement, everyone was looking around except Alex and her husband. He swept his arm around the room as he spoke. "This may well be Sandy's favorite room, although Dick and Bob spend a lot of time down here too. I think Sandy has read more than half the books in these bookcases."

Sandy nodded. "I counted on New Years' Eve. I've read two books shy of three quarters of our library."

Bob smiled, looking at Jess and the others. "I don't think any of the rest of you have been down here, have you?" They shook their heads.

Alex went to the basement fridge and opened it. "If you want something different to drink, we've got cans of juice and pop over here."

Harry was standing by the window and looking out again. Bill went and stood by Harry, carrying some pizza and a glass of iced tea. Carole's Dad joined him, and they glanced at each other. "Paul, the flames are advancing away from us so far, but we'll have to take turns watching."

Paul spoke quietly. "Okay."

For a little over a half an hour, they continued to eat and talked. Harry stayed by the windows. Sometime later, Harry got their attention with his "Rowwl."

Bill got up and looked. "Okay, everyone, the wind has shifted. The flames are moving toward us. Carry what food and drinks you can. We're moving again." He went to the display case and pulled the hidden lever. The secret door swung open. He touched a button, and the apartment's lights came on. "Everyone, it will be safe in here."

Bill didn't have to tell them twice. Inside, the ceiling wasn't as high as in the main basement. Sandy and Harry were the last to come in, and Sandy closed the door.

Alex got their attention while Bill started going through a routine they had discussed in a family meeting several years earlier. She appeared calm, but Bill and the boys could sense well-hidden tension in her. Bill's memory briefly flashed back to their hike in the Chocolate Mountains before they were married. Their love was merely growing then. Now, their love for one another held them tightly together emotionally and spiritually as she spoke. "Boys, let me explain to our guests what's going on." She paused. "I've rehearsed this in my mind, but I've always hoped I'd never have to say this." She paused again. "Since we live on the edge of a canyon, we've always known that brush-fire flames could come up the hill too fast for us to get away." She looked at her husband as he approached and took over.

"When I designed this house, this shelter was not in the plans. As construction began, heavy equipment was brought in to lay the foundation and place anchors in the hillside. Where we're standing was discovered on the first day. It was in the news for a few days. When this was discovered, it was quickly determined to be a relic of World War II. It was built in 1941 right after the Japanese bombed Pearl Harbor, and we subsequently got into the war. The army built several buildings, burying them in the hills above Los Angeles. Many people believed it entirely possible that the Japanese would come on across the Pacific and attack the West Coast."

Alex pointed at the furniture. "This will take a few minutes, so everyone can sit down." She remained standing beside him and put an arm around him while he continued.

"All of this was dusty and stuffy. It was a bunkhouse with a dozen bunks, a latrine, and a galley. The vents were clogged, and the septic tank was useless. We gave the furnishings to a local museum. I drew plans to bring the structure into the twenty-first century. This place has been here a long time, and it has endured countless fires and earthquakes." He took a breath and sighed. "While Alex was talking, I checked to see which of our ventilation shafts was furthest from the flames and smoke, and I started that fan. If the power goes out, we have a battery backup that will last for quite a while. If we're still here tomorrow, we have emergency food and water. There's also a relay to provide us with cell service and the Internet."

Alex continued their explanation. "Bill and I must ask you to forget that you have ever been here or even that this shelter exists. The world out there believes the army bunker was removed when the house was built. County records do not show that this exists anymore. Will all of you please promise to keep this a secret?"

Jess raised her hand. "If any member of my family ever tells anyone about this place, they will never hear from me again!"

Carole spoke louder than usual. "Me too!"

Trina nodded. "Amen!"

Alex smiled broadly. "That's a relief for us." She pointed. "The TV over there isn't as big as any of the others in the house, but it can keep us entertained. In addition to the Internet, there's a menu for five cameras. They are mounted outside to view various parts of our property. With them, we can keep track of the fire."

Bill offered another bit of information. "One more thing I should have told you. Although this apartment has been used by Harry and his mother more than we ever will, there's an emergency exit. Leaving from the galley, there's a slide that goes down the hill. At the bottom, there's an exit, and there's a passageway to another exit further away." He pointed. "Behind you through that door is a full bathroom with a separate relief station for Harry. He seldom uses it because he usually goes outside through the emergency exit." He pointed off to the left, away from where they had come in. "Through that door is a kitchen and eating area. The rectangles around the perimeter of this room are drawers that hold ten queen-size beds that are already made up, so that in emergencies like this one, everyone has a place to sleep. Boys, you and the other children work out how you will share the beds not used by your parents and your girlfriends." They nodded.

Alex and Bill were surprised at how calm everyone was throughout that time in their shelter. It turned out that Carole's Dad, Paul, has real talent as a comedian. Carole's Mom, Stella, played his straight woman. Maxine, Lona and Stella had questions about some of the movies that Alex had made. The three other fathers talked to Bill about the house and how it was anchored into the mountainside. They also had questions about the modifications that had been made to the shelter to bring it from the World War II era into the twenty-first century.

From time to time, the boys would go to the monitor to check to see what the different cameras were showing of the fire, and their girlfriends went with them. When all of them rolled the beds out of the walls, they were definitely tired.

21.
More Adventures

Sunday morning, Alex's phone rang. And she spoke quietly on her cell phone while she and Bill were still in bed. Hello?" She paused about thirty seconds. "No, there's no problem. Unless something happens between now and tomorrow noon, we'll expect you at 1:00 tomorrow afternoon." She paused. "That's right. Bye." Alex put away her cell. She got out of bed, found the control, and chose the TV's auxiliary menu. She switched from camera to camera.

With most of the others still dozing, Bill got out of bed and stood next to her. "What was that about?"

"We can talk about it later. We can go back into the house, and we Moms will fix breakfast." She raised her voice a little. "Okay, everyone, we can go back out into the house. Just please remember your promise." She turned back to Bill. "Tell everyone that asks we can go back down the hill in an hour or two, after we have breakfast." He nodded.

Bob approached them, and she turned to him. "Later, I want you three boys to change the linens and towels here in the shelter and get them laundered."

"Okay, Mom."

Bill started his shutdown routine for the shelter while the others got up and started getting organized. After everyone else was headed out into the basement, the boys started gathering up the bed linens and the towels.

It did not take long to have breakfast, and then it was time for the parents to surprise their kids. Paul told them about it. "Kids, we parents had lunch together two weeks ago, and we've come up with a surprise for all of you." He had everyone's attention as he continued. "Either tonight or tomorrow morning, each of us needs to pack a bag for Spring vacation. We won't be back until next Saturday, the day before Easter. We need to pack for cold and wet weather."

Sandy's eyes were big, and he had to know more. "Where are we going?"

Bill smiled. "Monday after lunch, we're all going to park in a secure area at Towne Center, near the entrance closest to American Rag. A bus will pick us up at 1:00, right after lunch, to take us to the airport. You'll find out where our first stop will be once we're on our way."

Alex looked up from the kitchen counter. "Those of us going to church this morning, we're going to the second service at 11:00. The rest are on their own today."

When they got home to the mountain house from church, everyone spent most of the afternoon cleaning the house thoroughly and doing laundry. The air still smelled of lingering smoke coming from remaining hot spots of the fire. All the burned area was more than a half-mile away except for their canyon. Smoke still lingered. After dinner, they packed their bags. Alex and Bill wouldn't even give the boys a hint as to where they were going. They simply told them they had to pack for cold and wet weather.

Just before Monday's lunch, there was a knock on the door. It was Abby and George, their old friends and former neighbors. Bill greeted them and shook George's hand. "Good morning, George! Good morning, Abby!" He looked down. "Good morning to you too, Tammie!"

"Rowwl."

Just then, Tammie's brother came into the mud room. "Rowwl." Harry greeted her and nuzzled her.

Bill led them into the great room. Alex was coming down the stairs. "Good morning! We're so glad that you two can house-sit this week. I think Harry will enjoy having his sister around for a few days."

Abby reached down and scratched Harry's head. "He looks so much like Sheila did."

Alex nodded. "I know. When Harry was injured in his scrap with the coyotes, his vet went ahead and sterilized him. We don't have to worry about Harry giving Tammie and you two any future challenges."

George smiled. "We love Tammie, but we didn't want her to have any kittens either, so the vet at the San Diego Zoo that you recommended fixed her right after she got settled at home with us. She and Beau are great companions."

"So, Beau is still pretty healthy?"

George smiled. "You wouldn't think he's a senior citizen in dog years."

Abby shook her head. "No. Our vet says Beau is doing fine. He and Tammy play constantly."

For lunch, Alex and Bill fixed BLTs and chocolate shakes for all, and then they headed down the mountain to meet the other three families. As they approached the mall's parking lot, Sandy touched his Dad's shoulder. "Will our van be okay parked here for a week?"

"Your Mom and I have paid the mall's management to have the mall's security watch our cars as part of their routine while we're gone. It's part of our rent of the secure area."

They pulled into an area near some trees about twenty yards from the American Rag store's delivery door, just as the other three cars also pulled up. A few minutes later, a small airport shuttle bus pulled up. Just a few more minutes later, they were on their way.

Bill spoke a little louder than he usually did because of the noises of the shuttle. "When we get to the airport, we're going to a private area where TSA security will check us out. Then we'll get on a chartered jet." He looked at his watch. "If we stay on our planned schedule, we'll be landing at the Monterey Regional Airport. If the weather cooperates, we'll be eating dinner while watching the sunset over Monterey Bay. Even if the weather doesn't cooperate, we parents are looking forward to talking about the future of all of our soon-to-be young-adult children."

Sandy's and Carole's faces lit up. She could barely contain her excitement. "Are we just going to explore the coastline, or are we going to spend some time at the aquarium?"

Stella smiled. "We'll take in as much of the area as we choose, Carole. You and Sandy can make all the stills and videos you want." Sandy's eyebrows went up. He was obviously glad that his future mother-in-law was so supportive.

Just over an hour after they took off, they were going through security in Monterey. As they got onto a shuttle bus, Bill saw Alex speak to the driver, and she nodded. Bill gave Alex a questioning look, and she spoke quietly. "I've asked the driver to take us to Salinas for some field-ripened strawberries before she takes us to our hotel."

Trina overheard Alex and nudged Dick. They were sitting behind them. "This is great! Fresh-picked strawberries!" Dick now gave his girlfriend a questioning look, so she went on. "They're not in the grocery stores yet down where we are, and even then, they'll have been under refrigeration, possibly for a couple of days."

About a half-hour later, our shuttle pulled over to a roadside stand. They all got out and stretched. When the stand's owner saw that they were going to buy a whole flat of berries, he let them pick out a flat, and then he emptied two more boxes of berries on top of the others in the flat. Back on the shuttle, they had a hard time resisting, but Lona pointed out to Trina and the others that they should probably wait until they could get the berries washed at the hotel.

It took them nearly an hour to get settled into their rooms at the Monterey Bay Beach Spa. The suites for the children each had three queen beds, and the parents got rooms with king beds. One of the bellhops took their flat of strawberries to the kitchen, where the berries were washed and put into bowls for each of the rooms. They snacked on them until they met in their private dining room overlooking the beach. The sun had almost set, and the shades of reds and pinks were impressive. There were tables for all nineteen of them.

By the time they finished their dinners and were working on their desserts the sky was getting dark. Alex stood up and turned towards the table with her sons and their girlfriends. "Tonight, we're going to talk about our kids who are graduating and their futures. Sandy, while Carole finishes her pie, why don't you start, telling about the scholarships you are Carole have, and what the two of you are going to be doing this coming September. I'm sure Carole will interrupt when she's ready." Carole nodded.

As Alex sat down, Sandy stood up. "Carole and I have accepted scholarships to U.C.L.A. I'm going to have dual majors in Mechanical Engineering and Photography. It looks like Dad and I will be working together some of the time after I get my bachelor's degree. My photography hobby will likely become an avocation that will occupy at least some of my time with Carole."

Carole stood up beside him. "We'll continue to have photography in common, although I will focus upon videography. During my second year, I'm supposed to begin an internship with Steve Leone. He will help me develop a career in cinematography."

That got the attention of Lona. "So, you will have a career in making movies, Carole?"

She nodded. "That's my dream. A few weeks ago, Sandy and I spent the day with the Johnsons, Trina, and Jess at the home of Steve and Michaela Leone. I'm sure Trina has told you about how she and Dick walked up and down the beach. Mr. Leone spent much of the afternoon helping Sandy and I improve our photography. That day I pretty much decided to make cinematography my career, especially after Sandy and I discussed it afterward."

Paul spoke up. "Sandy, I'd like to know more about where your mechanical engineering training is going to take you."

Sandy nodded. "Last year, I had a brainstorm while looking at some of my Dad's plans for housing developments. I realized that, with all the many floor plans for many houses, the walls had certain things in common. I basically asked if walls could be manufactured and be brought to a site to be assembled as houses. Dad said that, in Japan, many houses are assembled in this way. My dream is to design and set up such a factory."

"Wow!" Paul was impressed.

Carole and Sandy sat down.

Bill stood up. "Trina, since Dick is having another dessert, why don't you tell what you and Dick are going to be doing this coming fall?"

She stood up, smiling broadly. "We began to realize how much fun we can have together two Halloweens ago. I love working with my hands, making things that are useful and reliable. I just love working and playing with this amazing guy. I still don't know why I can always recognize him compared with Sandy and Bob, but I can. As we were walking on the beach in Santa Monica, Dick told me he was thinking about going to Triangle Tech in Pennsylvania. He and I have been offered scholarships to both Triangle Tech in Pennsylvania and to Los Angeles Trade Tech. We're going to move to Pennsylvania."

Dick stood up. "Ken Crain was the general contractor who built our house on the mountain. He and his wife, Wanda, have become friends of our family since it was built. A little over a week ago, when I told him I planned to go to Triangle Tech in Pittsburgh and wanted to help get Trina in, he made some calls. As of last Thursday, we both have full scholarships to get Associate in Arts degrees."

Jess' Mom, Maxine, surprised them with an outburst. "Way to go, you two!" Bob and Jess didn't expect that from his future mother-in law. He looked at Jess, and she winked.

Alex stood up again. "Okay, Bob, you and Jess, so who goes first?"

Jess nudged him, so he stood up. "It seems like ever since I took my earliest piano lessons, I've been interested in vocal music. Although I've got scholarships to both Juilliard School of Music and Temple University, I've chosen Temple because of its excellence in Choral music. When I have enough training, I want to start some contemporary chorales in Southern California. Jess is even more gifted than I am, however."

Jess stood up and kissed him on the cheek. "Thank you, lover, but I doubt that. I think all of us remember that, when I was a freshman, I was tiny and boyish. I got to play the part of Amahl in *Amahl and the Night Visitors* at Christmas. Bob became my voice coach, and that's how we first got to know one another. Someone – I don't know who – saw me three and a half years ago when I played Amahl, and they called a friend who is a professor at Temple University to tell them I was graduating this semester.

Bob says it was not him. Anyway, I'm covered for all expenses at Temple University in Philadelphia."

All of them applauded.

That night, before Sandy turned off the lights in the boy's room, the younger brothers of Carole and even Jess's older brother had already crashed. As Alex and Bill learned later, it was a life-changing conversation. In the darkness, the boys continued to talk softly as they always did. Bob had to say something about the scholarships' discussion. "After listening to everything this evening, I'm thinking Jess and I should get married before we move to Philadelphia. I'm open to having a triple wedding if you guys are."

The silence seemed to last forever, but was probably less than a minute. Dick spoke very quietly. "I can't believe I'm responding like this, Bob, but…." He paused about five more seconds. "Yeah. I'm in. I'm definitely and enthusiastically in. I want to spend the rest of my life with Trina and have a boatload of kids. How about you, Sandy?"

They could hear him chuckling softly. "Oh, yeah!!! The sooner that Carole and I get married, the better. Definitely better! Assuming we can get our future mates to go along, when shall we do it? The Fourth of July is a Monday this year. We could do it that Saturday. What do you guys think?" They agreed to ask the girls in private sometime while they were at the aquarium.

During breakfast on Tuesday in the same dining room, not one of the boys let on that they had been talking about their wedding the night before. At about 8:30, their shuttle/limo arranged through the hotel picked them up at the front of the hotel to take them to the aquarium.

As they arrived at the main entrance, Bill stood by the door of the shuttle/limo. "Let's meet at the Café at noon. We'll decide then whether to spend more time here or head down the coast. Okay?" Everyone nodded.

Bill took Alex's hand, and they walked towards the aquarium's biggest tank, a dozen steps behind Bob. Jess and Bob followed the signs towards the Open Sea Community Exhibit. They stood in awe, looking up into the aquarium's largest tank, through its 14.5-foot-high by 54-foot wide window. Bob took her hand, and they went up into the bleachers several rows. Alex and Bill stood nearby. When Bob and Carole sat down, he leaned closer to her and kissed her on the cheek. When she turned to kiss him back, he held up his index finger. Alex and Bill couldn't hear them talking, but they told them all about it later. Bob told her, "Last night, during our nightly boy-talk, we decided to ask our girlfriends if they were interested in having a triple wedding on the Fourth of July weekend."

Her eyes got bigger than he'd ever seen them before – or since. "Absolutely!" Then they kissed quite a bit longer. She asked softly and intensely. "Where?"

He shook his head. "The wedding day is not nearly as important to the groom as the marriage that begins on that day. It is the bride's day. The bride determines every aspect of the day right up until the wedding night begins. At that point, everything is mutually negotiable. Okay?" She nodded. "The three of you plan it," he continued, "and the three of us will be there – along with a few guests, of course."

They kissed again. Alex and Bill knew that something was up, but they didn't know what yet. They went up the stairs to a different area of the seating near the big window.

The rest of the morning, Jess and Bob continued to explore the various exhibits of the world-class aquarium. From what Alex and Bill learned later, they could hardly keep their hands off each other. They ran into Dick and Trina at the Kelp Forest Exhibit, and Jess took Carole aside. They whispered to one another for about a minute, and then Carole grabbed Sandy's hand as they joined Jess and Bob. Jess nodded, looking at Bob. "Carole's all for it."

Carole nodded. "I already talked with Trina about ten minutes ago, and she's in. We'll meet with your Mom for some girl-talk either Easter Sunday afternoon or right after."

With nineteen of them all meeting there in that little café, it was no place to begin talking about a wedding, and everyone knew it. Talking with one another in small groups, they decided that they wanted to spend the rest of the day at the aquarium. They agreed to meet at the entrance at 5:00.

Later, looking across the crowd, Bob saw Carole talking with Alex. Her eyes grew wider and nodded, then she turned to Bill and spoke quietly. "There's going to be a triple wedding. I know that further discussion will be soon." Bill was stunned.

As they left the café, Jess and Bob found themselves walking more slowly and talking quietly. They had not talked about whether they wanted to have kids. Jess told Alex about it during the girl-talk session that followed the week after Easter. When Alex told Bill, she said the conversation was like the one they had had a couple of decades earlier.

It went like this: Bob put his arm around her and squeezed. "Whether we do have children or not, I'll have a great time trying!" He kissed the top of her head, and she turned a subtle pink.

"I will too, definitely, but seriously...."

Bob continued. "I see at least three options. First, we can delay our education get our kids into school before pursuing our dreams. I'm not fond of that option. Second, we can leave everything to God's timing. In that situation, we would simply adapt and adjust as time passes. The third option is to do our best *not* to have kids until after we get the education we want, and with both of us getting our incomes started, then we have kids."

Jess nodded. "Let's talk more about this later."

Jess and Bob went back to the auditorium with the giant window again, sat in the back row, and made out for a while. They were very cautious to control what others could see as they took a few liberties with one another.

It was shortly after 5:00 when everyone got back to the shuttle/limo and headed back to the hotel. Most of them were pretty tired. Just before dinner, some of them met and talked about the various tourist traps they wanted to visit.

Just like the previous night, the younger boys crashed as soon as they crawled into bed. Jess' older brother, Jerry, was also tired, and started snoring softly a few minutes later. After they turned off the light, the triplets had guy-talk for a while. Somehow Bob knew about one of the questions that would reflect his being seen making out with Jess.

22.

The Prom

Most of Wednesday, it was watching Carole and Sandy day. Watching them pursue their passion for photography and videography was an entertainment supplement to everyone else seeing the coastline and making images with their cell phones. Their shuttle/limo dropped them off at the Pacific Grove Marine Gardens Park. It was cool and breezy, but there was plenty of sunshine interspersed with clouds. For Sandy and Carole, it was heaven on Earth.

Everyone walked along the coastline until they reached the historic Point Pinos Lighthouse. The exhibits there held their attention for most of them, while Carole and Sandy continued to do their thing outside. Jess and Bob employed their cell phones to record their future brother and sister-in-law recording their visit to the lighthouse for posterity. Later, Sandy told his brothers that he wasn't even aware of the others being around much of the time. All he saw was Carole and the historic lighthouse.

As they continued to make their way along the coast on foot, they were getting very hungry. It was shortly after noon when they reached the Asilomar State Conference Center. Bill took out his phone while the rest of them looked around for something more than a snack.

His phone call got great results. Their lifesaving shuttle arrived less than ten minutes after his phone call, as their shuttle/limo driver took them to a place called *Fandango*. When they saw the menu displayed outside the entrance, Alex spoke out. "Bill and I will pick up the entire lunch bill, so order what you want."

The boys have talked about that lunch a few times since. No one knows whether they had simply worked up an appetite by walking, or whether it was the ocean air, or whether it was the fabulous food. It might have been a combination or any or all those things. They were there nearly two hours. They ate more at that lunch than at any other meal while they were on that weeklong journey. The tab was big, but Alex and Bill didn't mind. Everyone only ate snacks that evening. On the airport shuttle the next day, when Trina said that if they ate at Fandango every day, she would quickly get fat, Jess said, "Yeah, but what a way to go!"

From the time they left the gate at the Monterey Bay airport until they disembarked at the private gate in San Francisco, it was just over an hour. The airport was such a busy maze, they had to work hard to keep everyone together. About forty-five minutes later, a local shuttle took them to *The Lodge at the Presidio*.

After checking in at the desk, everyone took their luggage to their rooms. They were anxious to begin exploring the city. They went back downstairs, and all of them agreed to meet back at the hotel at 6:00.

Alex and Bill had been there before, but the others had not. Alex learned a lot about that day during girl-talk the following week. She and Bill were thoroughly enjoying watching their boys grow into adulthood.

There at the Hotel, Alex and Bill watched as Jess and Bob took her two sisters, Sherrie and Chari with them as they took off exploring. They had promised it to the younger girls the previous day. It was probably better for both Jess and Bob that they could do little more than hold hands and occasionally hug with a light kiss. They decided that it was to be part of having family along with them as they explored the city.

All day Thursday, the smallest group exploring San Francisco was Carole and Sandy. They had the city to themselves for their photography and videography. Since their hotel looked out over Golden Gate Bridge, they decided to explore that area first, but only for about a half hour.

Elsewhere, Chari and Sherrie complained to Jess and Bob about how cold it was, and about how hard the wind was blowing. Jess and Bob were so focused on each other, the cold just didn't faze them. They got on a *Muni* bus and went to Fisherman's Wharf. It was just as cold there, but they could go inside. Since it was about lunch time, they went into *Eight Am*. The kids loved the food. Jess and Bob agreed that it did not compare with Fandango in Pacific Grove.

The girls kept telling Jess, however, that they wanted to ride the cable cars as far as they could. She pretended to be skeptical. Bob was willing to do anything or go anywhere with Jess, of course. She pretended to hesitate for almost a half-hour after lunch, but finally she said, "Oh, okay, kids," and she winked at Bob.

After taking a cable car from Fisherman's Wharf to Union Square, they let the girls pick one more line to ride. When the lovebirds looked back on that day in San Francisco, they agreed that exploring the city through the eyes of Sherrie and Chari was a good thing. They really had fun with them. The time flew by, and by taking a taxi, they got back to the hotel at the time agreed upon by the whole group.

After dinner that night, Sandy, Dick, and Bob could see that the other boys were ready to go to sleep wherever they were. They got the younger boys into their pajamas and into bed at a little after eight. Jerry decided to explore the hotel and said he would be back in an hour or so. On the other side of the suite from the beds, the boys grouped chairs into a circle to talk quietly. Sandy was still pumped up. "For Carole and me, we were so focused upon taking everything in and recording as much as possible, the day seemed to disappear amazingly fast."

Dick grinned. "We had great fun. We did everything with the boys from dance with street artists to play games while riding the cable cars. We had so much fun, we didn't even stop for lunch. You know me, and you know how much I need to eat in the middle of the day, but I was so focused upon having fun with Trina. Lunch didn't occur to me."

Bob told them about spending the day with Sherrie and Chari. Then he added, "I think that, by spending the day this way, Jess and I got a glimpse our future time when we have kids."

Dick had a similar experience. "Trina and I acted like kids all day, and the boys made it even more fun. I think Trina and I will be great parents, though I'm sure it won't be easy. The three of us can look back now and see how much of a challenge we were as triplets."

Sandy agreed. "There must have been times when the three of us gave our parents fits. I'm more in love with Carole than ever, and as soon as we have our training complete and have jobs, I hope she'll want to have a bunch of kids with me."

They continued talking into the wee hours of the morning before heading for bed, even after Jerry returned.

Friday morning, all of them became wine country tourists. A shuttle bus took them across the bay to a train station, and they spent the morning on a train excursion that concluded with lunch. In the afternoon, they took some horse-drawn carriages for a while. Alex, Carole, Trina, and Jess took one of the carriages just for them and had some extended "girl-talk" time. They didn't talk about it much afterwards, but that was normal. Evidently, they talked about the triple wedding almost exclusively.

When the carriage rides were over, each of the boys' girlfriends made a point of inviting their Moms to an upcoming planning session for the wedding. Bill and the triplets, along with the other dads, made jokes about getting left out of "secret" meetings. The younger children ignored them.

In the late afternoon, they took a ferry back to San Francisco, followed by a *Muni* bus ride back to the hotel. The younger children began to complain about our having to go home the next day.

Everyone was exhausted. After dinner, they looked forward to sleeping in before the flight home the next morning. As previously, when the boys turned off the lights, they had guy-talk, and this time they talked about what their girlfriends had shared about the wedding up to that point. Before they finally went to sleep, they agreed upon getting a stretch limo for Prom transportation. They also tossed around some other ideas for Prom, which they later talked about with Bill in his study at the mountain house.

Saturday morning, everyone went to the hotel dining room for breakfast. The hotel called it brunch. There was a buffet that served continuously from six in the morning to two in the afternoon. They were told about it when they had checked in, and they didn't think they could pass it up. Dick and Trina tried stuffed pizza waffles. Jess and Bob shared a crab omelet. Alex and

Bill couldn't help but rave about their French Toast Kebabs. Sandy and Carole had seconds of Japanese Cabbage Pancakes. All went back to the buffet two or three times, trying various international breakfast dishes.

It was a good thing that they had also decided not to dress for the trip home or pack until after breakfast. They ate far too much, so they needed an extended break before they left for the airport.

Although the flight home was short, the boys and their fiancées talked quite a bit. They had gotten to the place where they could talk about anything and everything with one another, as with Alex and Bill. There were some things they shared that were not typical of kids their age.

Alex and Bill overheard one conversation because they were sitting next to Jess. "Bob, during the girl-time in our carriage, one of us revealed that, in the sixth grade, she had promised her Mom not to have sex until after she was married. I think your Mom was a little surprised. Anyway, the three of us made a pact that we would honor that pledge between now and the wedding."

Bob nudged her. "Are you telling me that not all of you are virgins?"

"No comment." She kept her voice low. "You and your brothers should agree that we don't want any of our honeymoons to overlap. We want to go to separate destinations. We also think that we should all plan on getting together on our mutual anniversary at least once every three years."

Bob wasn't surprised. "That's a good idea. Our lives have been intertwined for the last two years, so it seems natural that we will still get together regularly." He took her hand and looked at her. "Before we get to the wedding, the Prom is coming up in a few weeks. We're going to rent a stretch limo for the six of us."

Jess smiled, and her voice rose a little with excitement. "That'll be great! Are we going to have dinner together first?"

Bob pressed his index finger to her lips. "It's not definite yet. I'm pushing for *The Castle*, but my brothers have other ideas. Do you have a honeymoon dream?"

"Do you?"

"I've a couple, based upon our mutual interests."

"I trust your judgment, Bob."

Her response evidently could not have been better for Bob! "In that case, Prom will be nothing in comparison with our honeymoon – of that, you can be certain!"

At that moment, Bill suddenly knew where their honeymoon would take place. He nudged Alex, and she nodded. Lots of arrangements would need to be made. The woman named Charlie, who had been Alex's manager since before she and Bill got married, would be the key. Bob would definitely need Charlie's help.

After they landed in Burbank, the same shuttle and the driver who had brought them to the airport almost a week earlier was waiting for them. When they got to their cars, the shuttle hung around long enough to be sure that all our vehicles started. Good-byes were brief because they would be in church together the next morning – the boys, Carole, Trina, and Jess joining Alex and Bill. Their twenty-minute drive up the mountain was quiet.

For the remaining few weeks of high school, it often seemed like all of them were caught in the middle of a tornado. From the time the boys got home from school until nearly midnight every night, Sandy was in the basement, studying, getting ready for finals and designing something that didn't interest the others.

After Jess and Bob got accepted to Temple University, he had gotten an idea. Before they graduated from college, he wanted to be part of a performance of a 16th-century motet by Thomas Tallis utilizing eight choirs. He had written to one of the professors, and the professor had told him that the written music would need to be digitized for printing out all the parts and individual scores. They only had half-dozen copies in the university's music library, and the motet was out of print.

When Bob was not at his computer working on that, he was working on getting ready to perform the piano solo in Gershwin's *Rhapsody in Blue* with the high school's orchestra. His arms frequently ached from the extra hours of practicing.

Dick was not particularly worried about finals. He only had one that was even moderately difficult. He seemed to spend every spare waking moment at home working on things in the workshop, outside, and (strangely) in the kitchen. As it turned out, Dick installed a new type of trash compacting unit under the counter near the pantry, along with modifications to their dumpster to receive the compacted trash and to keep animals out.

All three of the boys handled their finals fine, getting all A's. Bob was very pleased when the orchestra performed unusually well with him on Gershwin's Rhapsody. Myburbank.com gave it an excellent review.

Prom was the next night after the concert. The stretch limousine pulled into their home's parking area a few minutes early. The triplets were ready for nearly a half hour. Alex took pictures of them together and separately. The driver was a member of their church, and he told Alex and Bill all about the evening the following Sunday.

Down the mountain, Jess was the first girl they picked up. When the driver opened the door, Bob practically ran up the sidewalk. Maxine opened the door, and Bob went in. Jess was waiting. He was stunned and got a lump in his throat. He managed to say, "You look incredible!"

Turning a little pink, she curtsied slightly, saying, "Thank you, kind sir!" She was still a little pink when Dan took pictures of them. Bob handed him one of Sandy's cameras, and her Dad took some pictures with that one too. Bob felt like his feet weren't even on the ground as he walked her to the limo. The driver held the door for them.

Inside, Dick whistled, and Sandy smiled, saying, "Wow!" as Bob handed him his camera.

Jess turned a deeper shade of pink as she said, "Thank you, guys!"

They picked up Carole next. As they watched Sandy walking with Carole towards them, Bob told Dick and Jess, "She looks like a younger version of Mom."

Dick nodded. "She almost looks like Mom does in that picture of Mom and Dad in Paris before they got married."

As Sandy held Carole's hand while she got in, Dick repeated the compliment, while the rest of us nodded. Sandy grinned. "I agree!"

Carole's eyes swept all of them. "Thank you! I think that's about the nicest compliment I've ever had! Your Mom's a world-class beauty! Thank you!"

As Dick got out of the limo for Trina, Sandy handed him the camera. Dick said, "Yeah! Definitely!" He walked rapidly across the cobblestone walk and up onto Trina's porch. Lona was smiling broadly. Dick went inside, and for about five minutes, those in the stretch limo could faintly hear voices and laughter.

As they came out, Dick was smiling, but Trina seemed to be almost sparkling. As the chauffeur opened the door, Dick said, "Okay! We're all here! Let's get this party started!"

Before any of them could respond, Trina nearly shouted. "Whoa! Look at all of us! We're going to steal the prom!" From there to their dinner at *The Castle*, Trina was a firecracker that lit fuses in all of them. As Dick later described Trina's dress, "It was gloriously red and hot!"

Years later, even Sandy had trouble remembering what they ate at *The Castle*. They did have a dining room that was decorated in the theme of *The Gaardian Saga*, the movie franchise that had made the boys' Mom truly world famous.

When they first arrived at the Hilton ballroom and their Prom, quite a few people turned to look at them. How often do you see three guys who look totally identical, each escorting a girl who looks like they've stepped off the pages of *People Magazine*? Wendy Palm had put together remarkable dresses for the three girls. Alex got her money's worth.

Although Jess, Trina, and Carole all enjoyed the attention, they were getting, their unique dresses were also great conversation-starters with kids they hardly knew. Sandy, Dick, and Bob kept passing around the compact little camera throughout the night. Sandy told them later that he had to change the battery twice.

Realistically, the Prom was almost exactly like every other dance they had gone to since they started middle school. Yes, the kids were dressed fancier, and they had matured some, but the music was basically the same. There were countless pictures taken, and there were some videos. Jess hid a tiny 4K video camera in her hair. It sent its feed by Bluetooth to her cell phone, which was hidden under her dress with the ringer silenced.

Following Bill's advice, Dick, Sandy, and Bob did not assume that it would be the best night of their lives. They simply relaxed and had fun. Sometimes Jess and Bob made out while they were dancing. They both enjoyed it, but they were both a little self-conscious also. The others did the same.

It was the first time Bob had ever danced with Carole or Trina. All six of them knew, of course, when they switched partners. It is doubtful that anyone else noticed when they made the switches. Although Jess and Bob danced as though they were one person with two parts, the others were different kinds of experiences.

Carole was reserved and graceful. As Bob would tell Jess a few days later, Carole flowed with the music. It was though the music was a river of sound, and Carole floated above it. The boys followed her. They were with her, but except for Sandy, the other two kept space between them.

Trina let the music control her, with moves that were synchronized with every beat. Sometimes the boys weren't wasn't sure whether the music was controlling Trina, or whether somehow Trina was controlling or directing the music. As a musician, from Bob's point of view, Trina was part of the band. When Bob later described it to Jess, she responded by saying that she saw Trina dancing with him, but it was as though the two of them were in different rooms.

At midnight, the triplets looked at each other without looking at their watches. As planned, they headed for the limo. Bob spoke quietly to Jess as they walked. "I feel more cemented to you even more now. Does that even make sense? It's hard to describe."

She kissed him on the cheek. "I'm not sure the word I'd use is 'cemented,' but it seems like you and I have become one in every way but one, and that will come after the wedding ceremony."

He leaned over and kissed her without missing a step. "It seems like such a long time into the future.

Until the limo got to Trina's, the six of them continued to make out. It did not take as long to take the girls home as it did to pick them up. When the boys got out at the house, Sandy handed the driver an envelope full of cash. It was almost 1:00 AM.

They assumed that Alex and Bill were asleep, but they weren't. Dick held a finger to his lips, and they tried to be as quiet as possible. Each of them took a quick shower and headed for bed. When Bob turned off the light, he said, "When Jess and I danced, it seemed like we were one body, totally synchronized."

In the darkness, Dick spoke quietly. "Jess is a smooth dancer, but I made it a point to keep a gap between us."

"Me too." Sandy was thoughtful. "Carole and I think alike, so much that we didn't give our moves much thought. Trina's another matter, however."

Dick started to laugh and silenced himself. "The love of my life is filled with fire and energy. When I danced with Jess and Carole it was like I was in the eye of a hurricane. I knew that when I went back to dancing with Trina, it would be a time of boundless energy, except during the slow dances. Slow dances with my future bride were like an adventure in sexuality."

Sandy was still thoughtful. "I knew better than to try a slow dance with Trina, but she almost wore me out with her energy."

"Me too. When Trina and I danced, I think she was in a world of her own." The boys turned over and went to sleep.

At 8:30 AM, Bill turned on their lights. He spoke louder than necessary. "Rise and shine, guys! Breakfast will be ready in fifteen, and we're leaving for church in just over an hour! Come on! Rise and shine!"

Dick was still so exhausted that when his Dad twice said, 'rise and shine,' he mentally resolved never to say that to his kids. On the other hand, they could smell bacon, which was probably baking in the oven. When their Mom does it that way, it seems like all of breakfast is better for the boys.

Bill looked over at Dick as he took a forkful of pancake and syrup. "So, did you boys try trading partners for some of the dances?"

Dick almost choked and swallowed some juice. "We did, and we talked about it some before we went to sleep last night."

Bob nodded. "Jess and I danced as one person, Trina was a hurricane in her own world, and Carole flowed with the music."

Sandy put down his coffee. "Yes, my Carole is peacefully flowing as she dances, even when the music is moving faster. Trina is like dancing with fire, and Jess seems to soar above the music."

Dick was grinning. I agree with my brothers."

23.
Triple Wedding

Graduation was almost like a minor detail in the triplets' final year of high school. Receiving their diplomas was like a pause in that spring's excitement. There were several funny conversations where people confused one of the boys with another, but they had all decided in advance not to correct anyone and go with the flow. Paula Lewis, the girl whom Sandy had had a crush on in middle school, flirted with Bob like crazy. Jess was nearby, and Bob managed to secretly wink at her while he enjoyed Paula's flirting on Sandy's behalf. Jess understood what Bob was doing.

In their guy-talk that night, they shared those conversations they had had after the graduation ceremony. Sandy was surprised about Paula's flirting. "She and I have hardly spoken to each other in over two years. Furthermore, I was surprised on your behalf, Dick. Both Beth Robertson and Rita McLaughlin thought I was you. Both spoke about how much they enjoyed dancing with you when we were in the eighth grade."

"Really! Beth is still a bookworm, and I've never thought we had anything in common. Rita's another matter. She's been dating Jim Edmonds for more than three years now, but if they had broken up a couple of years ago, I might have made a play for her." The guy talk went on for a couple of hours as they shared other conversations they had had.

With graduation behind, the rest of June flew past them rapidly. The boys spent a lot of time making sure their honeymoons were going to come off as planned. Until the rehearsal dinner, none of them knew much about the wedding ceremony itself except the date.

Almost every night, Alex brought Bill up to date on the preparations for the wedding. They both reflected on their sons' growing maturity and pending nuptials. Their nightly pillow talk became special in that way, as they remembered their own wedding and honeymoon.

The boys saw their girlfriends almost every day during the second half of June, but on the day before the wedding, none of the girls would talk to them about it except in general terms. The wedding rehearsal was almost a relief in the sense that all the details of the wedding day were brought into sharp focus.

The wedding was truly the beginning of Alex and Bill's futures. The grooms all had their own tuxedoes since before the prom, so there was no question regarding what they would wear.

The ceremony itself was smooth and long. The triplets discovered something new that they had in common. They were all unafraid to cry, and none of them tried to wipe their tears away. For Bob, Jess was the most beautiful bride he had ever seen. He also realized that his brothers were moreover marrying incredible women.

Carole looked like she had stepped off a magazine cover. Both Jess and Trina were almost envious of Carole's wedding dress. An old friend of her Dad's had been in the three-day war with him and wanted to show his gratitude for saving her Dad's life. The dress had been worn by someone in the royal family of the British Isles. It was loaned for Carole's use.

Trina simply looked incredibly exotic. Trina wouldn't say exactly where her wedding dress came from. It had a plunging neckline and a moderately long train. She would only say that it was given to her by a family friend.

Jess wore her mother's wedding dress because Maxine insisted, and because Jess wanted to avoid family tension on her day she had dreamed about. It had lots of lace with heart appliques.

The only thing that was unusual about the ceremony was at the beginning. The six of them had memorized their vows, and they took turns reciting portions of their vows without their pastor having to prompt them. Each was best man for each other's weddings. Their fiancées were the same for one another.

The rest of the ceremony was typical. Finally, the pastor said, "Ladies and gentlemen, I now present to you Sandy and Carole Johnson, Bob and Jess Johnson, and Dick and Trina Johnson."

Whenever the media learns of a multiple wedding, they want to cover it, and this wedding was no exception. The grooms being the triplet sons of a celebrity made the event even more newsworthy. The wedding photographer was Peter Duvall, the same man who also had been the photographer for Alex and Bill when they got married in La Jolla. The wedding took place in the Wayfarer's Chapel in Rancho Palos Verde Hills, which is south of Los Angeles and overlooking the harbor. The church is a small glass church built in the middle of a grove of large redwood trees. It was perfect for this wedding because only the four families were in the audience. Peter placed cameras, well hidden, throughout both the glass worship chapel and the reception ballroom down the hill from of the church at the hotel. The media were kept out of the chapel, but at the hotel, they were not restricted.

The reception was at the bottom of the hill. On the harbor side of the chapel was in the Westin Hotel ballroom. The grooms and their brides had been rehearsing for the first dance even longer than they had rehearsed for their vows. The entire "first dance" had been choreographed by a friend of Alex's, Jill St. John, who had choreographed the dancing for several movies. Sandy called out, "Let's do Christian rock!"

Carole, Dick, Trina, Jess, and Bob responded together. "Amen!"

The six walked onto the dance floor as couples. Sandy led off by dancing eight beats as choreographed by Jill. Then Dick and Bob joined him for eight beats of the same pattern and stopped. Carole led off the brides with a different routine, mostly synchronized with Jess and Trina. With brides and grooms facing one another, they broke into a routine that lasted just over five more minutes.

That wasn't the end of the routine. Bob looked at his brothers. "Let's merge our families!"

Dick and Sandy chanted together, "Absolutely!"

The grooms went and took the hands of their new mothers in law, the brides took the hands of their new fathers in law, and they all foxtrotted to the old classic "Love Is a Many Splendored Thing." Jill's choreography for that part was simpler, and the parents had no problems with the familiar step.

After the reception, the triplets and their brides took off in three different directions. Peter Duvall and his staff released official wedding photos and a wedding video to the media within a few hours after the three couples had left on their honeymoons. Alex and Bill remained well into the night, talking with both the guests and the media.

Jess and Bob took off for a musical honeymoon in New York City that Alex's manager, Charlie, had helped Bob arrange. On their first morning in the Bridal Suite of their hotel, they ate breakfast in bed. They could see the city below them through the window. "I wonder," Jess asked, "where the others are. You and your brothers have been so secretive about where we were going. You would only tell us that there were to be three separate honeymoons. I can see where we are, obviously, but where are the others?"

Bob gazed at his incredibly beautiful bride. "I'll tell you after I tell you once more, Jess, that I love you unconditionally, passionately, and forever." They had a lingering kiss, after which they finally broke for air.

"Actually, you'll have to admit that, until the wedding rehearsal, my brothers and I knew virtually nothing about our wedding day, just as our brides haven't known the details of the honeymoons. Still, okay, here's the scoop. If everything is going according to plan, last night Dick and Trina landed at Jackson Hole Airport in Wyoming. They will spend the next two weeks exploring Grand Teton National Park and Yellowstone National Park. Dick decided not to do too much planning except getting reservations for hotels and a car."

Jess nodded. "So, what are they going to do after the honeymoon?"

"Trina didn't tell you?" Jess shook her head. "On the Internet, they found a house near Triangle Tech in Pittsburgh, and after exploring all the pictures, videos, and virtual reality, they purchased it. Dick wired the down payment, and they'll sign the final paperwork when they get there. They'll have two years of work at the tech school, and then they'll have internships."

"What about Carole and Sandy? Where are they now?"

"Last night, they took a short flight to Las Vegas, where they spent the night in a huge bridal suite at the Four Seasons Hotel and Casino. Today they'll rent a car and drive from Vegas to the Grand Canyon's North Rim. It's a long drive, but that place is supposed to be really worth it – much better than the South Rim."

"And after their honeymoon? Carole didn't tell me anything either, although we know they'll be going to U.C.L.A. Are they going to buy that condo in Westwood?"

Bob nodded. "Just like Dick, Sandy provided a down payment last week to the realtor." Bob took Jess' hand. "Let's go take a shower together. We were too tired last night."

She smiled and kissed him on the cheek. "I'm ready anytime you are."

That first evening in New York City, they took in a special performance of the Philharmonic at the old Radio City Music Hall. They took in the New York Philharmonic twice, and they took in four different Broadway musicals – all while being typical tourists taking in the sights and sounds of the city during the day. That went on for nearly two weeks. Each morning they went on the Internet to shop for a place to live in Philadelphia after their honeymoon. Eventually, they bought a townhouse about a mile from Temple University. They completed their purchase using a combination of their phones and the Internet.

They also arranged to take delivery on a car from a dealer in New Jersey, which they drove south to their new home at the end of their honeymoon. They would tell Alex and Bill all about it the following Christmas.

Twenty-three days after the wedding, Bob parked their car in the garage, which was attached to their first home. "We can take in our luggage later. Let's first see what the situation is inside." At the back door, Bob took out a slip of paper, looked at it, and then pushed numbers on a keypad. There was a soft click, and the door was unlocked. "Okay, my love, put your arms around my neck."

As she complied, Bob picked her up and carried her inside. As he put Jess down, they kissed, and she did a slow pivot, taking in the kitchen and beyond. "We've got a lot of work to do!"

Bob had a wry smile. There were boxes piled high everywhere. He took her hand. "Let's check out the rest of our first home."

They walked through the dining area into the living room. Jess shook her head. "We may not get to it today, but I don't like the way the furniture we ordered is arranged, do you?"

"Nope! Those delivering the furniture were only guessing as to where things should go. It looks like the movers put everything from our houses that aren't clothing here temporarily. All the pictures and knickknacks are probably in here, don't you think?"

"Probably." Jess scowled. "I almost hate to see what our master bedroom looks like, but let's go upstairs and see." The master bedroom was easier to get arranged. With their honeymoon over, they were highly motivated to get that part of their lives on a solid footing.

By the end of that first day, they had a start on their cookware and dishes in the kitchen, but it was three days before they prepared their first meal there. To complicate things further, their classes at Temple University started the following Monday.

Bob decided before he graduated from high school, he was going to pursue a Master of Music in Choral Conducting. Taking a slightly different path, Jess decided to pursue a Master of Music in Vocal Performance. First, however, they both needed to pursue Bachelor of Arts degrees in Music. They had decided to go ahead and buy their first home instead of rent one because they knew they would be there five to seven years. During that time, they could build equity instead of simply surrendering rent money each month to a landlord. They knew it would be their best choice in the long haul.

Jess and Bob have great memories of their first years of marriage. They were firm in their decision not to have a family until they got their basic degrees in music. They pushed themselves to achieve their goal as quickly as possible. When they came back to California for that first Christmas, they all talked about it.

All arrived at the house on the mountain in the afternoon of December 20th. Sandy and Carole only had to drive in from Westwood, but the rest rented cars. Jess and Bob had an appointment before they could go up the mountain. They headed into Los Angeles and to the Los Angeles Music Center complex. The guest conductor during the holiday season was Logan Swanson of the Fort Worth Symphony.

He had written to Bob, asking to see him when he and Jess went home for Christmas. After they parked, they made their way to Walt Disney Concert Hall. There was no one on the stage, but Logan Swanson was sitting in the front row of the orchestra section of seats. "Mr. Swanson?"

He stood up. "Yes! Are you Bob Johnson?"

"Yes, sir. This is my wife, Jess." They all shook hands.

The conductor pointed. "Let's go to the Green Room. We can talk more comfortably there." He led the way. Once they each had a bottle of water, they sat down. The conductor was cordial. "I'm glad I can connect with the two of you while you are home for the holidays. Bob, I've seen pictures of the house where you grew up and where your parents still live. You have quite a view up there!"

He nodded. "Yes, sir. Jess' parents live at the bottom of the grade in La Cañada Flintridge."

"Okay. I wanted to see you, Bob, because the Dean of the Music Department there at Temple, James Matheson, is an old friend of mine."

"Yes, sir, he told me. He said that you have a job you want me to do."

"Yes. Last August, Jim and I took our wives to the Bahamas, and I asked him for a favor. I told him that on the Fourth of July weekend of this year, I am conducting the New York Philharmonic, and that one of the pieces to be performed is Mahler's Second Symphony. The last movement requires a chorus."

"Yes, sir, I'm familiar with Mahler's Second. I think it is one of the most dramatic pieces written in the late Romantic Era."

Logan nodded. "That it is. I told your Dean that I wanted him to pick one of his conducting students to rehearse the chorus for me. Jim picked you."

Bob was stunned. "I'm only a freshman!"

"So, I understand. If you agree to do this, here's what will happen. There are several youth choirs in the New York City area. Most of them will start rehearsing the music next month in their own locations. The three weekends prior to the Fourth of July weekend, the different youth choirs will all meet at a church in Brooklyn, which is large enough to accommodate them and which has the amenities that we need. You will rehearse them as a combined chorus. We don't know yet how many exactly will be in the chorus, but it will be at least a hundred. It will possibly be many more than that, perhaps double or even triple that."

Jess was smiling. "Wow!"

"Bob, on those three weekends, you and Jess will drive north to Brooklyn on Friday afternoon, spend the night at a hotel paid for in advance, rehearse the choir on Saturday morning, and return home Saturday afternoon. After the Fourth, you'll get a small stipend. What do you say, will you do it?"

Bob glanced at Jess, who nodded. He also nodded. "We'll be glad to. By any chance, can Jess and I get tickets to one of the performances?"

"Of course! The Fourth is a Monday. There will be performances Saturday evening, Sunday afternoon, and Monday evening. The Monday evening performance will be outside and include fireworks."

Afterwards, as Jess and Bob got in the car to go towards La Cañada Flintridge, he was in a daze. "Jess, this is an incredible blessing!"

"Yes! Praise God! I'm at least a year older than the seniors in the youth choirs, but I don't think there'll be any harm in rehearsing with them."

"Definitely!"

It was late afternoon, with the sun low in the sky, when their rental car joined the other cars parked near our mountain house. Inside, after leaving their shoes in the mud room, they went in and joined the rest of them. Most of the four families were scattered in the great room, but a few were in the basement. Bob nudged Jess and pointed up towards the cathedral ceiling. Harry was lounging there, his eyes wide open. Jess smiled. "Hi, Harry!"

"Rowwl."

That first evening home, Bill and Alex had hired caterers so that they could visit with the rest of us the whole time. As the sun was setting, Bill said grace, and as they were starting on their plates of food, Bill called out. "Okay, everyone, our families will all be in the area for a week or so, I'd like the boys to answer one question. Of all the things you may want to share with us while we're here for Christmas, I want each of you to pick one thing that you want all of us to know right now."

Dick grinned. "Trina and I are expecting our first addition to our family in June!" They beamed.

There was a chorus of congratulations in between forkfuls of food.

Carole put her fork down and looked at Sandy, who nodded. "Sandy and I are scheduled to lead some photo tours."

Mom smiled. "Really! Where to?"

Sandy had some excitement in his voice. "Carole and I are working with a travel agency over in Westwood. During Spring break, we'll lead a photo tour of secret tourist spots in Hawaii. In June, we're leading a photo tour of Alaska. Next December, if all goes as planned, we're going to join a photo expedition previously planned to New Zealand and on to Antarctica. In each case, a tour guide will lead the group, and we will provide photography training and support."

Bob nudged Jess. "Someday, I want us to go to New Zealand and Australia."

Bill smiled. "Your Mom and I are going to go down there next year, if we can work it into our schedule. Bob, you and Jess landed in Burbank three hours ago, but you just got here, way after the others What gives?"

Jess touched his hand that she would answer. "During this holiday season, the guest conductor for the L.A. Philharmonic is Logan Swanson from Fort Worth. Next July, he'll be guest conducting the New York Philharmonic. He contacted Bob, and we met him this afternoon. The Fourth of July weekend, the New York Philharmonic is going to offer three performances of Mahler's Second Symphony, which is often recognized as the 'Resurrection Symphony.' The last movement uses a chorus, and Bob is going to rehearse a choir of teenagers from all over that area on the three weekends prior to those performances. The Fourth is going to be on a Monday, and Bob and I will have tickets to that outdoor performance, which will have fireworks afterward."

"Trina, let's go up there and join Bob and Jess." Dick was emphatic.

"Maybe, but we'll have our baby to bring with us."

He nodded. "True. We'll have to play it by ear."

"Boys," Alex said, "This week, you and the girls will be with their parents on Christmas Day and New Year's Eve, and you'll be here with your wives on Christmas Eve and on New Year's Day. We parents want to be fair with each other, dividing time between families." She glanced up. "It looks like Harry is going to come down and greet us. We can have desserts later."

Some of them took their plates and cups to the caterers in the kitchen, while Harry began making the rounds and purring. Carole and Sandy took pictures and video of Harry greeting the rest of them, then they handed their cameras to Jess and Bob, and they made pictures and video of Sandy and Carole with Harry.

As Jess worked with the cameras, Bob had to say something. "Guys, as great as married life is, I have missed our sessions of guy talk. How about you, Dick?"

He nodded. "Definitely. Trina and I talk about anything and everything, but I miss the connection with my brothers. Sandy?"

He smiled. "I'm glad you two have brought this up. A couple of evenings when Carole and I have been enjoying sunsets, she has caught me looking like...."

She touched his arm. "He looks like he's lost in another world, and not just when we're enjoying sunsets. Sometimes, when Sandy is reading, he'll put the book down, swallow some tea or coffee, and have a blank stare. I've asked him about it, and we've discussed it several times. I'm glad that you and Dick feel the same way, Bob."

He nodded. "I think the best way to satisfy this hunger is with maybe a phone conversation on weekends, as regularly as we can."

Their Dad was obviously curious. "When your Mom and I have been apart, we have often arranged Skype conversations. I enjoy looking at your mother when I'm talking with her."

Dick and Sandy were shaking their heads, and Dick smiled at him. "We know how much you and Mom have enjoyed video calls, but prior to now, most of our guy conversations have been in the dark, after we turn off the light at night but before we've gone to sleep. We don't need to see each other."

It was nearly midnight when things wound down. Jess and Bob decided to spend their first night of vacation there on the mountain, while Sandy, Dick, and their wives went to be with their other families. After the wedding, Alex and Bill had re-decorated the room that had been the boys' room. The twin-sized beds were gone, replaced by a California-king-sized bed.

In the doorway, Jess and Bob stood there, taking it in. Jess glanced up at him. "Bob, we're used to a queen-size, so we could almost get lost in this California King. I guess we can enjoy looking for each other."

He leaned down to kiss her. "It'll be my pleasure, I'm sure!"

Because of the time-zone difference, the next morning Jess and Bob were wide awake before 5:00 AM. About twenty minutes after 6:00 they began to smell bacon. When they went downstairs and into the kitchen, there was plenty of food on the counter. Alex turned to look from the stove. "Good morning you two! There's bacon and melon already fixed and ready. What'll it be? Just eggs and regular toast or French toast?"

Jess' face lit up. "I haven't had French toast since our brunch in San Francisco before the wedding! I'll have some! What about you, Bob?"

"I'll join you. Where's Dad, Mom?"

"He fed Harry, and then he took a call from Francis Johns and is in the study. I'm sure he hears our voices and will join us as soon as he can."

"And here I am!" Bill came into the kitchen. "Good morning, love birds! I hope you slept well – that's the first time that bed has been slept in."

Jess greeted him with a kiss on his cheek. "Yes, we slept well, but the bed is so huge! We could almost get lost! It felt like a foam bed. Is it?"

Bill nodded. "Yes. It was a bed-in-a-box. Your Mom and I had fun wrestling with it when we let it out of its box to expand. It was compressed to less than half its current size, and as it expanded, it had a mind of its own."

"That's for sure!" Alex took several slices of French toast off the griddle to put them on a platter. "It would have been easier if at least one of you was here to wrestle with it. Jess, did you notice the platform?"

She nodded. "Yes! I didn't notice it last night, but this morning, I noticed the drawers under the bed. I guess, since it is a guest room, the drawers make it unnecessary to have a dresser in there."

"That's right. Your Dad designed a pivot lift for the mattress, so that you can step in under the bed to get at all the contents of the drawers from the middle. The mattress platform is counterweighted, so it lifts easily. What are you two going to do today?" She sat down at the counter with the others.

"Bob and I want to go shopping at the mall. When we first started dating, one of our dates was a shopping date. I learned how amazingly patient Bob is with me as I shop."

"I think Bob and his brothers get that from their Dad. Countless times, Bill and I have gone shopping together, and after several hours, we've bought nothing. That's online. Sometimes I'll put on a prosthetic nose and chin with a wig, and we'll go down the mountain to the mall. I've never been recognized."

24.

Young Marrieds

On the mountain, Christmas always seemed more like Christmas when there was snow on the ground. Jess and Bob stood by the windows of the great room on Christmas Eve afternoon, watching Harry roll in the snow and chase a fox down the embankment. "I wish we were making a video of this," Jess almost whispered.

"Me too."

"What?" Carole joined them. "Wow! The trouble is, by the time I get my camera, this moment will be gone!"

Sandy came up behind them. "So! Harry's chasing down a possible meal in the snow! I've always loved watching him doing it."

Bill walked up and handed Sandy a camera. "You left this in the mud room, son."

Sandy grinned. "Thanks, Dad!" He turned on the camera, steadied himself against a post, and began shooting while Harry chased another fox.

By late morning, all of them were there, and they simply enjoyed one another's company. It was, overall a great and memorable day during which absolutely nothing happened that was unusual. They drank lots of hot chocolate and hot mulled cider.

For the first time, the boys' wives got to taste and enjoy the special cookies that Alex made every Christmas. Carole bit into one dusted with powdered sugar and chewed. Her eyes got big. "What are these called, Mom?"

"Those are called pfeffernüsse. They are small spice cookies, popular in Germany, Denmark, and The Netherlands, as well as among ethnic Mennonites here in North America. My Mom got the recipe from a Mennonite woman she knew. Those white crisp cookies with a molded animal on the tops are actually biscuits but called Springerle cookies. They're also popular in Germany."

Jess picked up one of those white creations. "They're delicious! They taste a little like licorice. They're harder and crisper than I expected."

Trina nodded. "My Mom taught me to make Springerles too. That's anise flavor, I think. They keep almost forever without spoiling in a cookie jar."

Later in the media theater they watched "It's a Wonderful Life" while eating dinner they held in their laps. They opened presents and exchanged lots of kisses and hugs. With wives now part of the boys' lives, their sense of family was richer and fuller.

Jess said it best when they had finished opening their presents. "I didn't know it when I was in high school, but now I realize something. Before I married Bob, my family, my sense of direction, my sense of purpose, and my life were incomplete."

Alex nodded. "Our sensed of family for Bill and I was incomplete without our son's wives and future children."

They all nodded. Bill smiled and looked at Alex. "Sheila would have enjoyed all of this."

"Yes." Alex's eyes got misty.

Later, they headed down the grade for a worship service that concluded at midnight. That church, filled to capacity that night, has a tradition going back more than a half century. At the stroke of midnight, the organist starts playing the introduction to Handel's "Hallelujah Chorus." The words are projected on the screens, and everyone sings along as best they can. As they were leaving the church, Bob told Sandy and Dick that he would call them with a conference call the next night at 11:00 PM.

Once again, it was nearly midnight when things wound down. Jess and Bob spent the night there on the mountain. In the doorway, they stood there, taking it in. Jess glanced up at him. "Bob, as I told your Dad and Mom, we're used to the queen-sized bed at home, but as I expected, I feel lost in this California King."

Bob nodded. "I feel the same, though I associate this room with the three twin beds that used to be in here for me and my brothers. What time are your parents expecting us tomorrow morning?"

"My family won't open their presents until we get there, so we had better get there by seven. Let's take a shower and go straight to bed."

"I can never argue with that idea."

The next morning, Bob and Jess planned to go in her parents' front door quietly, but it made no difference. Jess' two younger sisters opened the door before Jess put her key in the lock. Their greeting was practically unison. "Merry Christmas, Jess! Merry Christmas, Bob!"

They hugged one another. "Merry Christmas, Sherrie! Chari!"

Jess' older brother, Jerry, came around the corner. "Merry Christmas, sis, Bob!"

"Merry Christmas!" Bob shook his hand. "When do you finish your bachelor's degree?"

"Next year, probably."

"I smell breakfast cooking!" Jess took Bob's hand. "Let's see what Mom is fixing," They headed for the kitchen.

Maxine looked at them from the oven. "Merry Christmas! The spam and waffles will stay hot in the oven while we open our presents. Let's do what everyone has wanted to do since dawn." She called out. "Dan! It's time to open presents!"

Faintly they heard his voice. "I'll be right there."

The openings went fast. Bob enjoyed watching Jess as she played around with her sisters and brother. Maxine was more subdued, but she watched her children intently as they expressed their glee with each present. Dan was quieter.

A half-hour later, they were wolfing down breakfast, laughing, and joking around. Bob looked at his mother-in-law. "Mom, I didn't get to spend much time with you and Dad over that Spring Break trip. I've been looking forward to spending today here." Jess secretly touched his hand beneath the table and squeezed it.

Dan sipped some coffee. "I really loved your wedding. Did you get the pictures I took and sent to you by email?" They both nodded, and as Bob was about to speak, he continued. "I understand that you and Jess are both pursuing bachelor's degrees in music."

"Yes, sir. Jess is focused upon singing performance; I'm centered upon conducting."

He nodded. "So, Bob, how's life in Philadelphia? Maxine talks to Jess, but I want to hear the details from your perspective."

"After our honeymoon, we drove south in our new car from New Jersey and pulled up to our new house that we'd purchased online."

Jess touched my arm. "Bob carried me over the threshold from the garage into our kitchen very romantically, but we could immediately see that we had a lot of work to do."

Maxine raised her eyebrows. "What kind of work?"

Jess laughed. "The kitchen was piled almost floor to ceiling with boxes, and there were similar piles all over the house. The movers placed our furniture we'd shipped from California, and delivery men put new furniture we'd ordered at our place too. They probably thought they'd placed things logically, but neither Bob nor I liked it."

"Jess and I started with the master bedroom upstairs and worked down from there. The first few days we ate out." Bob and Jess went on to tell them a little about their first semester.

Bob really enjoyed that day being with Jess' family. That house is much smaller than the house on the mountain, but then most homes are. After spending a day with Sherrie and Chari in San Francisco, Bob enjoyed spending Christmas Day with them. That evening, after the girls went to bed, the rest of them continued to talk until later.

Finally, Bob looked at his watch. "I've got to make that conference call with my brothers."

Jess nodded. "Okay. You can do that in the bedroom. Why don't you tell Mom and Dad and Jerry about that routine?" She looked at the others. "I think you'll find this interesting."

Bob was a little embarrassed, but he needn't have been. "As triplets, back in our grade-school days, we would go to bed, turn off the light, and then talked for a while. We called it 'boy-talk. Until the wedding, we did our nightly boy-talk every night. Since then we've missed it. I've told Dick and Sandy that I would set up a conference call tonight at 11:00, and it is about that now. If all of you will please excuse me, I'll see you in the morning." He gave Jess a quick kiss, got up, and went to the guest room.

After closing the door, he took out his cell and set up the conference. "Hi, guys! Jess is helping her Mom do some late chores while we talk. I've had a fantastic day. Dick, how was today for you?"

"I'm not sure Trina's Dad likes me. Mario is quiet and moody. He isn't very outgoing, like Lona. They seem to have a good marriage, though. They are consumed with having their first grandchild. I wouldn't be surprised if Trina and I have another within a year after our first."

Bob was enthusiastic. "Fantastic! What about you, Sandy? How was the day with Carole's parents?"

"I get along with Paul and Stella fine. From the time we went to Mammoth, when Carole and I did night photography with Harry, Carole's parents have insisted that I call them by their first names. Every time I see them, they ask about Harry. Carole and I are going to take them up the mountain to see Harry and our folks later this week. When we go back to Westwood after New Year's, I've got a lot to work on with our web site, and Carol's putting the finishing touches on a photo tour to Antarctica. Bob, how are you and Jess doing at Temple University?"

"After our honeymoon, we moved into a house not far from the campus. It took some work getting moved in, but we like it."

"Did you buy the house or rent?"

"We decided to buy it because we figure we'll be there for at least four or five years."

Jess snuck in quietly and went straight to the bathroom to start her nightly routine while Bob continued to talk. His conference call with his brothers went on for another twenty minutes or so.

The triplets decided to make the very most of that week between Christmas and New Year's because they were virtually certain they wouldn't all get together again until the following Christmas. Jess and Bob spent as many days on the mountain with Alex and Bill as they did at her folks' house with her family. His brothers did the same.

That included spending New Year's Eve in Burbank. Trish's brother went out and bought balloons and streamers to decorate the living room. As it often happens in Southern California during the winter, the weather was mild. Dan fired up their barbecue grill, and they had hamburgers and hot dogs along with all kinds of other foods.

Sherrie and Chari were almost asleep when the rest of them watched the ball drop in New York, bringing in the new year. Jess and her mother helped the girls crawl into bed while Dan, Jerry and Bob cleaned things up before heading towards bed themselves.

On New Year's Day, all four families naturally gathered at the mountain house in time for brunch because it could easily accommodate all four families at once. Alex and Bill had it catered. It was one of those rare occasions when the draperies in the great room were all closed. They watched football on a fifteen-foot-wide screen that Bill rented and put in front of the drapes. The projector was put on the staircase. Between the giant screen and the six-track sound, watching football was like being there.

They screamed and cheered until they were hoarse, and then they cheered some more. No one could later begin to remember the different kinds of pizza they ate, or how many kinds of buffalo wings and ribs they ate, or how many…. It was a great party for the four families. They watched football all day.

After dinner, they were finishing up pieces of mincemeat pie when Dick spoke between bites. "Sandy, Bob, since four of us are flying back east and home tomorrow, why don't we have a guy-talk session in the basement when we finish our dessert?"

Bob nodded. "That's a good idea. Until next Christmas, our guy-talk will have to be on the phone."

He looked at Sandy, who was nodding. "Carole and I will probably be here for next Christmas, but not before, I don't think." He looked at her, and she shook her head. A few minutes later, the triplets headed downstairs, and Harry followed them, purring. They sat on the floor next to the windows, and Harry laid down and continued to purr softly.

Bob scratched Harry's head. "Harry, I'm glad you're joining us this time. Dick, by this time next year, you'll have another mouth to feed."

"I'm glad that you and Jess are living within a few hour's drive from Trina and me. Sandy, with you and Carole living out here on the West Coast, you're not going to be able to help if we have problems."

"That's true, but during spring break or the summer, we can get good deals on travel when necessary because we work with a travel agency. Carole and I don't plan on having kids until we at least get our basic college degrees."

"Yeah," Bob said, "Jess and I are like you and Carol in that. We plan on waiting at least three more years before we start a family. I'm surprised, Dick, that you're comfortable with starting a family immediately."

"Yeah, I'm surprised too." He paused. "I think, now that the three of us are married adults, we should invite Dad to be a part of our guy-talk. What about it?"

Sandy nodded. "When we were growing up, we could approach Dad any time, and he would drop what he was doing and talk with us. I miss that. Dick?"

"I agree. To me, it will be especially good because I'm becoming a contractor, and Dad's an architect."

They talked nearly a half an hour before they went back upstairs and into the kitchen, where Alex and Bill were cleaning up. Bob said, "Dad, we've decided that, from this day forwards, we want you to be part of our guy-talk. Okay?"

Their Dad was thrilled. "Absolutely! I miss those days when you boys would approach me when I was working in the study." The triplets went on to talk about the session they had just had.

The next day, Sandy and Carole stayed through lunch to help Alex and Bill clean up the house while Dick, Trina, Jess, and Bob headed to the airport for early-morning flights back to the east coast. With the time difference, the four of them wanted to get home in time for dinner. It had to be Trina's last flight before the baby was to be born.

As Jess and Bob flew home, they talked about what was going to happen in the months ahead, even as they were taking off. As the flight attendants began pushing their beverage cart down the aisle, Jess opened up about how she had already started to make plans in her head. "Since Pittsburgh and Philadelphia are less than a five-hour drive away from each other, you and I are going to start spending a lot of weekends with Dick and Trina."

"I know. Dick told me that Trina will probably not take any classes during the summer, but in the Fall, they will arrange their classes so that at least one of them is available to take care of the baby all the time. They may hire a part-time nanny."

"Still, Trina may appreciate my being there with her on the weekends, Bob, and I'm sure Dick will appreciate your coming along as well. Do they have a Spring break at that trade school?"

He shrugged. "I don't know, but if they do, we can invite them to spend their spring break with us. We can reassess how things are going for them at that time." Dick and Trina had a similar conversation during their flight. Neither flight had a layover.

After Bob and Jess got back to Philadelphia, the following Sunday one of the church's families, Sam and Sandy Cruise, had kittens they were giving away. The kittens were in the Cruise' home, not far away from church. Bob wasn't particularly interested in having a pet to take care of, but Jess insisted that they go over to the Cruise's house to see the kittens. Snow was lightly falling.

The kittens were being kept in an old claw-foot bathtub in the garage attached to the house. Sam and Sandy Cruise were very friendly. Jess stooped down to look at them. "Wow! They're adorable, aren't they Bob?" He didn't answer, but stooped down to look at them. At one end of the tub, two of the kittens stayed together. Jess picked up both and handed Bob one. "Bob, this one's a female. What about that one?"

"It's a female, too."

"We need to have two so that they keep each other company while we're in classes during the day."

Bob knew Jess had her heart set on these two, but he pretended to be skeptical. "I'm not sure, Jess."

"Listen, Bob, you and your brothers raised Harry, who is ten or twelve times as big as these two will ever be. This will be a cinch."

He pretended forced smile. "I doubt it'll be a cinch, but okay. We'll stop at *Pets World* on the way home and get supplies."

She grinned. "Great! We'll put Faith and Hope in the back seat."

"Is that their names?" Sandy Cruise was smiling.

Jess nodded. "Yes, but I haven't decided which is which yet."

Bob and Jess got into their car with their new pets. "Since you decided on their names, why don't you let me decide which is which, Jess?"

"Okay." The pet store was only a few blocks away, and as they pulled into the parking lot, she touched his arm. "You keep our car warm while I run in."

Bob stopped by the door, and Jess jumped out and scurried in. There weren't a lot of cars in the lot, so he parked as close as he could and kept the engine running. Both kittens were a mix of calico and gray. One of them, mostly calico, crawled into the front-seat area and onto Bob's lap. She immediately settled in and started to purr. "Okay, girl, you are the first one to venture into the front seat, so we'll call you Faith." He stroked her with a finger.

About ten minutes later, Jess came out, put their supplies in through the rear door, and got back in the shotgun seat, shivering. "I see you've got one, but... Hi there! Which one are you?" The other kitten crawled onto her lap.

"That's Hope, and this one's Faith. Faith ventured into the front seat first. She's got the most calico fur. Hope has more gray hair."

"Okay. I didn't want them getting an urge to go while upstairs with the litter box being downstairs, so I got two self-cleaning litter boxes with litter. One is for the laundry room, and one is for under the shelf area at the end of the hall upstairs. I also got two self-dispensing water dishes and dry food dispensers, along with ten pounds of kitten food they recommended to us."

Bob started pulling out of the parking lot as she continued. "The litter boxes are cool. They strain the litter deposits into an enclosed container each time the box is used, and it only has to be emptied once every week to ten days, they said."

"Okay, Jess, but let's keep them in the laundry room most of the time for the first week or so, until we are sure they're both housebroken."

Bob needn't have worried. When classes started four days later, they let them have the run of the house while they were gone to classes.

Temple University in Philadelphia and Triangle Tech in Pittsburgh had Spring breaks the same week. Bob and Jess invited Dick and Trina to come and visit. Faith and Hope were nearly full-grown cats by the time Dick and Trina arrived. Since Trina was pregnant, she kept her distance from the cats because of the dangers of toxoplasmosis, which can be a danger due to contact with cat litter. Dick, being always playful, didn't hesitate to begin playing with them. "What are their names?"

Jess pointed. "Hope is the one over there dozing. She's mostly gray. You've got Faith. She's mostly orange."

Trina smiled. "Dick, I hope you'll always remember to wash your hands after playing with them. I won't be able to this time."

"Right. Faith is really fun to play with. I guess I'll catch up with Hope later."

It was a very busy week. Trina was well along in her pregnancy. It was fun for all of them to take a leisurely walking tour of the historical city, and they spread the audio guided tour out over three days. They listened to their tour guide's voice on their phones while they walked.

Dick opened up on the first day, as they walked along. "Bob, Jess, I never expected what has happened to Trina and me. At first, when we learned that we were going to have our first child in June, I tried to take it in stride. Even Trina's morning sickness didn't have much of an impact on me, or at least, I didn't think so."

Bob was seeing his brother differently. "So, what happened?"

"Fatherhood is creeping up on me, Bob. It's hard to describe, but I'm changing my attitude about a lot of things."

Trina giggled. "He's not exactly a different man, but he is a changed man. We're having just as much fun with life, but our fun is more serious."

Dick nodded. "Yeah. We know that our first is going to be a boy, and I've got all kinds of scenarios washing through my head, of things I want to do with him and teach him. I want to be a good father, like Dad, and always have time for him."

They paused in front of Betsy Ross House. Trina spoke more quietly, for some reason. "Before we go inside, let me just say that, since Christmas, I've been comparing my Mom with my mother-in-law. They are very different women, but I love them both. I want more than anything to be a good mom, and I've decided that I want to breast-feed him."

They listened to what the tour guide said about the Betsy Ross House, and then they went in. Betsy Ross House has a fascinating history. They were there nearly an hour.

After visiting Betsy Ross House and Independence Hall, Bob was curious about what was going to happen after the boy is born. "Trina, I assume you'll take some time off from school after your boy is born. Then what?"

Trina grinned. "Triangle Tech is such a great place! We're earning our Associate in Arts degrees as well as our vocational certifications. Beginning this summer, I'll be doing as much of my classroom coursework as I can. Dick will too. We've found wives of two of our classmates who will help us with childcare, and the deal we've made with them is pretty reasonable."

Jess looked at her. "Would you like Bob and me to come up and help one or two weekends a month?"

Trina's eyes got big. "That would be fantastic! Our second bedroom will be our boy's room when he's bigger, but we'll have the crib in our room for a while at first."

Their walking tour of the city was stretched out through the whole week, and then Dick and Trina went back to Pittsburgh on Saturday. Bob reminded Dick that their guy talk would be at 11:00 that night.

Jess and Bob began blocking out time on their calendar. They would not be able to go to Pittsburgh on the weekends of rehearsing the combined choirs for the Fourth of July weekend. The other weekends would be free for them to visit Pittsburgh.

On Memorial Day weekend, Jess and Bob decided to have a romantic getaway at the Hotel Hershey and explore the chocolate factory. It was only two hours away, but it was like being in another world. Bob gave a detailed description that Saturday night during the guy-talk. Almost a week later, Trina went into labor. Alex and Lona caught a flight from Burbank with one carry-on bag each, and they arrived in Pittsburgh just before midnight on Friday. They went straight to the hospital.

Jess and Bob made plans far in advance for this. After checking into a hotel less than a block from the hospital, they went and joined Dick, Alex, and Lona. They simply waited. Saturday morning at 3:46 AM, William Mario Johnson was born. William, of course, is his paternal grandfather's name. In the same way, Mario is his maternal grandfather's name. They would call him Billy.

After seeing the baby and congratulating his parents, Alex and Lona joined Jess and Bob as they went back to their hotel. Alex secured a suite because she and Lona planned to stay a week with their kids and a new grandchild. Bob and Jess got few hours' sleep before they headed home.

As they turned off the light, Jess spoke quietly. "Bob, I still want us to finish off our bachelor's degrees in three years. Do you still want to take classes throughout each summer and only go back to California for Christmas?"

In the darkness, Bob pulled her close and kissed her. "Absolutely! That's our goal, but let's not stress out about it. If it takes three years plus a semester, it'll be no problem. Do you still want to keep going until we get our masters' degrees?"

She kissed him back, and she did so a little more passionately. "Yes, but if we get pregnant, I'm still willing to put my master's degree on hold."

That didn't become necessary as time flew by. They picked up some required classes that summer and enjoyed the Fourth of July concert in New York. As they moved into the Fall semester, they began to see some future possibilities.

Meanwhile, during their second year of training, Dick and Trina began to accumulate praise from their instructors. Both developed their natural skills, and both were hard workers. Little Billy grew rapidly. Trina and Dick wanted to return to California in order to live closer to family, so Dick's goal was to become a licensed general contractor in California.

In the Spring of their second year, they celebrated Billy's birthday during a weekend visit from Jess and Bob. Dick and Trina told them about a phone call they had gotten. After countless prayers and hard work to complete their apprenticeships, one evening Dick's phone rang. The caller ID said it was Ken Crain. "Hello, Mr. Crain!"

"Hi, Dick! I understand the two of you have finished your apprenticeships. I'm calling to see if you two would be interested in working for me on a job in South Pasadena. Would you be interested?"

"I think so. Let me turn on the speaker so that Trina can get in on this." Dick pressed a button as Trina moved closer to him on their sofa as she nursed little Billy. "Okay, I've got Trina here now. You were saying that you have a job for us in South Pasadena?" Trina's eyes got bigger.

"Right. It is a 90-unit apartment complex that the owners may decide to market as condos rather than as rentals. We'll start laying the foundations in two months. Dick, I've been talking with your instructors and the master carpenters who have apprenticed you. I want you to be my chief framing contractor. You can take ten days to two weeks to vacation your way back home to the West Coast. Your parents will put the three of you up until you get your own place."

"That sounds great! You have work for Trina also?"

She leaned in closer. "Yes, Mr. Crain, I can do framing if you want me to, but that's not my area of expertise that I've developed."

"I know, Trina. I want you to oversee finish carpentry and cabinetry. You've got many people there at Triangle Tech saying how good you are."

Trina was beaming at this point. "That sounds great!"

"Out of the ninety units, eighty-eight will have four floor plans with mirror images of those plans. There will also be both a penthouse unit and a manager's unit. If the complex is marketed as condos instead of as rentals, the manager's unit will simply be another condo, but with three bedrooms. The cabinets are all factory-made, but there are more than a dozen trim variations. Are you renting there in Pittsburgh or do you own the place?"

"We own it. As we finished our apprenticeships a couple of weeks ago, I called the realtor who sold us this place that we would be moving out soon." He glanced at Trina. "We love it here, but we knew we might have to move on short notice. We can put our furniture into a pod, and have it shipped to storage in Pasadena or in La Cañada Flintridge."

"Good. As soon as you get here, we'll start the process of getting you two your California contracting licenses." I'll see you when you get here."

Jess and Bob came to Pittsburgh a few days later and spent a weekend helping them get ready to move. With the two carpenters no longer in Pittsburgh, Jess and Bob focused totally upon their schoolwork at Temple University.

Out in California, Sandy and Carole were working hard at U.C.L.A. most of the time. In addition to their classes, Sandy built a web page for Carole and Himself. His reviews of everything having to do with photography began to get more hits each day.

Carole posted videos and pictures from their photo expeditions, and those also began to get thousands of hits. During their junior year, they added light-hearted banter between the two of them regarding both their expeditions and their equipment.

It was just after Spring break during their senior year that Jess and Bob got a phone call that would change their lives forever. It was Jess' phone that rang as they were finishing breakfast one Saturday morning. The caller ID said it was from The Majestic Theater in New York. Jess put her phone on the kitchen counter and pressed the speaker button. "Hello?"

"Jess Johnson?"

"Yes."

"This is Akira Eng. I'm calling from The Majestic Theater in New York. How are you?"

I'm fine, thank you."

"Good. I'm going to be directing a revival of Lerner and Loewe's *Camelot*, which I hope will open in time for the holiday season in December. This theater is where it premiered back in 1960. The Majestic has hosted one revival since, and we have been holding tryouts here for the last two months. Steve Leone, Jim Matheson, and I were having lunch yesterday. Your Dean there at Temple University suggested that I call your husband about being the vocal coach for this production and to direct the music rehearsals. Steve Leone said I should ask you to try out for the part of Guenevere."

"This is Bob Johnson, Mr. Eng. Camelot is one of our favorites of the old musicals."

Jess was smiling. "I'm surprised that you don't have all the leads filled by now."

"The truth is, there are two that are available that are very qualified and have great voices and have fine reputations, but I'm not sure how either of them would fit in with the rest of the cast. How soon can the two of you come to New York? If you drive up here today, this evening at the theater would be great, as a time for us to meet and talk."

Jess and Bob nodded at each other, smiling. "We'll be there."

25.

Growth & Change

From the time they invited him, Bill truly enjoyed the guy-talk with his sons. He then shared virtually everything they told him with Alex. She was glad. "This is great, Bill. Sometimes, when I've had the girl-talk, I wanted to share everything the girls told me, but when I shared things with you, I felt uncomfortable. I was seeing their lives only from a female point of view. This is so much better!"

Bill agreed. "I can easily understand. It's great that you and I can discuss the lives of our sons and their wives with both perspectives. Has Temple University responded to your offer to make commercials and promotions for them?"

"Yes. Their trustees are going to discuss it at their next meeting. They have some financing to discuss, because I pointed out some avenues of promotion they had not considered." Alex and Bill went on to talk about a house he was going to design for Ken Crain to build in the Santa Barbara foothills.

When Jess and Bob went off to New York City to see about becoming part of a revival of *Camelot*, it turned out to be the break that every musician hopes for. For most of that weekend, Bob was the center of everyone's attention. After only a few hours, Akira Eng told him that he was the man he had been looking for to do the voice coaching and chorus direction for the production.

Bob wasn't sure. He thought the production deserved to have someone with more experience. What Akira Eng was proposing was daunting – almost overwhelming. Bob called his Mom repeatedly after that weekend to get her input.

It was Jess, however, who convinced him. On that weekend, late Saturday evening, Bob and Jess were getting ready to go back to Philadelphia when Akira Eng stopped them. "Jess, when I invited you two to come up here this weekend, I intended for you to try out for the part of Guenevere. I have not heard you sing, and the others have gone home. Bob, take the score and go to that piano. I want to hear Jess sing *Simple Joys of Maidenhood* as you accompany her. Jess, you know the song, don't you?"

"Sure! I was Bob's music student long before we got married. It was one of the songs we worked together on."

The director smiled. "Okay, let's hear it." Jess told Alex later during girl-talk that they went through it three times with the director, as he asked her to sing it in different ways.

Finally, after saying farewell to the director, they started driving south, while they discussed the possibilities constantly. As they were going south through New Jersey, they stopped for burgers. They were famished because they hadn't eaten since lunch. As they sat around the table, Bob was emphatic. "I'm too inexperienced to deal with something this big! It's overwhelming."

"You can do it, Bob. I know you can."

They got back to Philadelphia early the next morning, and they did not hear a word from Akira Eng for over three weeks. Then the director called and told Jess she would have the female lead in the production, but Akira wanted Bob to be the vocal coach and chorus director. Jess talked Bob into it.

That revival of Camelot turned out to be nearly the same length as the movie version, but the critics agreed it was better than all previous versions, both in the stage versions as well as the film version. Jess was a hit and was labeled a rising star. Akira Eng repeatedly told people that it was Bob who worked behind the scenes to fine-tune the performances of the singers.

Some things remained the same. Each weekend, at 11:00 PM Eastern Time and 8:00 PM Pacific Time on Saturday, the triplets and their Dad continued to have guy talk. A couple of times their Dad mentioned to them how much he looked forward to it. His sons have said that they look forward to it too.

In a similar way, every Christmas Eve, Jess, Trina, and Carole have girl-talk with Alex, in person, just as they do by phone the rest of the year. Interestingly, the girls' Moms all said that they didn't think they should join the group.

After a short vacation, Dick and Trina plunged into their work on the apartment complex. They left little Billy with Alex and Bill at the mountain house during the day. They returned each evening. They were more than willing to be free babysitters. They signed paperwork to have authority for medical decisions and took Billy to his doctors' appointments.

Harry seemed completely content with having the baby in the house. When Billy got fussy, Harry would go over to the crib, purring, and peer in. Harry's purr was almost hypnotic to Billy, keeping the baby's attention until Alex or Bill got there with a bottle or changed him. When Alex was working, Bill took over. He had done the same things when his sons were babies, when Sheila was there.

By Christmas, when Jess and Bob joined the rest of them, the apartment complex was almost half completed according to Ken Crain's schedule. Trina was very pregnant again, but she was still working, supervising a large crew of cabinet installers. Her license came in the mail, but Dick's was still being processed. The owners decided to sell the apartments as condominiums, and they took the penthouse unit.

Jess and Bob stayed only a couple of days because they had to get back to New York. Jess called Alex every morning for updates about Dick and Trina.

Three weeks later, Trina gave birth to a little girl, and she was named Maria Alexandra. With Billy now having a baby sister, Harry didn't seem to get much sleep. He was almost always in the nursery, sleeping beneath one of the cribs whenever he could sleep.

Late in the Spring, one Saturday morning, Dick's phone rang. It was Ken Crain. "Good morning, Dick. I'm calling to let you know that we've had our final inspection, and after I sign some paperwork today, the project is officially completed. If you and Trina still want to buy what would have been the manager's apartment, you two had better buy it. If not, it will publicly go on sale next Friday."

Dick was sitting in the kitchen finishing coffee, and Trina walked in. "Who's that, Dick?"

"It's Ken. The project's complete. If we still want the manager's unit, we need to buy it this week."

Trina's eyes became huge, and Alex turned towards them from loading the dishwasher. "Wow! That's fantastic!"

Trina nodded. "Tell Ken we'll talk to our bank Monday."

"Ken, we'll call our bank Monday. When you talk to the owners, tell them we'll take it."

"That's great! Tell your folks I'll come up later this week to see everybody and say hello to Harry." He hung up.

On Monday morning, Dick and Trina went to Bank of America and signed the paperwork. When they got back to the mountain house, there was a letter in the mail for Dick. He had his general contractor's license. He practically screamed, "Praise God!"

In New York City meanwhile, Jess and Bob settled into a routine. They had a rented apartment near the theater, which was occupied solely by Faith and Hope when they were not there. They took Sundays and Mondays off, with Jess' understudy, a woman named Helen Grayson, playing the part of Guinevere when Jess was off. They would take Faith and Hope south with them to the house, catch up on their mail, and relax except for going to church on Sunday morning.

Out on the West Coast, Sandy and Carole were continuing their classes at U.C.L.A. while having a thriving business in partnership with a travel agency in Westwood. Their business was thriving because of their doing two things. They were leading photo expeditions two or three times a year, and their Internet business was growing rapidly. Their subscribers paid a small fee each month with an automatic debit. In return, Carole and Sandy were doing equipment reviews and editorials on anything having to do with photography or videography.

During the first six months after launching their web page, the acquired several thousand subscribers. Furthermore, Sandy was often asked to lead classes on photography, and Carole did some modeling. They did not get much sleep because they were still managing to keep up with classes and getting good grades. In all of this, Sandy was a good husband. Carole's needs were his first priority.

During this time, Alex and Bill decided to join Carole and Sandy on their second photo expedition to Antarctica during the continent's summer, in January. Just before they were to leave with Carole and Sandy, the four families were having hot chocolate and cookies on Christmas Eve. Carole was sitting next to Alex, and she took her hand. "Mom, Dad, while Sandy takes you and twenty-six others to Antarctica next month, I'm going to have to stay home."

Alex turned to her. "What's going on?"

"I am too pregnant to fly." She smiled rather demurely. "Sandy and I are going to have twins late in April."

"Carole!" Mom hugged her. "Would you like me to stay home with you?"

Carole shook her head vigorously. "Oh! Thank you! No! Everything is fine, but the airlines won't let me fly now, and neither will my gynecologist. By the way, Dad," she looked at him, "Steve and Michaela Leone have signed up for this tour. Just like my husband, they want to photograph the southern polar lights – the *aurora australis*."

Five days later, they flew south. It was hard for Sandy to describe those nineteen days on the seventh continent during their weekly guy talk, which they continued to do even while Sandy, Alex, and Bill were down under. With seasons reversed, it was "summer" down there, of course, with temperatures somewhat like winters in northern Minnesota. Sandy and Carole both had previously said that being down there is almost addictive. Alex and Bill agreed.

As Alex and Bill joined Steve and Michaela in photographing the *aurora australis*, what all four of them noticed the most was the quiet. After they got back home to Southern California, they discussed the experience constantly. During guy talk, Sandy frequently talked about it too. When Jess talked to Alex about it during girl-talk, it was the same sentiment.

During guy talk while the others were down under, Dick reported that he had put in a bid for doing an upgrade of the West Covina Mall. Trina was updating their web page and checking email every day because they were getting nearly constant inquiries for remodeling kitchens, work that they thoroughly enjoyed doing together.

After returning from Antarctica, there was catching up to do, of course. Alex became the spokesmodel for American Rag Stores, when she was already producing and directing their commercials. As Alex told Jess one night, "I'm having just as much fun making these commercials as I ever did when I was acting in movies."

Bill was also still working as well. Harvard University hired him to teach graduate studies in architecture on the Internet. He also agreed to lead an in-person graduate-level workshop each summer at one of the locations he had previously designed or was working on.

Harry was getting old. They did not know how much longer he would live. Debby Donovan told them more than once that she was surprised that Harry had lived as long as he had. The vet also told them that Harry's niece, Sheila, had disappeared one night. They and local law enforcement had searched for over a week. Alex and Bill were more than a little intrigued by the name they gave to the kitten.

Sandy reported to the others during guy talk one Sunday, that with Carole scheduled to have the twins in late April, Alex began talking with her nearly every day. Bill talked to Paul about what was going on every week or so, and Alex frequently talked to Stella. After all, they were about to become grandparents for the first time. Alex and Bill could speak from experience.

The twins were born the second Saturday in April. Paul, Stella, Alex, and Bill were there with Sandy in the waiting room. Sandy said later that he tried to seem calm on the surface, but he knew his Mom could tell he was nervous. "Since all four of you are here, I think Carole would want me to tell you that we think that these two will be enough."

Bill raised his eyebrows, but he wasn't surprised. "Really?"

Sandy nodded. "Carole and I have looked at all the possibilities, and we're not planning on having any more after this. By the way, Dad, I haven't forgotten about building a manufactured homes factory with you. After you finish those sets you're working on, I'll show you some plans I have sketched in my spare time. Will it interfere with your teaching for Harvard?"

He shook his head. "I don't think so."

Alex nodded and said, "During the summer, I am going to be directing several commercials, as Bill works on set designs and teaches his Internet classes. This sounds like a good plan."

Alex looked over at Paul and Stella. "Bill and I are already enjoying being grandparents because of Dick and Trina's two children. What about you two?"

Alex and Bill chatted with Stella and Paul until a nurse came to tell them that they could see their new twin grandchildren. All the guy-talk and girl-talk that Saturday was about the twins.

After the twins were born, Alex realized that summer was not far away, and she wanted something special to happen. She and Bill discussed it constantly for days. Finally, Alex described it during girl-talk, and Bill did the same during guy-talk. While cooking dinner one evening, Alex touched the speaker button on her phone. "Call my manager, Charlie."

The connection only required a few seconds. "Hi Alex! I understand that the twins have been born!"

"Yes, they have, Charlie. I've got something I want you to do for me. It might be a little difficult."

"Shoot!"

"Bill and I want to treat our four families to the Fourth of July show at the Hollywood Bowl. I'll need at least twenty tickets, maybe more."

Charlie whistled. "That's a tall order, Alex, even for me!"

"I know, my friend. If you and your husband want to join us, you're welcome. It's all on our tab."

"Wow!" She paused. "I'll start working on it the first thing tomorrow. I can't make any promises though."

"I understand, Charlie."

Three days later, Alex's phone rang while she and Bill were eating lunch. She touched the speaker button. "Hi, Charlie! Were you successful?"

"Yes! Knowing you as long as I have, I got you a block of fifty seats. You can give away the seats you don't use and take them off your taxes."

"Excellent! We can talk later about you and your husband joining us."

"Right! We can work that out later. See ya!" She clicked off.

Once they had the tickets arranged for, Alex and Bill started making video phone calls. They had a hard time getting through to Bob and Jess. Since their Sunday performances were in the afternoon, they finally got through to Jess on a Sunday evening in the middle of June. Alex and Bill set up the call by the big video screen. "Hey, Jess! We were reading this morning that the show is still sold out through December!"

"Hi, Mom, Dad! Yes! Bob and I are getting a percentage of the box office, and we're doing great! The latest, however, is that we're going to be taking a leave of absence starting in November."

I responded, "Why? What's up?"

Bob came into view and sat down beside her. "Hi. As you know, we had put having a family on hold until after this show runs its course. Evidently, God has other plans for us."

"I'm pregnant!" Jess grinned.

"Congratulations!" Alex and Bill said together. Alex asked, "When are you due?"

Bob had a huge smile. "The doctor says it will probably be early March. We don't have an exact date yet."

His Dad nodded. "That's great. The reason we've been trying to contact you is that we've bought a block of seats for the Hollywood Bowl celebration of the Fourth of July. Do you think you can get a couple of days off for that?"

Jess nodded. "That would be great, but we'll have to ask Akira. That's a big weekend here in New York, too."

Alex nodded. "We understand. We hope you can make it. Have you talked to Sandy or Carole since their twins were born?"

Jess' eyes got big. "No! That's great! I'll call them after we end this call. Bob and I have been so wrapped up in the show that we've hardly talked to anyone in the outside world. This makes it even more important that Bob and I get there for the Fourth. I'll press Akira on this! How are Dick and Trina doing?"

Bill sat forward a little. "They're staying busy. We baby-sit Billy and Maria regularly. They've got helpful neighbors in that big condo complex, but they like to see us as often as possible. Harry treats them like kittens he must care for. He's like a feline grandfather to them, protecting them. It's cute."

Bob smiled. "Harry's getting up there in years, isn't he?"

Harry strolled over and sat in front of the screen. Bill put the phone on the table in front of the screen and turned the phone's camera towards him and towards the rest of them, who sat behind him. He purred. "Rowwl." Alex scratched Harry's head.

"Hi, Harry!" Bob waved.

"Rowwl." He sat down, facing the screen.

Jess also waved. "Now I've got to convince Akira to give us the Fourth off! My understudy is a woman named Helen Grayson. She says she knows you, Mom."

Alex nodded. "Yes, I know her. Helen has been taking your part on your days off, hasn't she?"

"Yeah. She does a great job."

"She's a fine talent. She has co-starred in quite a few Broadway productions, but she's never had a lead role. I'm sure Helen will enjoy doing the lead when you're on your leave of absence. Doing the role on the Fourth weekend would be a good run for her. Tell Akira that."

Jess nodded. "That sounds like a good idea, Mom.

As it turned out, Bob and Jess could join them for the Fourth at Hollywood Bowl, and Helen Grayson got positive reviews. On the Fourth, Trina and Dick announced that they were pregnant again, this time with fraternal twins due in late September.

On their way into the Bowl before the concert, Trina was definite, saying, "Four children will be enough for us. Both of us enjoy working." Dick smiled and nodded.

Surprisingly, Trina's Mom, Lona, spoke to Alex quietly while they were at the bowl and watching the fireworks. "I just want you to know, that ever since my granddaughter was born that I've been on the wagon. I'm going to AA meetings every week. Please pray for me."

She nodded. "Bill and I will pray for you every day, Lona. I'm proud of you. Are you aware of the Celebrate Recovery groups that meet in our La Cañada Flintridge area?" "It is a 12-step program like AA, but Christ-centered. I'm asking only to see if you are aware of it. I'm not pushing it, Lona."

She smiled. "I know, Alex, and thank you. I'll pray about it."

26.

Déjà vu

The demand for tickets to Camelot began to taper off, and Jess had an idea. She approached her director one Sunday afternoon. "I have an idea I want to run past you, Akira."

"What's that?"

"We all realize that this production will probably wind down soon. What about using our cast and instrumentalists to make a new movie version?"

Akira shook his head. "That's not my area of expertise, Jess. Simply filming a Broadway production and putting it on Blu-ray wouldn't even be profitable in our current economy."

Jess nodded. "I know that. I have something better in mind."

"Oh?"

"Steve and Michaela Leone are friends of my family. With your permission, I will ask them about the pros and cons of doing a full-blown movie musical on video."

Her director was visibly surprised. "That kind of thing hasn't been successfully done in several years. The previous movie version was only moderately successful. I don't have any problem with your talking with them about it, but don't be surprised if they do their best to discourage you."

When Jess got back to her apartment, Bob already had things packed for going south to their home in Philadelphia for two days. All they had to do is put Faith and Hope in the car and go. It was mid-afternoon, and they would be home for dinner. They didn't have to be back until noon on Tuesday.

As they left the George Washington Bridge and drove into New Jersey, Jess told Bob about her conversation with their director.

Bob was thoughtful. "I like the idea, but it is also a scary idea, Jess. The money required to produce a musical production with staff is mind boggling. I'd like to do it, but I'm not at all sure what Mr. & Mrs. Leone will say."

As Bob continued driving down Interstate 95, Jess took out her cell and scanned her directory. Finally, she touched a button. "Jess Johnson! What a nice surprise!"

"Hi, Mrs. Leone! Are you busy?"

"No, I'm just relaxing on our patio. When we finished lunch, Steve had some work to do, so he's inside. What's up? I understand that your production of *Camelot* is still just about sold out for every performance."

"We're still doing well, but we'll probably close down in the next six months to a year. That's why I'm calling to get an opinion from you and your husband."

"Oh? Tell me!"

"Akira Eng has given his blessing for me to ask you about the pros and cons of producing a movie musical. He says it is not his area of expertise, and he is doubtful. I'm wondering about using the same cast to make a new movie of *Camelot*."

"A movie musical has not been made in several years."

"Akira – Mr. Eng – pointed that out to me."

"It's an intriguing idea, as far as I'm concerned, but I want to discuss it with Steve. Can I call you back tomorrow?"

"Sure!"

"Talk to you tomorrow." They ended the call.

"Michaela says she will call me back tomorrow, Bob."

"Don't get your hopes up."

Alex and Bill heard all about it the next day, but they didn't hear about it from Jess or Bob. Michaela called them the next morning while they were having breakfast. Alex's cell rang, and the ID said it was Michaela. Alex put her phone on the counter between them and pressed the speaker button. "Hi, Michaela! It's good to hear your voice."

"Hi, you two! Steve and I have been talking all night about a phone call we got yesterday from your daughter-in-law, Jess."

"Really!" Alex was as surprised as Bill was.

For the next ten minutes, Michaela told them about Jess' call and Michaela's discussion of it with Steve. Her husband didn't think it was worth doing, but Michaela convinced him that she wanted to direct a production of the musical. Then Michaela dropped her bombshell. "Bill, you don't know the business as well as Alex, but I want the two of you to produce it and lasso some investors. I don't think any studio will take it on unless we can come up with some money to back it."

Bill looked at Alex, and she looked down at her phone. "Michaela, Bill and I will have to pray about it for a few days. I'll call you back, okay?"

"I know I'm offering something huge for you two to shoulder, so I guess I should expect you to pray about it. Can we talk about it later this week?"

"Sure, Michaela, I'll call you back then." Alex touched the button again. "Wow!"

"We can both say that repeatedly!"

By Wednesday, they had decided to go for it, and they also decided to put some of their own money into it – borrowing against up to half the value of their investments. They had already started building a factory in Wyoming to pre-fabricate super-insulated homes, with Sandy as a partner in that venture.

Alex began making phone calls to producer friends. When Alex and Bill said yes to Michaela and told her the budget she would have, she let out a nearly deafening shriek. It was her turn to say 'wow.' "That's great! That's even more than I hoped for! Hold on, Steve wants to get in on this." They heard whispering in the background.

The director came to the phone. "Hi. It sounds like you're ready to back this. I'll help Michaela get a studio involved. Meanwhile, I am thinking back to almost six years ago when the eight of you came over here and spent the day. Your daughter-in-law Carole is a gifted cinematographer with no experience in this kind of thing, of course. If Carole's interested, this would be a way for Carole to start getting such experience."

Looking at Alex, Bill nodded, and she smiled. "Right, Steve, I'll ask her today if I can contact her. She's in her last year for getting her Masters in cinematography. She and Bob will have their hands full with their twins, but Bill and I can help with that. She's due in March."

"I thought so. Today, Michaela and I will call your other son and daughter-in-law and tell them that we will start moving forward on this. I'll also call Akira. He's an old friend."

"That's great Steve." Bill was enthusiastic and could see that Alex was. "We'll talk again soon."

"Right."

They ended the call. Bill looked at Alex. "This being Monday, they'll be in classes all morning. Let's start trying to get hold of Carole and Sandy after lunch. If this works out, they will both have new careers as well as twins."

It turned out to be easier than Alex and Bill expected to get Sandy and Carole to shift their lives after graduation. On Friday, they drove over to spend the weekend with them. Carole was very pregnant and wanted to spend time with Alex anyway. After dinner, they relaxed in the great room, with Harry purring at their feet.

Sandy looked relieved. "This is great, Dad! Carole and I haven't made a lot of money with our tours, so it will be easy to cut back to one or two photo tours a year. I can continue to do photography equipment reviews for our Internet business, and Carole and I can hire someone to help us maintain our web site. This will give you and me plenty time to work out the kinks as we start our new business."

Carole nodded. "For the last several months, Sandy and I have been talking about the changes that might take place after the twins are born and we graduate. My gynecologist will induce labor during Spring break. From what you've told me Mom, there's no way production can get underway before the end of the summer, even ideally."

Alex smiled as she nodded. "That's right, Carole. Since your Dad and I are the producers, we can make all of it work out as conveniently as we can. If most of the cast members working with Jess sign on for the movie, the stage version will probably wind down on Labor Day. We'll play it by ear after that."

Bill had to get Sandy's attention. "As soon as you graduate, son, you're going to have to put your engineering expertise to work with the other engineers at our factory. You'll be on the Internet all day, every day. Our manufacturing equipment is being assembled in several places and shipped to our Wyoming location. I think we can start producing homes by midsummer. We're getting inquiries from contractors in fifteen states so far. Word is spreading fast after *Architectural Digest* published that article about our factory."

The remainder of the year often seemed impossibly full and busy. Blessings came to Alex and Bill from many directions. Dick and Trina established themselves in their new condo, both as a family and as a business centered on the Internet. The two of them began specializing in remodeling and restoring homes throughout the Los Angeles Basin. When they were at work, neighbors took care of their children.

The twins were born to Carole and Sandy in March, as planned. They sold their home in Westwood and moved into the mountain house temporarily in May. It was business as usual for Harry to watch the twins. Sandy and his Dad were on the Internet, working, nearly all day practically every day.

Carole joined Bob, Jess, Michaela, and others, in preparing to go into production on the movie at a location in southern Oregon. Virtually the entire cast of the stage production of *Camelot* signed on to be in the movie. Thanks to an investment in exchange for advertising by Sony, the digital movie was to be shot in 8K.

Sandy and Bill manufactured and sold temporary housing to the movie studio to house the cast and crew, where a little town was born because of the production. When word got out that the houses had almost no utility expenses, hundreds came from Portland, Eugene, and elsewhere to live in the new community and start businesses there. Sandy and Bill quickly developed buildings for small businesses. Once ordered and paid for, the buildings were shipped within a month.

One unexpected development was that Bob seemed born to the role of being a producer. He did call on Steve Leone for help from time to time, but Steve was there anyway, helping Michaela when she needed him. Bob was a natural at anticipating the needs of everyone in the cast and crew.

Alex and Bill start doing philanthropic work, raising money for various charities. Whenever they prayed together, they constantly thanked God for their successes and the successes of their sons and their daughters-in-law. All the extended family became part of churches where they were working, and they thrived.

Production in Oregon was suspended between the week before Christmas and the 5th of January. As usual, the triplets and their families came to the mountain house for Christmas Eve. It was by then a much larger clan, so Alex and Bill brought in their favorite caterers to prepare and serve the dinner. They also rented extra tables and chairs so that they could sit down to a formal Christmas dinner together. Some of the children made messes, but no one was concerned. The caterers did their jobs.

It was snowing outside in the late afternoon, and Harry was by the big windows, looking down. "Rowwl."

Bill walked towards him. "What is it Harry?" He looked down, and then he turned to his beloved wife. "Alex, you and I can go downstairs for this." He looked around the room. "I want everyone else to stay up here. You can watch if you want to." He looked down at their cat. "Watch, Harry!"

"Rowwl."

The others moved towards the windows as Alex and Bill walked towards the stairs, Alex was curious and spoke very softly as they walked to their spiral staircase. "What is it, Bill?"

He smiled and almost whispered. "You'll see. This just might be a very unusual blessing." They started down the stairs.

"What do you mean?"

"Do you remember Debby Donovan telling us that Cherrie got pregnant by one of the cheetahs?"

"I remember."

"This just could be one of the kittens."

"Animals don't escape from that zoo."

"You're probably right, but I remember when Sheila first appeared in the bushes outside my house in La Jolla. Cherrie inherited her leaping skills from her mother. We never found out how a cheetah gave birth to Sheila or where that mother came from, much less how Sheila came to arrive at my La Jolla house. It was a mystery that was never solved."

They went outside, and in the snow, they immediately began shivering. He pointed. "There she is."

There, hiding in the bushes, they could see a pair of orange eyes. Slowly, Alex and Bill moved forward until they could see a face that looked almost exactly like Sheila's when she was a kitten.

Alex was fascinated. She spoke in a stage whisper. "She looks like a miniature Shelia!"

"Rowwl."

They stooped down to see the kitten more closely, and the kitten started inching slowly towards them. As the kitten started to nuzzle Alex's hand, Bill heard himself softly saying, "All that God does, God does well."

Other Books by James J. Stewart Available on Amazon

Christian Inspiration, Study, and Poetry

Faith and Yosemite: Fourth Edition
[Christian poetry with pictures of Yosemite]

Faith Fuel
[Meditations on the Christian faith and life]

Lasting Love
[Short Biographical Sketches]

Living for Jesus
[A Gospels Study Guide for Couples and Small Groups]

Deliberately Growing Spiritually
[A five-year Bible reading program for spiritual transformation.]

Seed Thoughts for Christian Prayer and Meditation
[Workbook]

Single Sentence Sermons
[Workbook for growing faith]

Walking in Faith
[Much of the same poetry as Faith and Yosemite but without pictures]

Spiritually Growing Through Prayer
The focus is upon personal piety and spiritual growth through prayer.

In Jesus' Name
[Praying Effectively]

Christian Fiction

The Camera Doctors
[Two people meet on top a famous mountain, and romance ensues.]

Casting Lots
[Christian romance and adventure set in the near future]

Christian Romances in the Foothills
An anthology of Tom's Town,

Soul Mates, & The Camera Doctors

An Extensive Life
[The life story of a man who lived more than four hundred years.]

Empty Tomb, Full Hearts
[A Selection of Testimonies Among Those Who Saw the Risen Christ]

The Gaardian Saga
[Christian science fiction fantasy with God in a major role.]

A Nation Transformed
[A future tale of God intervening in the USA with miracles.

A Second Call to Serve
[A tenth-generation pastor and his second wife accept a call to build a church from scratch.]

Prayer Warriors
[Urban adventures in a near-future continuation of Casting Lots]

Soul Mates
[Romance, the same setting as Tom's Town]

This World Is Not My Home
[Two together since high school separate to find love with others.]

Tom's Town
[Small town life and Christian romance]

The Warrior and the Prophet
[God has surprises and blessings for newlyweds]

Yosemite Picture Books

Ever-Changing Yosemite Valley
[Yosemite Valley is a glacially carved valley. Moment by moment, scenes change.]

Faith and Yosemite Fourth Edition
[Pictures of Yosemite National Park, with poems about the Christian faith]

Portraits of El Capitan
[El Capitan rises 3000 feet above the floor of Yosemite Valley]

Portraits of Half Dome
[Half Dome marks the east end of Yosemite Valley]

A Sense of Wonder: Yosemite
[A Christian poem about Yosemite, illustrated with pictures]

Starlight Over Yosemite
[Large pictures of Yosemite taken at night]

Yosemite Textures and Shadows
[High definition photographs of Yosemite Valley, depicting all seasons, both day and night.]